JU WATCH ME

JUST WATCH ME

Lior Torenberg

SCRIBNER

London · New York · Amsterdam/Antwerp · Sydney/Melbourne · Toronto · New Delhi

This edition published in Great Britain by Scribner,
an imprint of Simon & Schuster UK Ltd, 2026

SCRIBNER and design are registered trademarks of The Gale Group, Inc.,
used under licence by Simon & Schuster Inc.

1 3 5 7 9 10 8 6 4 2

Simon & Schuster UK Ltd, 1st Floor
222 Gray's Inn Road, London WC1X 8HB

Simon & Schuster Australia, Sydney
Simon & Schuster India, New Delhi

www.simonandschuster.co.uk
www.simonandschuster.com.au
www.simonandschuster.co.in

A CIP catalogue record for this book is available from the British Library

The authorised representative in the EEA is Simon & Schuster Netherlands BV,
Herculesplein 96, 3584 AA Utrecht, Netherlands. info@simonandschuster.nl

Hardback ISBN: 978-1-3985-5185-5
Trade Paperback ISBN: 978-1-3985-5709-3
eBook ISBN: 978-1-57344-561-0
eAudio ISBN: 978-1-3985-5187-9

Typeset in Palatino by M Rules
Printed and Bound in the UK using 100% Renewable Electricity at CPI Group (UK) Ltd

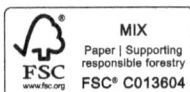

MIX
Paper | Supporting
responsible forestry
FSC
www.fsc.org   FSC® C013604

JUST
WATCH
ME

MONDAY

LiveCast Ranking: 530,204

A guy comes in, early thirties with a suit on. Good-looking in a Listerine-clean sort of way. A bit heavy on the hair product. I slip the apron around my neck and let the straps dangle around my ankles.

"Can I have the Doctor Clean Green with almond butter instead of peanut butter?"

"Sure," I say. "Almond butter will be three dollars and fifty cents extra."

"What?" he says. "Are you kidding me?"

"I'm not kidding, I'm sorry."

"I was here yesterday and they did it for free," he says, and if I wasn't on Nik's bad side I'd gladly avoid charging for the swap. Give the customer something for free and they'll give you a bigger tip.

"I'm sorry," I say, trying to actually look it. "Do you still want to substitute the almond butter?"

"What's your problem?" he asks. "Three and a half dollars for a swap. I'm not even adding anything. That's fucking insane. I fucking hate this city," he says.

I want to laugh. I want to commiserate. It is fucking insane, but so is paying nearly twenty dollars for a smoothie. The livelihood of this store is predicated on the existence of this man, who doesn't blink before spending my hourly salary on a sixteen-ounce beverage.

"Is your manager here? Hello?" He calls behind me into the back room, which is empty, but then he takes out his phone, and I know precisely what he's doing. Online reviews are exclusively written by people like him. I'm no stranger to the low-carb outrage of American Psycho drones on their lunch breaks. I either give this guy what he wants and risk getting fired, or he leaves a bad review and I'm definitely getting fired.

"Hey," I say, but he doesn't look up. Just keeps moving his fingers across his phone screen. I swear, every shift here takes a week off my life. "Sir," I say a little louder, a little more pissy. If I'm screwed either way, then there's no reason to put up with being treated like this by a man whose leather briefcase is worth more than my kidneys on the black market. Anger flashes across my front brain. It gains texture, and heft. I blink hard but it won't go away. The man's fingers keep typing.

"Hey," I yell. He looks up from his phone. I throw the jar of almond butter at him. "Whatever, okay? Just take it."

He catches the jar in one hand and looks at me, his other thumb paused over his phone as I take off my apron and toss it to the ground.

"Want to get a drink?" I ask.

"What? No."

"Fine," I say, and leave the store.

When I'm halfway home I slow from a run to a jog, to a walk, and then a standstill. Impulsive little shit. I am so screwed. I have to get back to our storefront in Grand Central Terminal before Nik looks at the cameras and notices that I'm gone. I've put him through way too much in the six weeks since I started at Juice Body. But then my phone is ringing, and it's him. Because of course it is. That man has eyes on the backs of his eyes and cameras everywhere else.

"Hey," I answer. There's yelling. I pull the phone away from my ear.

"Dell, you are done."

"Nik, the guy—"

"I don't care if the guy tried to shoot up the store. You cannot leave."

"I can't leave if someone tries to shoot up the store?"

."Enough! This isn't my problem anymore!"

"I'm sorry I was late for work, it was just a few minutes, and—"

"Late for work? You think I'm calling about 'late for work'? You threw your apron on the ground and left! No one is in the store right now, the front door is unlocked. Anyone could come and take whatever they want! Am I supposed to drive back from the Hamptons to close the store? Is that what you want me to do?"

"No, I can do it. I can—"

"Do you think Juice Body is a joke? Do you think my livelihood is a joke?"

"I'm going back now, Nik. I'll be there in a second, I swear. Are you coming in tomorrow? Let's talk about this in person," I say. I can't lose this job. I get paid seventeen dollars an hour plus tips to put crap in a blender and press a button.

"Dell. Listen to me. I told you: no more warnings. I know you have a lot going on with your family, with your sister in the hospital, and I've let a lot of things go since you started here last month. But I can't do it anymore. I'm on vacation, for god's sake. I called Krishell and she's heading to the store. You are no longer part of the Juice Body family; this isn't how family treats each other. You're done."

The mention of Daisy makes me grip my fists around nothing. "I'm done? I'm done?" I say. "You're basically pulling the plug on my sister, Nik. You know that."

"I've heard it before," Nik says. "I'm sorry, Dell. No more chances."

"Can I at least come talk to you about this in person? I'll have to pick up my paycheck, anyway. When are you coming back, Nik? I'll come by tomorrow and we can talk? Don't do this to us. Hello?"

•   •   •

It's five flights of stairs to my Hell's Kitchen lair, a matchbox apartment with barely enough room for a single match: strike me against the wall and watch me burn. I walk slowly, and not just because the stairs are crooked and old and I have to be careful. I'm drained—emotionally, physically, psychically—and I can't stand up straight because of the pain in my abdomen.

Lately, my stomach has been a blimp between most meals, tight and tender to the touch. A riptide of pain that drags my appetite far, far away from me. Which is just as well since my grocery budget has been nonexistent. And I don't have insurance, so I'm sure as shit not taking myself to the doctor. But I don't mind the pain right now, as I trudge upward. I want to be out of breath. I want my lungs to sear and my calves to revolt.

I let myself into Lee's apartment, which is right next to mine but holds a different atmosphere. They're on their laptop on the couch. The couch is L-shaped and plush, but they don't slump. Their posture is excellent. The walls have art on them—not online prints framed for cheap, but real art. Their laptop is a MacBook Pro, the newest edition. They wave and point at their headphones to let me know they're in a meeting.

"Why are you always in meetings?" I say. "You're a data scientist. You shouldn't have to talk to anyone except your computer, and me." They shush me again.

I go to their bathroom and chew several pastel Tums from their medicine cabinet. I'm an antacid connoisseur and assorted fruit flavor Tums are my favorite. Gaviscon is a close second, as long as it's not the grape flavor. Pepto Bismol tastes like viscous, minty yogurt.

I open Lee's fridge and eat an organic strawberry, tossing the stem into the sink. My stomach is still a raging gash but I'm starving, and I need something to do while I wait. I reach past the organic pumpkin seed granola, candied ginger, and vegan chickpea puffs for the bag of

Chex Mix at the back of the cupboard, picking out the pretzels one by one. Carbs help settle my gut. Sometimes.

"Will you stop raiding my kitchen?" they say, swatting the bag out of my hands after they close their laptop. But they're smiling, they're always smiling. That's what I like most about them, and also what pisses me off the most. It's also why I'm not desperately trying to find another apartment. I like listening to their footsteps through the wall, their shower coming on, the noise from their TV. I like hearing their unrelenting, unrealized plans to quit their job and start a software company or a coffee shop or an organic farm or an Airbnb empire or whatever it is that week, even though I often have no idea what they're talking about. I like knocking on the wall that adjoins our apartments to say good night.

"Last time, I promise," I say, grabbing the Chex Mix back. "I just got fired."

"From Juice Box?"

"Juice Body."

"What did you do?" they ask.

"Why are you saying that like it's my fault?"

"Was it?"

"I mean, this guy was being an absolute toe so I gave him a jar of almond butter."

"You what?"

"I don't want to talk about it."

We smoke on Lee's fire escape and watch the sun flame blue over the Hudson River. Lee leans forward to take a hit, their head tilted down, the back of their neck the color of summer sand. I like when they wear their hair up like this, in that tiny sprig of a ponytail at the base of their neck. Down below, on the street, everyone oozes into each other. The glass buildings crackle and shimmer pink in the sun.

"Hear me out," I say. "I'd be a sick receptionist."

"Seriously—"

"Or an inside sales rep, or a business development rep, or whatever those telemarketing jobs are called nowadays."

"I'm not getting you another interview to bail on or half-ass," Lee says. "It's not a good look."

"That was last month. I've changed since then."

"They keep records, you know. Files on people they interview. Or the people they don't interview. The people who don't show up to interviews."

"Again: last month."

Lee laughs. "You have your shit together now? It doesn't take a month. It takes years. You have to stay at a job and grow and learn and get promoted and all of that. No one hands you things. It takes time."

"I don't have time," I say.

Lee wiggles their naked toes. "Okay, drama."

"Having a desk job doesn't mean you have your shit together," I say. "It just means you have a flat ass from sitting all day."

The only thing sadder than taking out massive private student loans for a useless undergraduate degree is taking out massive private student loans for an incomplete useless undergraduate degree. If I had gone on academic leave instead of dropping out, like my mom begged me to, I wouldn't have to start paying my loans yet on top of everything else. But I don't want to go back to NYU at the end of the summer, or even in a year. If I do go back to school, it'll be somewhere no one knows me. Somewhere I can be whoever I want. My reputation spit shined, my nail beds clean.

·   ·   ·

String of Hearts succulent longs for love & liberation, $30

Healthy, sober, employed Plumeria you can take home to your parents, $38

Sexy Mimosa Pudica looking for match. Moderately famous, discretion needed, $25

My apartment is small and made smaller by the matriarchy of plants stationed inside of it. I can grow anything: Chinese money plants and spider plants and peace lilies. Air plants and African violets and fattened-up jades. I buy buds at the hardware store for mega-cheap, propagate them, and sell them for nasty multiples of what I paid. I have a handful of grow lamps that I bought at Home Depot for $36.99 each—an investment that paid off quickly. I trick the heliotropes, sun-seeking animals. And people go nuts for plants. In a good month, I can make up to a thousand dollars. It's so tasty it almost feels like a scam.

If I had a bigger place, propagating and selling is all I would do, an army of breeding mothers. Except that I wouldn't, because it's more work than it seems, and if I'm being honest, the plants have started to scare me. They stick their grubby tendrils in my underwear drawer, stretch their shoots up to my lofted bed, and stroke my feet while I'm sleeping. It's not right to have them jungle up like this in a zero-hundred-square-foot apartment. My arms get tired from watering this variegated mess, overfragrant and darkening my already-dark apartment. I post some new listings online.

Attractive, mature Monstera not religious but a little holey, $75
Unique, educated Rattlesnake Plant seeks intelligent companionship, $50
Jalapeño pepper plant doesn't always play nice, $15

Then I switch tabs to LiveCast. I love watching people talk to their cameras. It does something for me, always has. And I'm not the only one. LiveCast has over 240 million monthly users. If that's not evidence of a loneliness epidemic, then I don't know what is. The most popular live streams are of people playing first-person shooter games or doing mukbangs of themselves eating forty-seven Korean mozzarella corn dogs. But I don't watch those. I like the "Just Chatting" section where people sit in front of their computers and talk or fold their laundry or go for a walk with their cameras on. They keep me company when I can't fall asleep. The featured "Just Chatting" broadcast on the home page is some dude doing a streamathon for charity titled "IM OFFICIALLY HOMELESS #SAD." He seems to be in some sort of college dorm. He's already raised half a million dollars and he's not even hot, or homeless.

I click in: dark blond hair and a rookie stache. He's talking about some golf tournament to over a thousand viewers, myself included. He's been streaming for twenty-one days straight. It seems like every hour or so he does a spiel about how he's raising money to help rebuild his family home after a hurricane hit Florida last summer. His goal is six hundred thousand dollars and he's nearly there after three weeks of streaming every waking moment of his life. Donation after donation comes in—some as small as five cents and some as big as five hundred dollars—and all he does is sit there picking his nose. There's no way to know what he's even using the money for. Was there even a hurricane in Florida last summer? Won't there be another one next summer?

I'm too high for this.

An online search tells me that the average LiveCast streamer makes between one cent and one dollar per viewer per hour. A wide range, but impressive when you think about it. To make what I was making at Juice Body, I would only need seventeen viewers giving me a dollar an hour, or thirty-four viewers giving me fifty cents an hour, or sixty-eight viewers giving me twenty-five cents an hour. Etcetera. The most popular streamers have viewer counts in the hundreds of thousands, and donations are just one part of the equation. There are monthly subscription fees, exclusive content, merchandise, ad revenue, affiliate deals. People actually do this for a living.

I change the stream to an adult woman with pigtails talking about conspiracy theories, and turn the light off so that my windowless studio apartment is pitch-black except for my screen. I throw my laptop onto my lofted bed and climb up after it. I can't actually watch streams up here because my laptop doesn't have the ceiling clearance to fully open, but I can put it next to me with the screen half-closed and listen, which is often enough to knock me out. I also don't have the clearance to sleep on my side comfortably, but I've gotten used to taking naps and sleeping on my back, and in the mornings I can reach my tongue out and lick the dew right off the ceiling.

• • •

The toxins swishing around my skull aren't letting up, even with this streamer droning on and on about how reptoid lizard people live in tunnels underneath Denver International Airport. I open my mom's texts from today, yesterday, the week before: all unanswered.

> You have to come with me to visit Daisy soon
> Dell?
> You can't keep avoiding us
> I forgive you, you know
> Do you forgive me?

I hate hospitals. I hate everything about them.

I worked three days this week, so my Juice Body paycheck should be a little over four hundred dollars. By this time in the month I should have more squirreled away, but I just re-upped on plants and got square with Lee for all the takeout they've spotted me lately. I have one thousand dollars in my checking account and I need to triple that by the end of the week or else I'll be booted from this rathole. And as much as I hate it, it does serve to protect me from the elements.

Lee would lend me the money, but I'd never ask. Takeout, maybe, but not thousands of dollars. There's my mom, but she's been spending everything she has on Daisy's hospital bills. And if I do ask her for anything, she'll just pressure me to move home like she has ever since I dropped out of school.

Screw this.

I jump out of bed and open my laptop to look for jobs. I need to be able to buy food. I need to have a place to sleep. An art museum is hiring a receptionist at a plush salary of twenty-two dollars an hour, but they require applicants to speak more than one language. Why? They don't even specify which one. There's a guest services associate gig at European Wax Center—aka, a receptionist job—but they require applicants to have two years of customer service experience. The Container Store has part-time job openings, but they ask that employees conduct "frequent lifting and occasional reaching, stooping, kneeling, crouching, and ladder climbing," which makes me tired just reading it. And besides, that listing already has over seven hundred applicants.

I rage quit out of my job search tab. Before I can overthink it, I open LiveCast and click the red button in the corner that reads: "Start Stream."

There I am, ghost of a ghost, acne scars lit up by the glow of the screen.

"Mirror, mirror, on the wall," I whisper.

No one is in my stream but me. My LiveCast ranking is 530,204 out of 680,302. Seems I get a boost just for being online right now while everyone else is working. Finding streams is simple. There's "Talk Shows," "Fitness," "Travel," "Just Chatting," and a category for nearly every video game ever made. Viewers click into a category and it shows all the live broadcasts, how many viewers they have, and their ranking. It only takes a couple of minutes for someone to find and join my stream. A real, actual person. The chat box directly to the right of my stream lights up.

l0st3560 has signed on
l0st3560: hi

"Hi," I say. I open and close my mouth like a thick-necked goose.

l0st3560 has signed off

Shit.

The chat box is empty again, stagnant. I rename my stream "wec-lome to the jungle #plantcorner" and wait. I rename my stream "Late-night chitchat xx" and wait. Every couple of minutes I try something new, rubbing my brain cells together to see if they'll give off smoke. Finally I give in and type "my sister is in a coma #lol"

A couple of viewers appear, their names scratching at my screen. My LiveCast rank goes from 530,204 to 522,084. Really? That's the one that worked?

I clear my throat. "Hey, fuckers, welcome to my nightmare."

The chat box lights up again.

karnie_vibes: hey!!!!
excelsior404: hi mademoiselle_dell

"Nice to meet me, isn't it?" I say. Mademoiselle_dell. I made this screen name years ago, who knows why. But it works, it fits, and this is my stream: no one can fire me for having a bad personality. Once I settle into this particular persona, the words come faster and easier than I thought possible.

excelsior404: lol ya i found u on the New Streams page
excelsior404: whats ur deal
excelsior404: your sister is in a coma?

"So you can read. Congratulations, excelsior404. Did I say that right?"

> **karnie_vibes:** lol burn
> **excelsior404:** no
> **excelsior404:** its like "excel-see-er" not "a-cell-seer"

"I don't care."

> **karnie_vibes:** lol burn
> **jackofnotrades1** has signed on

Another one. Three whole viewers, and none of them have left yet. "Welcome aboard, Jack. How are you doing this fine night?"

> **jackofnotrades1:** my name isn't jack lol
> **jackofnotrades1:** its Rohan

"That's confusing."

> **jackofnotrades1:** its a saying
> **karnie_vibes:** lmaooooo
> **jackofnotrades1:** jack of all trades
> **excelsior404:** i get it
> **jackofnotrades1:** ^___^
> **jackofnotrades1:** tits?

I bare my teeth and grimace at the camera. I like the way I look in the light of my laptop: feral eyes, glimmering canines, wild hair. Wolf girl.

> **excelsior404:** what happened to your sister
> **burr9ty** has signed on

"Welcome to my stream, all you mercenaries, missionaries, and misfits."

burr9ty: hi

"The thing is, I'm supposed to be having the time of my conventionally attractive life. But my sister is in a coma." The words leave behind a sour, bilious taste.

jackofnotrades1: zoinks
excelsior404: what happened?
karnie_vibes: oh no :(

"She's been in the hospital for a few weeks and her doctors want to shut off her life support. In a couple of days actually. On Sunday."

excelsior404: this sunday?

"Yeah, basically. My mom and I want to put her on private life support, but that shit is crazy. Like, two thousand dollars a day crazy. We got so many different quotes and even the cheapest ones were in the thousands. She was showing some positive signs, some improvement. We think she could have a breakthrough soon, but the doctors are obsessed with freeing up her bed. It's just tough, because we're broke, so that's why I'm here." I rub the base of my throat, soothing it.

excelsior404: whats ur fundraising goal?

"Fourteen thousand dollars to put my sister on private life support for a week," I say, and it's solidified. "I'm not delusional, okay? Some families keep their loved ones around for decades. Obviously that's insane. But with Daisy, it's barely been seven weeks—not even two months." My eyes feel wet all of a sudden, gross, like eggs soft boiled in their shells. It's an obscene, unreachable goal, in more ways than one. "Just one more week, and then we'll go from there. If she doesn't wake up at that point, that's on her."

burr9ty: how do we know its for ur sister

"What kind of proof do you want? A doctor's note? A copy of my medical bills?"

burr9ty has signed off

"That's the spirit. Anyone else want my sister to croak?"

karnie_vibes: no :)
karnie_vibes: i mean
karnie_vibes: no :(
excelsior404: where r u?

"New York City."

excelsior404: same!!
jackofnotrades1: i went to the zoo there like 10 yrs ago
jackofnotrades1: there was a snow leopard
excelsior404: nice ive been to the zoo
karnie_vibes: that's cool

"So, what should we do? Should we chat? Anyone know any good jokes? Should we do an apartment tour?" I pick up my laptop and spin around in a circle. "This is the sweet life in the big apple, ladies and gentlemonsters."

karnie_vibes: i'm in vancouver
excelsior404: where do u live in the city?

I angle the camera toward the army of plants colonizing every corner of the room. "Anyone want to buy a plant? I'm selling them online."

karnie_vibes: nice
excelsior404: drop a link

I copy and paste the link to my listings in the stream chat.

"Meet my plants. That one stinks: Stinker. That one's called Prego on account of its big-belly leaves. This one is Stage Five Clinger. That one's got thorns sticking out of it? Stabby. That one is Eeyore. Majorly depressed."

saxophone22: lol depression isn't funny
burr9ty has signed on

"My mom got me a big red prayer plant as a housewarming gift when I first moved in. I freaked when I realized I could sell it for sixty dollars online. I've been chasing that high ever since, I'll be honest. I've carefully cultivated this creepy coven over the past couple of months."

crabbybob: i cant grow plants
crabbybob: its sooo hard sheeesh
burr9ty: its not that hard? lol

"It's not rocket surgery, anyway. Plants reproduce sexually or asexually, which is cool. Some female plants even have eggs. But propagation is different. With most plants, you can just cut off a stem with leaves and stick it in water for a couple of weeks. With other plants, you have to divide up the root structure. With something like a succulent, you can just plant a whole-ass leaf. I picked up some succulents the other day from Home Depot." I gesture at the empty cardboard box still on the floor by my bed. "Twenty for forty dollars and I'm going to sell them for ten dollars each."

excelsior04: Hi Odelia Danvers

"What the fuck?"

excelsior404: ur online listings r tied to ur account lol it says ur name
burr9ty: does anyone call you OD
burr9ty: like overdose

I go into the chat history and delete my original message.

"It's Dell to you. Mademoiselle Dell. Unless you donate, or buy one of these plants, in which case you can call me whatever you want. Except Odelia. Negatory."

Odelia. All inviting up front, shriveled at the tail end.

karnie_vibes: do you ship to vancouver

"If you pay for shipping, I'll send a plant to the moon for you."

karnie_vibes: lol how would i get it from the moon
excelsior404: i'll give u $5 if u eat those jalapenos

I put the laptop back down on my desk and lift up the jalapeño plant. It's pretty and lush, an outgrowth of peppers like tiny red dog boners.

"Five dollars a pepper?"

excelsior404: no just $5

"Anyone else want to get in on this?"

crabbybob: hi everyone!!!!
jackofnotrades1: hi crabbybob
jackofnotrades1: ok

jackofnotrades1: ill donate $5 if you eat all of them
karnie_vibes: lol

"Crabbybob, keep up. Are you in or are you out?"

crabbybob: lol
crabbybob: ummmmmm
crabbybob: no
excelsior404: ill donate $10 if u eat all of them

"Good."

I'm currently selling this plant for fifteen dollars. There are five peppers on it. I can eat them all now, make a couple bucks, give it another month or so for the peppers to grow back, and then sell the plant for the same price later. It's child's play. "You've got a deal, excelsior404, if that is your real name."

excelsior404: its not lol

•　　•　　•

I pick the first pepper off its stem. There is no resistance, just a quick and cool snap. I put it in my mouth and chew. A touch of spice, like black pepper, gathers in my right cheek like a spank. I swallow everything, including the seeds and stem. The pain is there, but it's minimal. The real pain will hit my stomach in ten minutes or so, when the pepper pulp reaches my digestive tract. I eat the second jalapeño, the third, the fourth. The pain doesn't accumulate but rather stays at a manageable wavelength, flames licking gently at the roof of my mouth. When I get to the last pepper, I rip it off its stem with a snarl, sending seeds flying everywhere. Little white projectiles. Soon the plant is picked dry. I swirl the hot saliva around my mouth and swallow that, too, warming and acidic.

I cough, and that's when I feel it: a little rattle in my left ear. The tiniest pinprick, an ever-slight distortion in the sounds around me.

karnie_vibes has donated $5

"Thanks, slut."

jackofnotrades1 has donated $5
excelsior404 has donated $10
cindyrella has donated $1

"You know the phrase 'every dollar counts' isn't literal, right, cindyrella?"

I try to get whatever it is out of my ear with my pinkie nail, and then a pencil eraser, and then the tip of the pencil.

crabbybob has donated $2

"Nice one, crabbybob. Is that what you tip at restaurants, too?"

I look at my LiveCast balance: twenty-three dollars, redeemable at any time to a connected bank account. That's grocery money. Even if Nik doesn't give me my paycheck, I can eat this week. And I made more in ten minutes than I make in an hour at work. I'm good at this, I think. I cradle the feeling, keep it close. I'm good at this.

crabbybob: nooo way
jackofnotrades1: u have to tip 10–20% at restaurants
excelsior404: don't tip 10% pls
excelsior404: i was a waiter
karnie_vibes: same
karnie_vibes: i worked at a coffee shop lolol
jackofnotrades1: i'm not tipping 10% for coffee
synthzorth: is ur sister in the hospital
synthzorth: live stream a visit

I lean my head to the left and shake it. What's in there, a jalapeño seed?

"What about the rest of you: donating or loitering? I don't like loitering. It provokes me."

synthzorth: i'm not donating

"You're not donating? You've decided?"

synthzorth: ya i'm just here to watch

"Blocked," I say, pressing the button by synthzorth's screen name.

karnie_vibes: damn thats savage

"I'm not doing this for fun," I say. "I mean, who am I kidding? Eating jalapeños was pretty fun."

cindyrella: jalapenos aren't even spicy
cindyrella: they're only a 2,500 on the scoville scale

"Nerd-to-English translation?"

cindyrella: it's the number of drops of water you need to not taste a drop of pure pepper or hot sauce
cindyrella: anything over 100,000 is actually spicy
cindyrella: like a habanero

"How much would you pay to watch me eat a habanero?"

cindyrella: i wouldn't
karnie_vibes: nooooo
excelsior404: $10

"Good."

• • •

It's easy to shoplift at Whole Foods. Security guards are stationed by the entrance but during the after-work rush, they wouldn't know where to look: moshing hordes of the living dead, cans of seltzer smuggled in the pockets of a coat, a bar of chocolate slipped into a back pocket. This is especially true at the Bryant Park location with its briefcased midtownies and the steady slam of clumsy tourists. An average-looking white woman of medium height can slip in and out with ease.

Habaneros. Where are the habaneros? I downloaded the LiveCast app on my phone before I left the house so I could take my stream with me on a little field trip. I hold my phone in front of me as I walk so my viewers can see what I'm seeing. If this were a regular day, I would go to the hot food section upstairs and eat one or two falafels while I pretended to look around. Then I would get an energy drink from the fridge and finish it as I roamed the aisles. I would throw out the empty can in the women's bathroom, then wander and stuff items into my bag at random: prepackaged sushi, pockmarked cubes of pepperjack cheese, teriyaki seaweed snacks. When I was done, I would walk right past security and emerge into the havoc of Sixth Avenue.

But today is different. I have people with me, operatives I can talk to through the walkie-talkie of my phone as I do recon. My LiveCast rank jumps from 522,084 to 515,842.

cindyrella: OMG whole foods is da bomb
jackofnotrades1: thats wher i get my shampoo and conditioner
jackofnotrades1: where

"Over and out. We're going in."

karnie_vibes: whole foods is too boojee
excelsior404: *bougie

karnie_vibes: i spell it like that on purpose
karnie_vibes: its ironic
excelsior404: u say over and out at the end of a sentence not the beginning

"Maybe I was being ironic, too."

No habaneros in the produce aisle. I stop an employee and he says they don't stock them at this location.

I should just go. But to leave the store, I have to pass the fridges by the cash register, and the sight of the cold drinks drenched in condensation makes my mouth water. I nab a Pink Lady Apple Kombucha and take another lap around the store to finish it.

karnie_vibes: dont get caught!!!
jackofnotrades1: check out the snack aisle
jackofnotrades1: they have terra chips
jackofnotrades1: i love that shit
cindyrella: OMG barf

Presently, I find myself alone in the nut and grain aisle. A rare occasion I mark by opening the brazil nut dispenser and allowing two perfect, fattened nuts to dribble into my palm. I've never had a brazil nut before. They're oily and tender. I grab a premade caprese sandwich from the deli section and head out, chittering with my viewers as if nothing out of the ordinary is happening, because it isn't. I shoplift all the time. The only difference is that now I have an audience cheering me on.

But then a hand appears on my shoulder. "Come with me," a security guard says, and I want to bolt. My plan has always been to bolt. Store security can't follow you out, so of course you run. And I'm so close, mere steps from being outside, but his arm on my shoulder is stiff, and his eyes are more tired than angry, so I let him lead me to the back of the store through a door marked "Employees Only."

✳   ✳   ✳

Inside the employee lounge are an oppressively clean tile floor and a magnet-free fridge. There are two employees at the lunch table. They pause their conversation to stare at me. The security guard leads me through a door marked "Security" where another guard waits, a woman. Her name tag says "Kels" and the man holding my arm is "Jiro." Kels glances at me before looking back at a five-by-five grid of screens, a vari-colored chaos of security footage that must cover every aisle of the store. And there's the nut and grain aisle, in the top left corner. My empty kombucha bottle is a bright pink beacon on the shelf. My phone is now deep in my back pocket. My viewers can't see but they can hear everything. And part of me is happy to have someone here for this: witnesses, spectators.

"What's your name?" Jiro asks me as he sits down beside Kels.

"Mary," I say.

"Mary what?"

"Mary J. Blige."

"Can I see your ID?"

"I don't have any," I say. Jiro and Kels look at each other.

"You don't have anything with your name on it?" he asks.

"No."

"Why not?"

"I don't carry ID with me. I prefer to lay low."

"Is that right?" Jiro asks. "So, what's in the bag, MJB?"

"This bag?" I ask, pointing to the bulging canvas bag on my shoulder.

"Correct."

Perhaps I should be more nervous, alone in this back room with two security guards. But this doesn't feel so much good-cop/bad-cop as tired-cop/bored-cop, and my viewers embolden me. They're all listening, and if I'm fucked, then I might as well put on a good show.

Kels has been silent this entire time, her arms crossed over her siz-able chest, her eyes glazed over.

"Hey," I say. "This was a mistake. I just started walking out by accident. I'll pay for everything."

"Why don't you show us what's in the bag first?"

I take the sandwich out and toss it to Jiro. It hits his shin and falls to the ground. He looks at it but doesn't pick it up.

"Anything else?" he asks.

"No."

"And what did you say your name was?"

"I didn't."

He looks at Kels. "Go ahead and call NYPD."

"Wait, hold on," I say. "Why are you calling the police? I thought we were talking it out."

"Our system runs facial recognition software, and we have camera footage of you shoplifting a dozen times in the last two months, at three different Whole Foods. And you won't tell us your name. I call that petit larceny and possession of stolen goods. And lying about your identity to law enforcement, which can get you charged with perjury or a misdemeanor."

"Are you law enforcement? Really? Supermarket security counts as law enforcement?"

"Ma'am—"

"Are you two paid enough for this? I mean, come on. Fifteen dollars an hour to call the police on people who walk out with, like, some bok choy?"

"Twenty-five dollars an hour," Kels says.

"Shit. That's awesome."

"Could be worse." Kels grunts. She gets up with effort and leaves the room.

"Are you going to call the police?" I ask Jiro. "Is she going to call the police?"

He nods and takes his phone out, starts playing a block matching game. His phone emits bubbly zings and whooshes, a mélange of celebratory sound effects, as he clears away rows of fruit jelly cubes.

I cross my arms and eye the clock on the wall. If I still had a job at Juice Body, I would be late for work. "So, what now?"

"We wait."

"You actually expect me to wait here?"

"I'm afraid so."

"Can I at least eat then?" I ask, gesturing toward the caprese sandwich on the floor. He shrugs. I pick it up and lean against the wall by the door, unwrapping the plastic. My back pocket vibrates with message after message. I take a bite and watch Jiro play his game, the flamboyant shapes and colors reflected in his eyeballs. He beats a level and his phone lets out a celebration jingle and a deep-voiced "Oh yeah." I take advantage of his distraction and scoot over slightly so that I can just graze the door behind my back. I guide my elbow to the door handle, testing my weight against it.

"Want a bite?" I hold the sandwich out to Jiro. He shakes his head but doesn't look up. "Suit yourself." I press down lightly on the door handle again. It's not locked. I just have to go for it. Press down hard and sprint out.

Three, two, one.

Three, two, one.

Three, two and a half.

I whip the door open. Jiro is up in an instant. I can hear his footsteps and the manic jingling of the keys on his belt behind me. He reaches for me, but I chuck the rest of my sandwich at his head and slip past him, out of the employee lounge and into the store, past a dozen carts and swinging baskets and too-slow shoppers. And then I'm out. I'm on Sixth Avenue and the police aren't here yet, but they will be soon. They'll have plenty of pictures of me from the security footage. But they won't have my name, that's what matters. I'll just never go back to

Whole Foods again. It's a pity, but it's doable. They didn't have what I needed anyway.

I disappear into the mob of Times Square and reemerge a few blocks away in Hell's Kitchen, strobe lights of adrenaline flashing across my brain. I check in with my viewers, and it's no longer just five or six stragglers, but thirty whole people in here. How did that happen? My LiveCast ranking has gone up to 440,382. I scroll up and read through the chats.

> **burr9ty:** is she gonna be okay
> **trutherdare:** 0.0
> **trutherdare:** omg
> **burr9ty:** bet
> **cindyrella:** i hate brazil nuts
> **burr9ty:** almonds r the best
> **cindyrella:** top 5 maybe
> **cindyrella:** i like pistachios
> **burr9ty:** shes running
> **trutherdare:** OMG
> **trutherdare:** OMG OMG
> **jimpix:** hi everyone

I read up on a hundred messages as I catch my breath, emboldened, heartened. There are about 700,000 streamers on LiveCast and, according to the rankings, I'm now in the mid-400,000s. That's impressive for half a day of streaming. More than impressive. The higher my ranking, the more viewers I'll have coming in, the more money. Not that I should index on today's performance. The algorithm could be manipulating me as a first-day streamer, giving me a taste of momentum and upward mobility so I keep coming back and striving for more.

LiveCast rankings are fairly opaque: an internet search reveals a complicated algorithm that includes not just viewer count but chat velocity, donation percentage, returning versus new viewers, viewer watch duration, drop rate, and a handful of other metrics. I don't have that many viewers, but I still managed to jump over 200,000 spots today. That's pretty dope.

"Hello, new friends, new enemies. Where did you all come from?"

karnie_vibes: i shared ur stream w my group chats!!!
crabbybob: i told my friends to watch
crabbybob: because ur insano

"I'm doing great, thanks for asking, crabbybob. I appreciate your concern. Bummed they didn't have habaneros. But otherwise I'm swell."

trutherdare: ARE YOU OKAY

"Yeah, well. I don't like running. I don't like sweating. And I'm still hungry. All I've eaten today is a bite of a shitty sandwich and some snacks."

excelsior404 has donated $10
excelsior404: legend

"Legend, no. Maybe."

excelsior404: steal from the rich and give to yourself?

"I'm not going to spend fifteen dollars on a sandwich while I'm raising money for a good cause. Consider the optics."

excelsior404: lmao
trutherdare: ^_^
excelsior404: consider them considered

I go to the dollar pizza joint on my block and buy two plain slices and a Diet Coke ($3.50). I shovel the pizza into my maw with one hand while keeping the camera on me with the other. My stomach tumbles like a dishwasher after all that gluten and dairy and oil, but I don't mind. Camera trained on my open mouth full of tomato sauce and doughy cud, I feel like I'm sharing a meal with friends. It's nothing like Nik watching me on his baby monitor at Juice Body as I slurp down free surplus smoothies after a customer has left the store. The line between surveillance and communion is thin but strong: not a knife's edge but a discernible, navigable border.

•   •   •

(!) You have a new private message

I see the notification banner pop up at the top of my LiveCast tab. I click to open the private message in a pop-up. I split my screen so I can see my stream, my stream chat, and my private messages at the same time.

> **excelsior404:** hey Dell
> **excelsior404:** what's up
> **mademoiselle_dell:** u know what's up
> **mademoiselle_dell:** ur in my stream
> **excelsior404:** lol okay
> **excelsior404:** just wanted to say hi
> **excelsior404:** im glad you didnt get arrested
> **mademoiselle_dell:** hi
> **excelsior404:** what's up
> **excelsior404:** im looking for something good to watch
> **excelsior404:** do you have any recs
> **mademoiselle_dell:** no
> **excelsior404:** do you watch much tv?
> **excelsior404:** or movies
> **mademoiselle_dell:** no
> **excelsior404:** lol okay one word answers
> **excelsior404:** rude
> **mademoiselle_dell:** u like when im rude
> **mademoiselle_dell:** thats why u follow me
> **excelsior404:** lol yeah i guess
> **excelsior404:** whats ur favorite tv show

> **excelsior404:** or like top five
> **mademoiselle_dell:** no
> **excelsior404:** aw youre not even going to share one? :(

I click into excelsior404's profile. His picture is an anime-style avatar. Following: lots of male streamers in tank tops and backward hats, lots of political accounts calling for the end of white genocide. Account created: twelve years ago. Followers: zero. No streams of his own, but it seems that this guy basically lives here.

> **excelsior404:** im curious about you
> **mademoiselle_dell:** i cant multitask
> **mademoiselle_dell:** i cant read my private chats and my stream chat at the same time
> **excelsior404:** oh yeah i get it
> **excelsior404:** no rush
> **excelsior404:** i just wanted to learn more about you and your sister
> **mademoiselle_dell:** not now
> **excelsior404:** ok ok ill message you when youre less busy
> **excelsior404:** and youll answer then
> **excelsior404:** because i looked you up and i found some interesting things
> **excelsior404:** that you probably don't want your other viewers to know
> **excelsior404:** talk to you later :)
> **mademoiselle_dell:** ok lol
> **mademoiselle_dell:** bye bye beta boy

• • •

I try not to be home much now that it's summer. The air in my apartment is thick and warm, the walls moist with condensation. A greenhouse for my flowering queens, air thick with estrogen and progesterone. Here's the deal with my place: it's a steal by Manhattan standards. Sixteen hundred for a studio is unheard of, and so I snagged it super-quick when I left the NYU dorms toward the end of the spring semester. But here's the real deal with my place: it doesn't have windows, and it doesn't have a bathroom. Just a lonely stainless steel sink, like in a jail cell. My mom would have an aneurysm. This Lilliputian kingdom consists of a lofted bed with a desk underneath, a dresser, a mini fridge, and a microwave — and plants. Far too many plants. There's no shared bathroom in the hall, either. It's an illegal unit, which is to say, it was carved out of Lee's apartment. I live in what was once their closet: the brackets are still there from the shelf rods, and I can see the faintest outline of where the doorframe was painted over. I can brush my teeth and get drinking water in here, but not much else.

When I first moved in, the landlord suggested that I get a twenty-dollar monthly membership to the 24-hour gym on the ground level so I could use their bathroom whenever I wanted. I'm not going to lie, I did that for a whole month. But I was used to it from dorm life, so it wasn't so bad, and ironically, I got in great shape going up and down the five flights of stairs to the gym so often. But one day I ran down to take a shit and found that the gym was closed for renovations. I didn't know what to do. Find a restaurant that would let me use their bathroom? Go back to my apartment and shit in a hat, a bucket, a bowl?

That's how I met Lee. I ran back up the stairs and banged on their apartment door. They answered in a sports bra and overalls, towering over me with their brassy green eyes and toothy smile. They had on a set of knuckle rings that said "FUZZ."

"You have my bathroom," I said to them.

"What?"

"I live next door and my bathroom is in your apartment."

"No, it's not."

"I don't have time to explain. Can I use your bathroom?"

They considered me for a moment, and then stepped aside to let me through. I locked myself in their bathroom for half an hour, luxuriating in the first nonpublic bathroom I'd used in four weeks.

Afterward, they came over to see my place and they laughed and laughed and laughed until I had no choice but to laugh, too. We confirmed that it was true: my apartment was their bedroom's original walk-in closet. Exhibiting a suspicious level of grace and neighborly trust, they gave me their spare key so I could use their bathroom whenever I needed to.

"Cancel that idiotic gym membership," they said, and so I did. I have a hard time doing what anyone tells me to do, but not with Lee. They have a way about them, blunt like me but you can tell that they give a shit. Plus, we were on the same antidepressants in high school so I know our brain chemistry is somewhat compatible.

• • •

"What do you want to know?" I ask my viewers. I chug a quarter bottle of Pepto Bismol as my stomach churns and cramps. Both my laptop and I are propped on our sides, laying nose-to-nose on the floor.

> **pklrik:** idk
> **pklrik:** is ur sister dead yet

Everything is about Daisy. She's all my mom talks about, all she thinks about. And after months of Daisy I finally had the chance to have one good thing that had nothing to do with her. My goal should've been three thousand dollars for this month's rent and expenses, not fourteen thousand for life support. Christ on a cracker. And if I don't meet that goal, am I still allowed to use that money on my own shit that needs seeing to? I should've given "Late-night chitchat xx" a few more minutes.

> **jimpix:** i feel like they cant just kill her no?
> **jimpix:** if theres brain activity

"A certain level of brain activity can still constitute a persistent vegetative state."

cindyrella: OMG sad :(
burr9ty: move her 2 a different hospital
cindyrella: id be so sad if my sister was in a persistent vegetative state

"My mom and I called like every hospital in a three-hundred-mile radius. Do you know how much it costs for a hospital to keep someone on life support? It's an insane number, like, ten thousand dollars a day. And my sister—she was breathing on her own for a while, and then she stopped, and that's not a good sign. Obviously. Doctors like to see improvement. But that doesn't mean she isn't still in there, fighting to get better and wake up. Her hand moved. She reached for me. But nobody listened."

saxophone22: but if they said shes a vegetable than shes dead
saxophone22: brain dead

"You're brain dead."

saxophone22: i'm just saying
crabbybob: sheeeeeesh
cindyrella: what happens after a week of home care
cindyrella: if she doesnt get better :((((

"I don't know, cindyrella. Maybe we try for another week, or we make an executive decision. But either way, it'll be our choice, my mom and me, not the hospital's."

saxophone22: every1 wants their family to be alive
saxophone22: but the doctors know best

"Doctors know best? What are you, twelve? Do your parents know best, too? Do the police know best? Did you know that one in twenty adults have been misdiagnosed by a doctor? And that one in three of those misdiagnoses led to serious injury or death? You can't just say shit. Well, you can, but not here."

I click the "Block" button by his name. Gone.

excelsior404: legend

My fingers go to the "Block" button by excelsior404's name but stop. He's given me twenty dollars so far. More than anyone else.

Just one more week. Just one more week. That has been my mantra for the past few months. The world record for longest coma before waking belongs to a woman named Annie Shapiro at twenty-nine years. Daisy wasn't even at eight weeks when Dr. Dole said the hospital wanted to take her off of life support. This is Daisy we're talking about, Daisy who used to sleep until noon on weekends in middle school. Mom would say she was growing and needed the sleep. So we'd have breakfast together on Sundays, blueberry pancakes, and Daisy would microwave hers when she finally waddled downstairs in the early afternoon, and the smell of butter and maple syrup would fill the house again.

Elaine Esposito did thirty-seven years—the world record for longest coma before giving up the ghost. Elaine and Annie, their families were held hostage by "just one more week." And for one of them, it worked out.

Daisy was breathing on her own until week three, then she needed a ventilator. At four weeks, she wrinkled up her forehead and cleared her throat. Then, more recently, we were in her hospital room and Dr. Dole was telling us how her condition wasn't improving as they'd hoped, and her right hand went berserk, totally twitched out and nearly slapped my knee. Dr. Dole said those things can happen, even if a person is gone. He really said those words. But he's wrong. The timing was too excellent. Too Daisy.

My mom and I went to the hospital every day for a while. We

played with Daisy's toes. Plucked her eyebrows. Even sang "She Will Be Loved" by Maroon 5, the song she most detested. We could tell that she was in there, on the cusp of waking. And then Dr. Dole and the rest of the ghouls at Mount Babel Hospital were done with her. They spelled it out for us: the only option is private life support—setting up a room for her at my mom's house with part- or full-time care. The cost for a single day could support me for an entire month.

Damn it, Daisy.

> **jimpix:** if my sister were a vegetable
> **jimpix:** she would be asparagus
> **jimpix:** because i hate her
> **cindyrella:** lol OMG

• • •

Sometimes my stomach hurts most when it's empty, and sometimes it hurts most when I eat. Today it's the latter, and when the pain from lunch finally abates, I am ravenous again. On top of my mini fridge I have a bag of cinnamon pecan granola I stole from work last week. Otherwise, my rations are gone. In my fridge is half a bottle of generic ginger ale and my cache of single-serving condiments taken from fast-food establishments: ketchup, mayo, mustard, relish; a creamy circle of Jif and a few crusted rectangles of Smucker's grape jelly; Kikkoman soy sauce packets and a suspiciously hardened packet of Ken's ranch dressing; a single-serving maple syrup; three packets of Wendy's sweet-and-sour dipping sauce, six packets of McDonald's honey mustard, and four packets of Burger King garlic sauce. I peel back a miniscule container of grape jelly and suck down its contents like an oyster.

> **crabbybob:** queen shit
> **redtimepolice:** strawberry jelly > grape jelly

I throat fistfuls of granola, oats dropping everywhere, as I chat with my viewers. During my shifts at Juice Body, I could drink free smoothies all day and that would keep me full throughout the night until my next shift. And I could take home all the blackened, sugar-bruised bananas I wanted. Once I took home a barely expired jar of organic, crunchy peanut butter, and that lasted me ages. I would love another gig like that.

Thirty-two, thirty-three, thirty-four unique viewers today. A handful of viewers have been with me the entire time since I started the stream. I feel a cool kinship with them, a sliver of affinity. My LiveCast ranking has dropped a little since the Whole Foods escapade, but only by a hundred spots or so.

If I could get to one hundred viewers, the money would start to add up fast. Using Daisy's story like this feels tender, like fussing with an infected tooth. But I imagine calling my mom and telling her I did it, I can pay for Daisy's private life support, we don't have to worry anymore. I imagine telling her to call up the in-home care service and have them bring all their beeping machines and tubes and wires over. Telling her to go pick up Daisy, that it's happening, that we can have one more week. That it's up to us now. We're in control.

I stick my pinkie nail into my ear as far as it will go, trying to get that damn seed out. It's deep in my ear canal, and ticklish, skittering around like a bug. I click on "Kim Danvers" on my phone and send my mom a text. This is the first time I've initiated contact with her since we were last in the hospital together.

Hey

She calls me immediately. I don't pick up. Soon I get a text.

We have to talk about checking out grave site etc. Call me back.

I turn my phone's sound off and toss it up onto my lofted bed, safely out of reach.

✹   ✹   ✹

I think I've finally gotten the seed out of my ear, but then the sensation comes back. With everything I've stuck in there over the last hour, I worry I've pushed the seed deeper into my brain hole. I imagine it catching hold and sprouting, growing leaves and sinking its hoary roots deep into my gray matter. An impossibly dense root structure hugging my brain, wrapping itself tighter and tighter. And if a stem were to grow out of my ear? And if it were thick enough? I could pull it out, slowly, slowly, until I was holding my silken brain in my hands, and I could remove those pesky roots one by one with tweezers. The trouble would be getting my brain back into my skull. Reverse mummification. But I don't need to think about that now, or ever. I need to focus on the real and present danger here: the army of plants crowding my apartment.

I get an offer online for my String of Hearts. Most people try to negotiate, but this person offers full price: thirty dollars. A guy named Casper with a private profile. I can only see his picture, which is a highly filtered pencil drawing of his face.

"Hold up. Is this one of you creeps?" I ask my viewers. It's close to midnight and there are seventeen people in here with me. Some from before, plus a number of new names.

karnie_vibes: j'accuse!!!

"Is this one of you trying to buy my plants online?" I ask, even though I know it's not likely. I deleted the listing link minutes after I posted it, and only three or four viewers were on my stream at the time.

crabbybob: no hahaaa
jackdaw2000: what plants?
crabbybob: i dont want anymore plants
crabbybob: they're toxic to my cat
karnie_vibes: no i live in vancouver

"Do you work for the tourism board, Karnie Vibes? I swear to god."

I respond to Casper and try to upsell him some of my other plants at a discounted rate, but he's not interested, which is unusual. There are two types of plant people: 1) those who use phrases like "plant mom" and "plant dad," and 2) those who are more committed to aesthetics and home decor than nurturing a source of life. Both of them are jazzed about a deal. The type of person who would trawl the internet in the middle of the night, who would travel across a city to adopt a new green member of the family, has a level of obsessionality. But this guy only wants the one plant, and he'll be here in twenty minutes.

"What kind of asshole does a plant pickup at midnight?" I ask. And I can hear my mom's self-satisfied retort in my head: "An asshole."

She rarely curses, except when I curse, and then she responds in kind, almost as if to make fun of me. But bad words have always sounded strange in her mouth. Muffled, like she can't quite fit them between her teeth. And she certainly wouldn't condone what I'm doing now: giving a stranger my address, meeting them alone in the middle of the night. This guy could be double my size and armed. I'm aware of that, and it's not that I think I'm invincible. It's more so that I don't care, and I need the cash.

xinfected_botx: maybe he's an insomniac
xinfected_botx: i online shop at night
crabbybob: ^^^
jackdaw2000: i love online shopping
jackdaw2000: not for plants though just sneakers

"He better not be drunk or something."

karnie_vibes: r u going to meet him alone???

"I mean, I'll bring you all with me on my phone. So you can call the police if anything shady goes down."

MSRN273: where do u live?

"I'm not giving you my address, so you'll have to tell the police to circle the city and look for a girl in green sweats with a big ass."

jackofnotrades1: show us your ass
karnie_vibes: ew perv

When Casper buzzes my apartment, I put my viewers in my back pocket and head downstairs. With my phone positioned just so, my viewers can pick up my audio and see everything going on behind me. Casper waves from the other side of the building's glass door. He's a tall guy, young looking, no older than thirty. Sober from the looks of him. His face is sheltered beneath his hat and hoodie, his eyes are shadowed in the pit of his head. His shirt has a great big orange moon on it that seems to glow in the dark. He seems normal enough, whatever that means. I pop the door open with my hip and he moves out of the way to let me out.

"Casper, yeah?"

"Sup," he says. I give him the plant and he hands me the cash.

"Thanks," I say, wadding the bills into my bra. "Have a good one." He looks behind me up the stairs and then looks up toward the windows on the building's exterior.

"Are you having a good night?" he asks.

"Hm?"

"This is a cool building. When was it built, the 1930s? 1940s? How long have you lived here?"

"Not long," I say, taking a step back in the doorway. "Let me know if you want to buy any more plants."

"See you later, Odelia."

I let the door close. He stands there on the other side with the plant in his hands, smiling at me. He's barely looked at the plant once. Hasn't examined the leaves or the soil or anything. This fucking guy. I can still feel him standing there as I climb up the stairs back to my place. But my viewers are in my back pocket watching him watch me, and at least that's something.

I feel rich with over sixty dollars in my bank account from my stream and the plant sale. Pre-stomach issues I would have blown it all on chicken wings or something. But for now I leave it in my LiveCast account. I want to see that number grow. Tomorrow, I'll pick up my four hundred dollar paycheck from Nik and add it to the thousand dollars I had beforehand. Not bad.

"What did you gremlins eat for dinner?" I ask my viewers, sitting cross-legged on the floor with my laptop open in front of me.

jackofnotrades1: quesadilla ^__^
crabbybob: sprite

"Sprite isn't a food. It's hardly a soda."

crabbybob: i'm going to eat later. it's early for me
crabbybob: 4pm
burr9ty: i dont eat at night i do intermittent fasting
jackofnotrades1: can u pose for a screenshot?

I turn my camera off. My viewers can hear me, but they can't see me. The rules of a marathon livestream are negotiable, but the general agreement is this: you can mute your audio or turn off your camera if you need to, just not both at once. There are no real breaks in a marathon.

"I'm not a camgirl, you dork. Do you want to get blocked?"

jackofnotrades1: no

"Prove your fealty and I'll turn my camera back on."

> **pklrik:** what is fealty
> **jackdaw2000:** i dont have the energy to cook dinner tonight
> **cindyrella:** i'm eating chicken tortilla soup

"Pklrik, it's a word you'd know if you studied for your English test tomorrow."

> **pklrik:** i don't have an english test tomorrow
> **pklrik:** i have one next week tho

"Are you serious?"

> **pklrik:** yes
> **pklrik:** im in 9th grade
> **jackdaw2000:** how old r ninth graders?
> **jackdaw2000:** 13?
> **pklrik:** wtf no im 15

I turn my camera back on: "Y'all are getting me off topic. Should I block jackofnotrades1?"

> **crabbybob:** oh sheeeeeesh
> **jackofnotrades1:** no i want to stay

"It's not up to me, it's up to everyone else. Should I give him the boot?"

> **pklrik:** give him the boot
> **chillnessa:** la bota
> **chillnessa:** that means the boot in spanish
> **jackofnotrades1:** can i stay plz
> **jackofnotrades1** has donated $1

"Fine, you're safe for today."

redtimepolice: lmaooooo simp

"Says the guy who has been watching my stream in silence for the past half hour."

redtimepolice: :D
karnie_vibes has signed off

The words simmer in my stream chat. Karnie_vibes has been here since the beginning. I try to refocus on the viewers who are here, who have stayed up with me so late into the night. I chat with them until three in the morning before I switch my feed to my phone and bring it to bed with me. Normally, I knock on Lee's wall to let them know I'm going to sleep, but not tonight. I picture my viewers closing their eyes and drifting off alongside me. My phone vibrates every time a chat comes in, a soothing ripple.

I dream of my plants. The crack of their spines as they stretch and grow, puffy with retained fluid, stretch marks along their stems. I know they want to join me up in my lofted bed. I'm lucky they haven't learned to climb the ladder yet, unroot themselves and launch. I feed them, water them, create for them an artificial sun. They shouldn't hate me as much as they do. But plants can sense things. I lean over the side of my bed and watch them dance in the dark. I want to shut my eyes, but I can't. They entwine their limbs and orgy all night, sleepless and hurting.

There was a big carob tree in my grandma's backyard. It shed oblong brown pods in the sticky Florida heat, like dried and flattened bananas. The pods were thick under my fingers, easily torn open. The seeds inside were smooth and brown, like almonds, or buttons. Daisy was always braver than me, wilder in the good ways. She would pop the seeds in her mouth, gnaw on the pods. She said they tasted like chocolate, but I didn't believe her, and I refused to put something so unappealing in my body. We'd gather the pods and bring them to my grandma, who would grind them into a fine powder to use as sweetener in the gravelly, health-conscious cookies she baked for us before she passed when I was in eleventh grade.

My mom never liked staying at Grandma's, but she took us anyway each summer for a week or two, because of all the space. Daisy was the one who loved to be outside, who climbed the carob trees. She was the one who cartwheeled across the front yard, careened off the diving board. I open a carob pod and she is inside, the smallest seed. I try to pick her up but she flies out of my hands and lodges herself in the divot at the base of my throat, embedding herself in my flesh.

TUESDAY

LiveCast Ranking: 440,601

I jolt awake and clutch my phone to my chest, hoping its irregular vibrations will quiet my heart rate. It's five in the morning and I'm a summer slug wrapped too tightly in my sheets. I shove them off and open my stream. Zero viewers. My LiveCast rank has dropped to 480,892. I catch up on the chats I missed, which are just inane enough to be interesting.

> **karnie_vibes:** i once slept for an entire weekend
> **pklrik:** no u didn't
> **karnie_vibes:** yes i did!!!
> **karnie_vibes:** i had the flu
> **karnie_vibes:** every time i woke up i took nyquil and went back to sleep
> **pklrik:** u didn't sleep for the whole weekend if u woke up to take nyquil

Viewer history: karnie_vibes came back for half an hour a little after I went to bed. That's nice. Pklrik shouldn't be up so late, though, seeing as he's an actual child. I shouldn't be up so late, either, but sometimes the morning seeps into night for me, and I'm too afraid to go back to sleep now that I know Daisy is waiting for me there.

At this time of morning, time unbundles itself. I doze in and out, never reaching the right depth. Around eight thirty, my first viewer of the day joins: excelsior404. I move the phone away from my face and get out of bed.

A string of texts come in from my mom, one after the other, wrapping around my finger and turning it purple.

How are you, Dell?

Let's talk when you have time

Please don't ignore me

Don't make me worry about you too

I eat handfuls of granola and chase them down with a shot of Pepto Bismol to get ahead of the stomach pain, which never actually works. Not really. Then I switch my stream to my phone and head out to see a man about a check. I usually jump the turnstile at the subway station, but I'm feeling flush this morning. I swipe in ($2.90) and take the train across town. The ride is just long enough to let the nerves set in. The closer I get to Juice Body, the tetchier I feel, lymph nodes swollen underneath my armpits and neck.

Maybe Nik will have a change of heart and hire me back. More likely, I'll have to grovel. I'm not above that, at least I wasn't before I started streaming, but I can't imagine doing it now. I have a reputation to uphold, viewers to entertain. Or mademoiselle_dell does, at least. Eleven viewers join during my trip to Juice Body and my LiveCast rank is slightly higher than it was this morning, but I still have work to do to get back to where I left off last night.

"I talked to my boss last week about how I really need to focus on raising money for Daisy. I gave him enough notice and did everything I could not to leave him hanging. But he's withholding my last paycheck, that motherfucker, because he couldn't replace me in time and had to change his vacation plans."

xinfected_botx: omg what an asshole

jackofnotrades1: this^^^

xinfected_botx: dont worry my boss is an asshole too

"Why would I worry?"

Audio on. Phone in my back pocket facing behind me. I've given my viewers the very special mission of letting me know if Nik checks me out as I'm leaving his office. Not a great job, but someone has to do it.

Krishell isn't working the register, thankfully. It's some new guy. Did Nik replace me already? New guy starts to say something, but I walk past him, past the storage closet and into the manager's back office where Nik is seated at his desk. His face is always pink, but it reddens when he sees me. He raises an eyebrow.

"What are you doing here?" he asks.

"How was the Hamptons? How were the Hamptons?"

"Beautiful. It was a beautiful time with my family that I had to cut short to come back and work because of you."

"That's why I wanted to come in and talk to you."

"Dell. You push me. You push me too far," he says. "I know you're going through a lot and I want to support you, but there is a limit."

"Can't we just have a conversation?"

"No. I have work to do."

"Is that guy my replacement?" I say.

"Who?"

"The guy at the front?"

Nik shakes his head slowly. "That's Johnny. My nephew. He's worked here for the last four years. You worked with him. He was one of the people who trained you when you started."

"Johnny? The guy with the huge mole on his nose?"

"He got his mole removed six months ago."

"I didn't recognize him without it."

"This isn't how family acts. We don't forget each other when we get a mole removed."

"It won't happen again, I promise. If he gets another mole removed, I'll notice," I say. "Please, Nik. I love this job. I love working here."

"I'm done with this conversation," he says. "Thank you for coming to see me, but it was not necessary. I've given you chance after chance these past few weeks. No one has ever gotten as many chances as you, Dell. As I said on the phone, you're no longer a part of the Juice Body family."

"Right," I say. A pit yawns open in my gut and stays open. Free food. Very solid hourly pay. A semi-walkable commute from my apartment. And Nik's not a bad guy, either. He hired me, after all, when he had absolutely no reason to. And he's given me plenty of second, third, fourth chances. And now he's looking at me with his eyes glazed over and his thoughts elsewhere.

"That's it then?" I ask. "You're just done?"

"That's it," he says. "I've learned my lesson with you. It's taken me time, but I've learned it. And I'm not going to be made a fool of again."

I'm not hurt, I'm furious. I don't want my job back, I want to jump on his desk and curb stomp his computer. I want to chuck my feces at the wall like a monkey girl, skyrocket my ranking, and make fuck-you money.

I can grovel, but it seems that mademoiselle_dell can't.

"I'll just ask one more time: Are you going to give me my paycheck or not?" I say.

"Your paycheck?"

"Yeah. I worked Monday, Tuesday, and Thursday last week."

"Do you know when my wife and I planned this trip? Over a year ago. We planned it over a year ago. A week in the Hamptons. Just a week away together. It's not too much to ask. But then I look at the security camera: you're throwing peanut butter at customers! The store is empty! So I leave my vacation and drive back and now I have to figure out who is taking your shifts so I can drive right back tonight and my wife won't divorce me again."

"It was almond butter."

"What?"

"It doesn't matter."

"Let's call it even, Dell."

"No," I say. "You owe me four hundred dollars."

"I don't owe you anything," he says. "You have no respect for me or the rest of the Juice Body family."

"You can't not pay people. Are you serious?" I say. "Are you actually fucking serious?"

He doesn't yell back. Doesn't curse me out. He just sits there.

"I've never been anything but kind to you, Dell. Understanding. I've been patient. And you took advantage of all of it. I'm truly sorry about your sister, but that's just the way it is."

"If you're taking food out of my mouth then you're just giving me a reason to eat you," I growl and throw the door shut behind me. Johnny says hello from behind the register and I flip him the double bird.

Fury gathers in my ankles and propels me home, the seed in my ear rattling with each step. I take out my phone and catch up on chats. Fifteen viewers. According to them, Nik didn't check out my ass when I left, he went right back to whatever he was doing. Math, probably. Nerd.

My viewers mirror my energy, adding their own four-letter words to the pileup of anger. You'd think it would feel weird venting to people I don't know online, but it doesn't. It reminds me of childhood, the sleepovers I never had. Staying up past my bedtime on websites like Chatroulette and Omegle, keeping the lights off in my bedroom in case my mom or Daisy walked by. Those websites that connected you with a stranger, usually a strange cock. But besides the genitalia, you knew everyone online was as lonely and bored as you were. There was something nice about that. Intimate, even. You can be anyone you want on the internet.

burr9ty: no one fucks w mademoiselle_dell
cindyrella: >:(

Four hundred dollars that I'm never going to see. That was a solid gig—better than the work-study job I had at the NYU cafeteria before I dropped out where I had to add red food dye to the meatloaf to make it look bloody and fresh. Nik paid me pretty well to put grassy-smelling gunk in a blender, and no one noticed if I added bee pollen to their smoothie instead of spirulina. And as grim as the "Juice Body family" shtick was, it worked. People showed up. People liked each other. And as much as I rolled my eyes at the forced camaraderie, it resulted in a less-than-shitty work environment, which is high praise for a minimum wage job. I hate that I'm getting kicked out of this particular home.

cindyrella: i cant believe he would do that to your sister!!

Altogether my ant-like existence costs three thousand dollars a month to maintain. And all of my bills—rent, phone, internet, utilities, student loans, credit card—are due in less than a week. If I don't make rent again, my landlord is absolutely going to give me the boot.

I check online but I don't have any offers on my plants. I have nearly three hundred dollars' worth of furious roots sitting at my place, brooding and taking up space. The issue is that it's summer, and all the richy-rich NYU and Columbia kids are home. In September, they'll be back in droves to deck out their drab dorms with plant decor, but in the summer it's just the locals. And the locals, in my experience, don't give a fuck. There's no use propagating more plants when demand is this low. I discount all of my plant prices one by one.

kirk_equivalent: where are we going next
kirk_equivalent: whats the deal (.)(.)

I grip my stinging stomach and breathe through my nose. I have $1,000 in my bank account, $34 in my LiveCast account, another $30 from my plant sale, and six days until I have to make rent and pay my bills. My rent is $1,600—my paycheck would've put me close—then utilities are $250 on top of that, including wifi and my phone bill. My student loans are $720 a month and my credit card payments are around $400. I can't bridge that gap with $1 and $2 donations. But that was for eating jalapeños. And that was before I tripled my viewer count with my escapade at Whole Foods.

According to cindyrella, habaneros are "actually" spicy. I'm sure I've had them before in some form. I'm not too worried about the spice level, but I still want to get a little high before I voluntarily pop one in my mouth.

· · ·

New Voice Message, 12:03 PM
Hey, Dell, it's Mom. Are you okay? I haven't heard from you in a while, so I have to assume you're okay or else I'll drive myself nuts. We used to talk more often, when you were in college. Freshman year you used to come home on weekends. You let me know how your classes were going and everything. That was nice. Not that we have to do that now, it's just something I remember. I've been thinking a lot about when you first went to college. How excited you were. NYU was an expensive school, and you needed to take out loans, but you wanted to go and that was that. You're so good at making your mind up about things. Maybe you've made your mind up about me, about screening my calls and texts. That's fine. I know how to take a hint. I'm not trying to bother you. It's the other way around. I'm wrecked, I'm going crazy, and I know you are, too. I'm here if you need me. Maybe I need you, too, but I won't put that on you. That's not how being a parent works. So, I'm here if you need me. And I'll try to give you space, if that's what you want. But not too much, okay? Not now. Call me.

· · ·

New Voice Message, 12:17 PM

I was just thinking about when I dropped you off at college and how god-awful it was to find parking in the city. Do you remember your first dorm? It was a forced quadruple. I was so mad, but you weren't mad. That's what I remember. The room was only supposed to have two beds but they replaced them both with bunk beds. Do you remember that? Really, the room was barely big enough for two people to begin with, and they decided to squeeze in four. I know that housing is expensive to build in the city but my god. You had to share two dressers between the four of you. I mean, really. It was bad. The other parents and I were all upset, and the other girls were, too. One of the dads went down to the housing office to yell at them. With the tuition they charge, they really should give you all your own rooms. But you weren't bothered at all. I was impressed with you. I thought: my daughter is so cool. Do you remember that? Anyway. That's all I wanted to say. I'll let you go.

I knock on Lee's door. They answer in a button-down shirt and plaid pajama pants: their Zoom-meeting mullet. I have my laptop in tow, and I turn it around to face them as the door opens.

"Say hello to my friends."

They lean forward and evaluate the screen, squinting at their reflection. "What is this?"

"I'm streaming. I'm a streamer now."

"These are your friends? There are like fifteen people in here," they say. Then, to my viewers: "You're all her friends? Really?"

The chat goes wild for Lee. I step into their apartment and put my laptop down on the kitchen counter.

"My mom-ager from my so-called Juice Body 'family' won't give me my last paycheck."

"What?" they say. "Why?"

"I don't know. For everything I've put him through, apparently. I don't know what to do."

"I mean, nothing, right? What can you do?"

"Bad answer." I roll my eyes.

"What do you want me to say? You're not going to sue him or any-thing. What is there to do?"

"I don't know," I say, then shake my head. "I'm just annoyed. Lis-ten: this streaming thing. I started yesterday and I've already climbed one hundred thousand spots in the LiveCast ranking."

"That's cool. Can we put them away for a little while? Your friends?"

"Oh, no. I can't. It's a streamathon."

"Like, all the time?" they ask. "And this is to make money? Do you have to pay taxes on that income?" Lee waves at my laptop, which is perched like a bird and chirping on the kitchen counter. "It's kind of creepy."

"You're being an absolute buzzkill today," I say, and I mean it. Lee can be terribly pragmatic about things. This is useful in the long-term but terribly boring when it comes down to it.

"God, I know. Lunch made me so tired."

"I'm eating habaneros on my stream later."

"No shit. When?"

"Like, five or six o'clock, maybe a bit earlier. I have to figure out where to buy some."

"Come hang after?" they ask.

"I'd have to bring my stream."

"Right, well. Have fun," they say. They start to walk back toward their bedroom, where their office is, then turn back toward me: "Did you need anything?"

"What? Like what?"

"I don't know. You knocked. You usually let yourself in—"

"I was holding my laptop."

"I was just wondering."

"No, I don't need anything."

"Okay." They shrug.

"It smells like food in here. What did you make?" I ask.

"I ordered lunch. I had pho."

"Soup?"

"Yeah."

"Soup with pasta in it?"

"It's not pasta, it's noodles. Rice noodles."

"Do you want to smoke?"

Lee laughs. "That depends. Can we ditch your friends?"

I shrug, meaning no. Lee goes to their room and comes back with a perfectly rolled joint pinched between their slender fingers for me. "Enjoy your playdate. Let me know when it's over."

"Are you sure?"

"Sorry, I have a meeting soon, and I'm not ready for my close-up."

I don't generally like to smoke alone, but it doesn't feel like I'm alone today. I hotbox my apartment and chat with my viewers. I introduced them to Lee as my friends, which isn't true, but it isn't untrue, either. They like me, and I like the company. By midday my viewer count reaches twenty. LiveCast Ranking: 419,548. Some viewers only stay for a minute or two and others have been hanging out since yesterday. The ones who hop in and out don't get to me much, but when one of my OGs leave—cindyrella, karnie_vibes, jackofnotrades1—it feels like sandpaper chafing against my temples.

crabbybob: brb grabbing dinner
crabbybob has signed off

How long does it take to eat dinner—fifteen minutes? Half an hour? When a viewer finally logs back on, I unclench my toes a little.

pklrik: who was that earlier

"That's my neighbor."

redtimepolice: she cute
trutherdare: free weed from ur neighbor? 0.0 lucky
trutherdare: my neighbor farts all day LOL
trutherdare: i can hear it trhoguh the wall

"Lee probably farts all day."

excelsior404: r they ur sister's friend too?
trutherdare: *through

"What? No. I mean, no. Lee doesn't know my sister. They've never met."

burr9ty: is ur sister in nyc too

"Yeah. Down the street. Lots of good hospitals here."

burr9ty: which one

"Bro."

burr9ty: r u going to visit

"That's kind of personal, isn't it?" I chug some more Pepto Bismol. "Maybe. Probably. Whatever. God. My stomach hurts when I eat and it hurts when I don't. It's fucked."

chickenleggy: eat some oatmeal
anomalous_donkey: you should visit her :D

"Oatmeal is for ascetics and people who have given up on joy. You know what's terrible for ulcers? Spicy food."

karnie_vibes: death by habo
excelsior404: u have an ulcer?

"That's my theory. No way to confirm it without going to a doctor, though."

xinfected_botx: im a doctor

"No, you're not."

xinfected_botx: a dermatologist

"That's not a doctor."

jimpix: its a doctor for pimples
xinfected_botx: ffs

"Careful," I say. There's no window I can open to vent out the marijuana smell in my room. Some of it seeps out underneath my front door, but otherwise it's here with me for weeks after I smoke, absorbed into my sheets and clinging to my clothes. I blink underwater, my high cresting gently in the space between my eyebrows. "What do you think the weed smoke does to my plants?"

karnie_vibes: what if u made habanero oatmeal
pklrik: that would be so bad
pklrik: or good with cheese
hot_pat_of_butter: your plants would be like: why are you burning our friends?
pklrik: like grits

"Ew, grits. Who thought that was an appetizing name for food?"

xinfected_botx: omg its hot pat!
xinfected_botx: no f'ing way

chickenleggy: OMG
hot_pat_of_butter: hi everyone
chickenleggy: HI HOT PAT
redtimepolice: hi hot pat my name is rachel
jackofnotrades1: whos a simp now

"What's your deal, hot_pat_of_butter?" I ask.

redtimepolice: hot pat is the shit!!!!
redtimepolice: stfu rohan

I click into this guy's profile, hot_pat_of_butter. He has nearly a million viewers—840,832, to be exact—and his LiveCast ranking is an outrageous 55. Top one hundred. Two shining digits. What is he doing in my stream?

"Some of us were born to be streamers and others were born to be viewers. Hot Pat, I'm glad you've accepted your place in the circle of things."

hot_pat_of_butter: lol happy to be here
chicknleggy: IM DYING
hot_pat_of_butter: you were on my discover page
hot_pat_of_butter: it said you were eating habaneros today in the stream description
chickenleggy: IM DEAD

I look through his profile. This guy has built a whole brand out of eating spicy food. He goes around the world doing challenges: a chili-eating contest in Hunan, China; the spiciest curry in the world in Montclair, New Jersey; a hot jerky competition in Ontario, Canada. The picture on his profile page is a stylized animation of himself—red hair, overlarge white teeth—surrounded by a neon ring of fire. I don't have a profile picture right now. Just a grayed out question mark.

Over eight hundred thousand followers. Which is wild because it means his viewer count is multiples of that. Out of all of the people that come and go in a given day, only a small percentage will actually take the trouble to click "Subscribe" on a streamer's page when they can just as easily bookmark streams or find them in their "Keep Watching" section. What subscribing means is that a streamer can email you directly or add you to their newsletter. Subscribers can also choose to give a monthly donation to a streamer in exchange for bonus content: exclusive streams, early access to merch, invitations to in-person meetups. I go to hot_pat_of_butter's subscription page and see that he has three subscription tiers—free, five dollars a month, and twenty dollars a month—each with their own unique offerings.

If just ten percent of his subscribers are on paid tiers . . . is he making hundreds of thousands of dollars a month on LiveCast just from eating spicy food? Could that be possible?

It is possible. Because subscriptions are just one part of the LiveCast moneymaking ecosystem. Ads, affiliate programs, donations, and more—there's millions of dollars for the taking.

So I'll ask again: What the hell is he doing in my stream?

• • •

My eyes are as red as planets, my lips cracked at the edges. I switch my stream to my phone and press my mouth as close to the camera as I can. "Get in, bitches, we're going shopping." I open my apartment door and the smoke rolls out around my feet. It's time for mademoiselle_dell and her posse to hit the road.

Walking to the grocery store with my phone in my hand is tricky. I try holding it directly in front of me so I can narrate my walk, but that's difficult in the city. A gang bang of noise and smells and activity. People walk into you, or you walk into them. So I hold my phone down at waist level and point it up at myself to create a spectacular double chin, and that works better.

The Latino supermarket isn't the closest supermarket to me, but it's the cheapest, and one of the most likely to have habaneros in stock. Plus, they sell Jarritos soda, and I love that shit.

chillnessa: btw if u dont want to eat a habanero today u dont have to

"I don't do anything I don't want to do," I say, although of course that's not true at all. When I was a senior in high school and Daisy was a sophomore, she and her idiot friends pulled the dumbest prank of all time. Somehow, they got ahold of the nail gun from shop class and used it to pin a bunch of lockers shut. I have to admit, it was funny for a second. No one could open their locker, and they couldn't figure out why. But then some kid needed his inhaler and it wasn't funny anymore. I knew it wasn't Daisy's idea. She had this one friend, this mean girl, that would come up with these half-wit ideas, and one of the lockers in question belonged to her ex-boyfriend. Still, I knew the nail gun was in Daisy's locker. So I got it out and pretended it was mine, pretended I had done it. I was already the queen of detention, and I was months away from graduation anyway. Daisy—everyone knew she could do no wrong. It was kind of annoying, how quickly the school administration and our mom accepted that I was the one who nailed the lockers shut. I got two weeks of suspension, and Daisy did my laundry for two whole months.

excelsior404: hows ur sister doing
anomalous_donkey: ^^^

I glance at my viewer list. Twenty-two now, including hot_pat_of_ butter. I'm hoping to have thirty viewers by the time I eat the habaneros. If I can get between one dollar and ten dollars from each of them, I can make a hundred dollars or more today and break 400,000 in the rankings.

"Fourteen thousand dollars to give Daisy another week, and we're not going to get there playing on easy mode," I say. "I have an idea: whoever donates the most today gets to pick what we do tomorrow."

pklrik: okay
pklrik: like truth or dare
jackofnotrades1: thats hot

"Nothing like that."

excelsior404: anything?

"No, not fucking anything. I'm not going to drink bleach."

anomalous_donkey: visit ur sister in the hospital

"Enough, okay. You actually want me to do that?" I say, and then: "You know what? I actually would drink bleach. I would. But it would have to be very little and it would have to be mixed with something, like orange juice. I could do it like a shot."

excelsior404: what would you do tomorrow for $50
excelsior404: if that was my highest donation today

"I would give you my social security number."

excelsior404: lol

"It can happen in an instant with these things. People wake up out of nowhere. Sometimes they're out for years and then they just open their eyes. Daisy's hand moved like crazy the last time I visited her."

jackdaw2000: thats scary

"No, it wasn't scary. It was the opposite of scary." Walking down the street, I make accidental eye contact with a man walking his teacup poodle who thinks I'm talking to him. "Daisy's doctor, his name is Dr. Dole. Isn't that hilarious? Like the pineapples?"

jackdaw2000: idgi

"Like the canned pineapple brand?"

chillnessa: no lo sé

"You'll just have to take my word for it then, about it being hilarious."

excelsior404: why is Daisy in a coma
excelsior404: what happened

I enter the store and make my way to the produce aisle. There beside the overripe, sun-bruised mangoes and waxy jicama are the habaneros. Ugly red chodes, wrinkly and pumpkin-looking. It's a shame to pay for something so small when I could easily stick it in my pocket. Plus, they're pricey: twenty dollars a pound. But I'm still a bit shaken from Whole Foods yesterday, so I put five in my basket.

excelsior404: ???

"She overdosed," I say. "She overdosed and didn't wake up." I don't like the produce aisle. All these fruits and vegetables, it creeps me out, reminds me of my plants back home. Something about vegetation, the fertile, over-green life. Heart-shaped apples conspiring in their crates, touched and touching each teeming hand. Slimy okra shivering and damp in its bin. Hairy-green carrots and oily bell peppers. It's like a morgue, or a nursery. "She overdosed and didn't wake up and I called her an ambulance and that's the story."

> **anomalous_donkey:** :O
> **anomalous_donkey:** damn
> **jackofnotrades1:** its good that u were there
> **cindyrella:** OMG ya :(((

"It doesn't matter."

> **crabbybob:** no seriously
> **crabbybob:** you probably saved her life

"Brain-dead people are called vegetables. Why is that? I guess cauliflowers kind of look like brains." I grimace and head to the snack aisle, where I belong.

> **jackofnotrades1:** hot peppers are actually fruits
> **crabbybob:** get bread and milk too

"You're going to squeeze me dry, crabbybob."

> **crabbybob:** its for the habaneros
> **crabbybob:** it helps with the spice
> **hot_pat_of_butter:** thats true
> **redtimepolice:** ily hot pat

"You say that like you're going to pay for my groceries. I need to get a lot of other crap, too, you know."

> **excelsior404** has donated $5
> **chillnessa** has donated $2

"That'll cover the bread and the milk. The habaneros are going to be more than that. Does someone want to buy me a soda?" I point the camera toward the Jarritos: mandarin, fruit punch, tamarind, lime, grapefruit, guava, pineapple, strawberry. Glass bottles lined up in a rainbow. "Which one should I get?"

> **chillnessa:** tamarind

"I've never had that one. Is it your treat?"

> **jackdaw2000:** what is a tamarind

"A fruit. Or a bean. Some kind of spice."

> **chillnessa:** jajajajaja

I pick up a tamarind soda ($1.99) and put it in my basket. I grab the cheapest container of instant coffee I can find ($6.28), two bottles of Pepto Bismol ($13.20), a loaf of bread ($2.88), and a half-gallon of milk ($3.27) that won't fit in my mini fridge. Including the habaneros, the total is around $37. That's more than what I made yesterday. But it's like when I buy my plant seedlings: I have to think about it as an investment.

I ask the cashier to smile for my fans and he gives a small, confused nod, head centered between the twin sentries of cigarettes and lotto tickets behind him. On the way out, I wink at the security cameras. God, how great would it be to get stopped this once, when I have an actual receipt on me.

• • •

> **(!) You have a new private message**
> **excelsior404:** hey
> **excelsior404:** is this a better time
> **excelsior404:** are you excited to eat the habaneros
> **mademoiselle_dell:** ya
> **excelsior404:** so cool that hot pat was in your channel

excelsior404: ive been watching his videos forever

excelsior404: i got really into him in like 2018

excelsior404: and i dont think he went super mainstream until 2021

excelsior404: anyway lol i wanted to ask you again

excelsior404: what would you do for $50 if i donated today

mademoiselle_dell: donate and find out

excelsior404: lol i want to know if its worth my while

mademoiselle_dell: what do u want

excelsior404: i dont want to say

excelsior404: hello?

excelsior404: i can see you on your stream

excelsior404: hello?

mademoiselle_dell: jesus fucking christ

mademoiselle_dell: relax

mademoiselle_dell: im walking home

excelsior404: i know youre bad at multitasking lol but i can see you on the screen

excelsior404: so i can tell when youre not answering me on purpose

mademoiselle_dell: bro

excelsior404: ive donated more than everyone else

excelsior404: just saying

excelsior404: you can be nicer to me lol :)

mademoiselle_dell: broooooo

excelsior404: how about an in-person meet up for $50

mademoiselle_dell: no

excelsior404: why not?

mademoiselle_dell: i dont want to meet up with u

mademoiselle_dell: do i really need to explain that

excelsior404: what like im a serial killer or something

excelsior404: thats a weird assumption and also rude

mademoiselle_dell: if u were a serial killer then at least u would be interesting

mademoiselle_dell: as it is im bored

mademoiselle_dell: also u only donated $25 so chill

excelsior404: ok lol wtf

mademoiselle_dell: if u dont like me then unfollow me

mademoiselle_dell: if u keep bothering me ill block u

excelsior404: i do like you

excelsior404: i wont keep bothering you

mademoiselle_dell: cool

excelsior404: i like the mean performance

excelsior404: but i know youre not mean
excelsior404: i just want to talk to you
excelsior404: dell?
excelsior404: can you answer for a second
mademoiselle_dell: what
excelsior404: i already told you i know everything
excelsior404: when I look you up everything is there
mademoiselle_dell: oh ya this again
mademoiselle_dell: whats ur point
excelsior404: when i look up daisy's name everything is there too
excelsior404: her social media accounts
excelsior404: news articles
excelsior404: its all right there
mademoiselle_dell: whats ur point
excelsior404: you know my point
mademoiselle_dell: i truly do not
excelsior404: -_____-
excelsior404: ok youre playing dumb
excelsior404: fine
excelsior404: just dont leave me hanging when i message you
excelsior404: thats all im asking

I try to keep my face blank. Excelsior404 is watching me right now. But so are more than thirty other people. I have to keep it together. I can look annoyed but not scared. I close my private messages and click into his LiveCast profile as I walk home. This fucking guy. No streams. No followers. No identifying information. I've got nothing on him.

Okay, it was a rookie mistake to post a link to my plant listings in my stream, but I barely had any viewers at the time. I could count them all on one hand. But excelsior404, he must have looked up my last name, looked up Daisy. There's things on the internet about us. A photo of our high school soccer team, me in the third row, second from the left, her directly in front of me, smiling with all her teeth. Daisy's byline in the school paper for an exposé on cafeteria food waste. On the second page of my search results: a winner interview from her middle school science fair. She demonstrated how clams can be used to detect water pollution because they close their shells when they encounter metals, pesticides, and other pollutants. She mentioned me in her interview, said I inspired her with my picky eating. I wouldn't eat clams. I called them stinky sea bugs. So, of course, she went down an internet search hole to exculpate them, and won a damn prize for it.

I should never have brought Daisy into this. Now excelsior404 is trying to, what—annoy me into giving him special treatment? Go on some quasi date with him? I could block him from my stream. That's what I should do. But he's also the one who gave me five dollars at the grocery store and twenty dollars yesterday. That's over half of my total earnings. I wait for another ding, another private message, but it doesn't come. My stomach is suddenly bloated and stinging, painful to the touch.

I know what my mom would say, if I were talking to her. She would tell me to take out a restraining order. Toss my laptop out the window while I'm at it, and my phone, too. Forget my Juice Body paycheck, forget my rent and bills, forget all of it. She would tell me to move back home with her, where she can oppress me with her own brand of attention. I'm reminded of a bindweed plant: alluring heart-shaped leaves that climb and smother and suffocate. Their taproot is so deep that you have to dig fourteen feet down into the earth just to get them out.

This is all so bizarre to begin with, this whole situation, and now I'm walking home with five fucking habaneros in my bag like a low-stakes drug mule, some creep watching me from my own handheld device.

I take the glass bottle of soda out of my bag and pop the top off on someone's concrete stoop. I drink it in the time it takes me to walk two blocks, then put the empty bottle down on someone else's concrete stoop. Tamarind. Whatever it is, it's not bad.

"Why are you here, huh?" I ask my viewers. "I know why I'm here. You know why I'm here. But why are you all here? I'd love to know."

karnie_vibes: to watch u eat habos!!

"But I'm not eating one yet. And you've been in my stream for hours today. Do you not have a life? And don't take that as an insult, because clearly I don't, either, I'm just curious."

> **karnie_vibes:** i like having a stream open while I work
> **racre001:** i just joined idk
> **cindyrella:** same karnie :))))

"Okay, got it. Got it. So you all have jobs and you have my stream open on another monitor? Like, I'm your not-so-chatty deskmate?"

> **cindyrella:** yeah i wfh and i like it
> **anomalous_donkey:** i like streams
> **anomalous_donkey:** it's like watching TV except it answers me

"Aren't you, like, twelve years old?"

> **cindyrella:** you're thinking of pklrik
> **pklrik:** i'm 15 -____-
> **pklrik:** i live in NM
> **redtimepolice:** o cool im 19
> **pklrik:** are you a senior in hs or older
> **redtimepolice:** older
> **redtimepolice:** i go to umass

"And Karnie Vibes is from Vancouver. I don't care. I'm going to eat some spicy shit, and I want you to look away from your work monitors and your geometry homework and give me your full, undivided, cult member attention."

> **jackdaw2000:** aye aye captain

"I said cult member, not ship crew. Don't mix my metaphors."

> **excelsior404:** yes queen

I wince. I hate that excelsior404 is here. I imagine him in one of those black-and-red gamer chairs, sitting in a dark room with his hands down his pants and his eyes on my stream. The type of guy that doesn't understand why women keep "friend-zoning" him. The type of guy who calls women "females" in a way that sounds like a slur. But there are over thirty other people in here for me to focus on. Thirty-eight, thirty-nine. I see them all as radiant, pulsing dollar bills. I walk up the five stories to my apartment and switch my stream to my computer. Then I dump the contents of my bag out onto the floor. The habaneros roll under the bed, toward the walls, and I gather them into my palms like volcanic bird's eggs, proffered to a hungry audience.

hot_pat_of_butter has signed off

My eyesight splinters. The words grow edges, press their fingers into my open sores. I hate when any of my viewers leave, but hot_pat_of_butter—he's the one who could actually change things for me. He's more than just a random name in my chat. In fact, he's more real than anyone else here, even me—he has the viewers and subscribers to prove it—and he chose to spend time in my stream for a little while. That meant something. And now that he's gone, my fingers and toes feel numb and tingly, deprived of oxygen.

Maybe he has to do his own stream or something. That's a good enough reason to leave. It's critical to stream at the same time every day. That's how you develop a consistent and loyal viewer base and maintain your ranking. I click into hot_pat_of_butter's profile and his last stream was yesterday evening, a couple hours later in the day. He rated and reviewed an array of limited edition hot Cheetos, a gift from Frito-Lay themselves. The flavors were Carolina Reaper, Tangy Chili Fusion, Nashville Hot, Xxtra Flamin' Hot, and Smoky Ghost Pepper. He ate the Cheetos with chopsticks, which is geeky as fuck. Just get your fingers dirty, get in there. He rated each bag of chips on a scale of one to a hundred, with ten different categories comprising ten points each. Seriously nerdy shit.

So, even if he's not streaming now, he could be preparing for a stream. Or he could have plans, out in the real world. Should I wait for him before eating the habaneros?

I click out of his stream and refocus on my face, my chat, my viewers. Forty-five of them now. My goal was forty. My goal was to break 400,000 and here I am at 394,293. And I got there all by myself, with the support of word-of-mouth from my viewers. I don't need hot_pat_of_butter. Mademoiselle_dell doesn't simp for anyone.

I change my stream name to "BURN AFTER EATING: HABANERO TASTE TEST." The more viewers I have, and the more they like me, the more I feel like I'm doing something good and important with my one untenable life.

"It's day two of this bullshit so we're upping the ante: a dollar a pepper from each of you. Nonnegotiable. And if I manage to eat all five habaneros, a five dollar tip. Does that sound fair? I think that sounds fair."

jackdaw2000: what if i already donated today

"Did I stutter? Did I mumble? Would you like me to repeat myself in song?"

trutherdare: LOL
trutherdare: mademoiselle_dell the musical
racre001: i would watch that
jackdaw2000: i didnt btw but i was just asking

"See that little 'Exit' button in the corner of your screen? If you're staying in my dungeon, you play by my rules, and my rules are one dollar a pepper. I'm not afraid of the 'Block' button. In fact, I love it. But I'm a merciful god at the end of the day. So just do your best."

barbistani: can u eat them with ur shirt off

"No."

barbistani has signed off
crabbybob: lol moving on

I pick up the smallest habanero and hold it up to the camera. This is a whole different game than jalapeños. We're not talking checkers versus chess, we're talking tic-tac-toe versus the Super Bowl. The plan is to eat the pepper quickly, everything except the stem. Chew as little as possible before I swallow it down with milk like a bulbous pill. The sooner I start the sooner it'll be over with. I take a deep breath as if I'm about to jump off a diving board, then take a bite of the pepper, getting to work. Hot liquid fills my mouth instantly, and I can't tell whether it's my own saliva or the pepper's juices or both. It's painful but not impossible, a wasp sting on my tongue that steadies me. But when I try to swallow, the heat inflames my throat and makes it close up. I cough like a motherfucker and reach for the milk, drinking straight out of the jug, willing my throat to work like it's supposed to. Finally, I get the first pepper down and I'm able to stop coughing.

chillnessa: estás bien?
l-nino9 has signed on

"Lee?"

l-nino9: hey dell
karnie_vibes: I can't watch lol
l-nino9: hey everyone
crabbybob: nod if ur okay

"I'm fucking dying," I say, giving two thumbs-up to the camera. It's hard to form words. A ball of fire has taken up residence behind my tonsils and my breath is overwarm. My skin is clammy and goose-pimpled, my stomach buckling strangely. This plant wants to destroy me. Even my teeth hurt. I eat a piece of bread and then another one. Lee shouldn't be here. I did tell them about my stream, but seeing their screen name pop up like this—it's unsettling. A slippage between worlds, a minor difference in gravity. I don't want them to see me like this, so unbound.

> **crabbybob:** r u the neighbor
> **l-nino9:** yeah
> **excelsior404:** hi Lee

I don't want them talking to Lee. I don't want them talking at all. Lee doesn't know about Daisy, and I want to keep it that way.

> **crabbybob:** sheeeesh

"Hey, turds. Pay attention to me."

I say the words and they come out right, but I'm elsewhere, willing my face to fade from a disastrous red back to its normal pallor. Willing my eyes to stay open and my nose to stop dripping. The pain in my mouth has evened out but isn't subsiding, and the seed in my ear is lit up like a struck match. The jalapeños were pleasant enough—condiment-level spice factor—but this is something else entirely, the mother spice, and I need to try not to panic. For a moment, the briefest moment, I consider signing off and ending my stream. I could pretend to have technical difficulties, call it a day, curl up in bed in the fetal position.

But my ranking is rising by the second as my chat blows up, and then hot_pat_of_butter signs back on and a smack of adrenaline lands me squarely back in my body.

＊　＊　＊

I bring my mouth up close to the camera and exhale, fogging up the lens. "You smell that? Pure heat, baby." I put the second habanero in my mouth and chew rapidly. The burn doesn't increase exponentially, but the sensation changes. It's no longer just heat in my mouth and throat but chills down my entire body, and a newfound lightheadedness. My guts start to shiver, begging me to stop. I take a glug of milk and swish it around my mouth with my head down, breathing out of my dripping nostrils.

"This is nothing like eating a jalapeño. My organs are throbbing."

hot_pat_of_butter: you're doing great!

"Shut up."

hot_pat_of_butter: capsaicin can do different things
hot_pat_of_butter: different peppers have different delivery methods
hot_pat_of_butter: like some weed can be a head high or a body high etc
hot_pat_of_butter: its the same with peppers

"Someone tell him to shut up."

crabbybob: oooo shots fired
chickenleggy: HI HOT PAT
hot_pat_of_butter: lol xD

Habanero number three. There is no numbness to the fire. It feels like pepper number one all over again. I wad a slice of bread into a ball and fist it into my mouth to let it soak up my saliva. Two more habaneros to go. It's been less than five minutes, which feels long and short at the same time. I blow my nose into the hem of my shirt and put pepper number four in my mouth, but I can't bring myself to chew. My body simply won't do it. I spit the pepper out and look at it, sucking in air between my gritted teeth to cool myself down. My eyes water and leak. I have to do it. I have to finish this. I put number four back in my mouth and stare directly into the camera. I close my eyes and chew. It's too much. I need to spit it out again. Instead, I grab the milk and forcibly swallow the overlarge chunks.

Chew. Swallow. Chew. Swallow. It's a prayer, this repetition.

My gut is an exploding star, a rippling howl. I'm more than a little afraid of the damage I'm doing to myself. One more. I'm almost done. Then I can crawl off and die in peace. I rip the fifth habanero into chunks and its chemical heat makes the tips of my fingers throb. I swallow each piece one by one with milk—no chewing at all. My mouth is sizzling and my throat is raw and tender. I try to talk but there's too much saliva in my mouth. I lean forward and spit it into my half-full cup of milk.

pklrik: eww
l-nino9: wtf dell
cindyrella has donated $5
jackdaw2000 has donated $5

"Hey, dickholes. We said one dollar a pepper and then another five dollars if I ate all five. That's ten dollars if you can't do the math yourself."

jackdaw2000: $5 is all i have :(

"That's not my problem."

karnie_vibes has donated $10

"Remember: the person who donates the most gets to pick what I do tomorrow."

jackofnotrades1 has donated $10
crabbybob has donated $11

"See that 'Donate' button in the corner of the page? I want you to visualize yourself clicking on it and giving me all your money. Really picture it like it's real, like it's happening. We're manifesting."

I-nino9: lolol
I-nino9: eyeroll

"Am I boring you, dear?"

I-nino9: I dont think anyone can call you boring
I-nino9: annoying yes but never boring

"Careful. I'll sic my hellhounds on you."

I-nino9 has donated $20

My LiveCast balance grows and grows by the second. I reached a peak of forty-seven viewers while streaming, including hot_pat_of_ butter, and a little less than half of them have donated—most actually gave the full requested amount. One hundred dollars, one ten, one twenty . . . the number climbs and stabilizes at $164.

excelsior404 has donated $50

Luckily my face is already red, or my viewers would see it light up like an alarm when excelsior404's name appears on my screen again. I had nearly forgotten he was here.

"Lords and ladylords, that's our highest donation so far, and as you may remember, the highest donor gets to choose what I do tomorrow. Anyone else want to step up to the bat?"

hot_pat_of_butter has donated $60
jackofnotrades1: hot pat is a god

Instantaneous relief. And not just that, but pride.

"Thanks, Hot Pat. Thanks, everyone. I appreciate you. Even though you made me do this today, I do appreciate you. Except cindyrella, because habaneros were her fucked-up idea in the first place, and I'm going to hold that grudge for the rest of my goddamn life, probably even past the grave, so prepare to be haunted, cindyrella. All of your contributions go a long way to help us reach our goal of fourteen thousand dollars to put my little sister on private life support."

> **excelsior404** has donated $75
> **jimpix:** WOAH
> **anomalous_donkey:** :O
> **hot_pat_of_butter** has donated $100
> **karnie_vibes:** bidding war!!
> **MSRN273:** fight fight fight
> **excelsior404** has donated $200

I make an involuntary gasp, a thin and croaking sound. And then: "Thanks."

> **anomalous_donkey:** baller
> **hot_pat_of_butter:** lol its all you
> **excelsior404:** so I get to pick what you do tomorrow

"Right, yeah. Yes. Does anyone have ideas for our generous boy?"

> **karnie_vibes:** 10 habaneros lol

"Don't even start, Karnie Vibes. I swear to god I will haunt you, too."

> **hot_pat_of_butter:** or something spicier
> **hot_pat_of_butter:** carolina reapers are the spiciest
> **hot_pat_of_butter:** the world record competition is later this week in nyc actually

xinfected_botx: are you entering
hot_pat_of_butter: no i prefer to watch and cheer on the contestants
xinfected_botx: mademoiselle_dell are you entering

"God, no. I have zero interest in doing that."

hot_pat_of_butter: how do you know if you've never tried
chillnessa: jajaja

"I've never tried to do a handstand, either, but I know I won't like it. Being upside down on purpose is a very weird human impulse."

excelsior404: tomorrow
trutherdare: 0.0
excelsior404: i'll give u $500 if u stick a habanero up your vag
excelsior404 has signed off

•   •   •

The pressure on my sphincter is unmanageable. I hobble-sprint out of my apartment and nearly knock down Lee's door trying to let myself in, it takes me so long to work the keys. Lee is in the kitchen making dinner. They start to say something, but I hold up my hand. I lock myself in their bathroom, take off my pants, and reach the toilet just in time. The most urgent shit of my life. Relentless and stinging. I close my eyes and open them again, refocusing on the lime-green U-shaped bath mat around the toilet. Why does Lee have that? It's such a elderly thing to have.

My stream is still on at my place, camera facing nothing, audio picking up nothing. I know this is going to tank my ranking. But I need a minute to process what the hell just went down.

Lee knocks on the door. "Are you alright?"

I answer with a courtesy flush. My stomach is digesting me from the inside out. I'm cold and shaky but not defeated. The adrenaline rush I feel is akin to a drug high, trippy and loud. My body is vibrating to a different frequency, and I know that by eating five raw habanero peppers I've done something that most people in the world can't or won't do. There's a satisfaction in that. And when the mass exodus from my gut slows down, I transfer my stream to my phone and check my LiveCast balance: $649. Ranking: 350,322.

> **kirk_equivalent:** that's nasty
> **racre001:** youre nasty
> **kirk_equivalent:** its also hot though
> **chickenleggy:** not as hot as HOT PAT!!!

Is that correct? I made $34 yesterday, and my viewers gave me another $7 at the supermarket today. That's $41. That would mean I made over $600 dollars in the last half hour.

Eating hot peppers. With excelsior404's $325 and $160 from hot_pat_of_butter, the math works out, but I don't believe it. Nearly $500 from those two idiots and a hundred bucks from everyone else. My daily pay after an eight-hour shift at Juice Body was $136 before tax. I've never made this much in a day. And for less than an hour of "work," it's astounding. My LiveCast balance is way more than the paycheck Nik is stiffing me on—though I do still want to get my hands on that.

It's not the money, it's the principle of the matter. And the money.

"I'm okay," I yell out to Lee, and from their response I can tell that they're still standing right outside the door. It's nice but also uncomfortable, and I wish they would go about their business as usual.

If I keep going at this rate, I can easily make rent. Daisy's hospital bills, not so much, but I made substantially more today than I made yesterday. And as long as my viewer count keeps growing, there's no reason to assume that pattern won't continue.

And if excelsior404 is serious about tomorrow . . . Well, he may be a creep, but five hundred dollars is no joke. It's not the kind of money

I know how to say no to, and I know that kind of show will do wonders for my ranking. I'm not afraid of inserting something in myself, per se. Doing it online is what worries me. LiveCast doesn't record my stream, but what if someone else does? What if they upload me to a porn site, or just plain old YouTube? What if the clip goes viral?

The thought of my mom watching me spread my legs on camera and insert a foreign object into myself makes me cackle. I get off the toilet and gaze into the bowl before flushing, looking for a tiny sliver, a small seed. Nothing. It's probably still in my ear, then. Or lodged in my brain. Already sprouting.

I flush and wash my face in the sink. I'm dehydrated, exhausted. I should answer my mom, but contact begets more contact with her, and it's not the type of contact I can deal with right now. I read through our older messages, which look a lot like our recent ones:

> Please come to the hospital with me. Your sister wants to see you
>
> Don't ignore me, Dell
>
> Be a good sister

I grab Tums from Lee's medicine cabinet and chew them six at a time.

Lee is busy at the stovetop with their back to me, all skin and stretch. They don't want to be on my stream but that's not really an option right now. I do, however, put my phone in my back pocket so my viewers can't see them. I watch them cook, chopping and dicing and grabbing things from the pantry. I watch their shoulders, smooth as pebbles, dance between the straps of their tank top, the smallest strip of lower back visible. They have a great body. I mean, they should, given how much they pay to go to the Equinox down the street. Last I checked it was close to three hundred dollars a month to access those hallowed halls, everyone gleaming and coated in Kiehl's. I walk up to them, tug on their earlobes. They smack my arm. I catch their fist in my hand and bite their knuckles.

"Animal." They laugh. "Did you destroy my bathroom?"

"You shouldn't let me come and go like this," I say, and I mean it. Sometimes—often—I feel like I'm taking advantage of Lee's hospitality, their openness. But I never feel bad enough to actually give them their key back. Besides, they like having me here. They've said so on multiple occasions. They grew up in a big, loud house and the living-alone thing can be a bit creepy and lonely, even in a big city.

"Why did that guy give you two hundred dollars? Jesus Christ," they ask.

"He has a crush on me. Or he wants to kill me. I haven't figured that out yet," I say. Excelsior404 left my stream after dropping his bombshell, so I can speak semi-freely.

"Are you going to do it?"

"What?" I hop up and sit on the counter. They hand me a wooden spoon to stir some kind of curry as they get provisions: cilantro, lime, yogurt. "Oh, you mean fuck myself with a pepper?"

They snort and reach past me to turn the stove off.

"Five hundred dollars," I say. "It's more than what Nik owes me, though I would still kill to actually get my paycheck."

"You're not going to do it, though, right?"

"Kill him?" I laugh.

"You could just try being nice," they say. "Just send him an apology and don't make excuses and ask politely for your paycheck. You could try it. The adult route."

"Why did you join my stream?"

It should have made me happy to have them there, but it's dangerous. All it would take is one mention of Daisy . . .

"You said you were eating habaneros. I wanted to watch."

"How did you even find my account?"

"It's the internet. I just looked up your name and peppers and Live-Cast," they say. "You're not going to do it, though, are you? That can't be healthy."

"Are you sure it isn't very, very healthy? Like a warming vaginal detox? Like a yoni egg?"

"Pitch it to Goop, I dare you."

"Did I tell you I have a seed stuck in my ear?" I say. They come over and look, shine their phone flashlight in my left ear and lean in so close their breath warms my temples. They can't find it. That doesn't mean it's not there.

Lee serves us bowls of curry. I'm not in the mood to eat with my stomach being such a mess and my mouth aching, but the curry is delicious, and the more I eat, the hungrier I get. Beef and waxy potatoes in a savory peanut sauce, fragrant and mild. Lee sits on the stool beside me, hunched over their own bowl, the knobs of their spine articulating elegantly against their T-shirt, and I want to reach out and run my hand along the ridges.

"You're good at it, you know," they say. "Streaming. You're funny."

"Why is your place always so clean?" I ask.

"Because I clean it," they say. "It would take you two seconds, you know. To clean your place."

"Two seconds is a big time commitment for me," I say. "And I have too many plants. I'd have to move them out of the way if I wanted to vacuum or something."

"You're a commitment-phobe."

"You think?" I ask.

"Maybe," they say. "I don't think I can watch you do that tomorrow."

"Yeah. I don't think you should."

"Or maybe I need to be there, so I can call you an ambulance if you need one."

"Don't worry," I say. "Everything's going to be okay."

"I shouldn't be worried about you?" they ask.

"No more than usual."

"I worry about you a lot," they say.

"Okay." I roll my eyes. "Chill. I've seen your medicine cabinet. I have a feeling your worries are all being pharmaceutically addressed." I get up to raid their fridge for dessert, but they shoo me away.

"You're an animal and a commitment-phobe and a thief," they say.

"And yet . . ." I wink, and let myself out.

Hey, Nik, I don't like how our conversation ended. I wanted to reach out and politely apologize

Like an adult

You've done a lot for me and I recognize that

Nik? Are you there?

I can come into the shop again and talk to you in person

I'll apologize to your cousin Johnny, too

You don't have to give me the silent treatment

I'm not asking you to give me another chance or anything

I just need my last paycheck. My rent and bills are due in a few days

You're just going to screen my texts?

I know you're on your phone all the time watching porn or whatever in the back office so I know you're getting my texts

I hope you develop a late-in-life soy allergy

And your favorite show is canceled

And your wife divorces you AGAIN

You fucking fuck!!!!

• • •

I peel off my sweaty clothes and toss them in my overfull laundry basket. Four dollars per washer, two dollars per dryer, lugging everything down and back up five flights of stairs. Making and unmaking a loft bed is also a nightmare. But I'm not dealing with that today. Or tomorrow. I'll never be as tidy as Lee, or as put together. I've accepted that. There's nothing to be done about it.

Now that my body—skin, mouth, stomach, lungs, throat—has mostly recovered from the habaneros, there are my plants to contend with. Slither and grow. Slither and grow. I have a handful left in my apartment. Seven big ladies plus twenty baby succulents. I log on to my listings page and discount them all by another couple bucks. I need to focus on moving this inventory before it moves me. Some of these vines are as thick as my wrist and I swear they're encroaching into more and more of my space every day. I keep forgetting to water these turds and yet they insist on growing. It must be something about the heat, the jungle humidity of my place in the summertime.

There's one plant in particular that scares me. It's so attractive: cute and pink and furry, its leaves contracting inward when I touch them. Mimosa pudica. Also known as the shame plant. According to the internet, it's a creeping plant known for its rapid movements. I like to stroke the small leaves and watch them contort. The seed in my brain throbs when I get close to it. The seed wants me to press my head into the soil, bury it like a bulb, suffocate. The salt of my tears and the sugar of my saliva nurturing the loam.

The seed wants out. I want it out, too. At least that we can agree on. It just has to grow a little more and come to term and then I'll be able to give it a good yank.

"Is anyone on here a doctor?" I ask my viewers. "Other than Infected Bot. Dermatologists don't count."

xinfected_botx: ffs

An even thirty viewers in my stream. About a third have dropped off since my pepper challenge of the day, which makes sense. But every time that number goes down, every time my ranking drops, I feel a twinge down my spine, something disagreeable and rotten. My favorites are still here, though: crabbybob, karnie_vibes, and even jackofno-trades1, though he's one perverted comment away from getting blocked.

> **chickenleggy:** I AM
> **chickenleggy:** borat NOT
> **pklrik:** my dad is
> **jimpix:** thats funny
> **jimpix:** about chickenleggy not ur dad
> **jimpix:** my wife is a doctor

"What kind of doctor are we talking?"

> **jimpix:** she's an orthotist

"Sounds fake."

> **kirk_equivalent:** yea sounds fake
> **pklrik:** my dad has a phd

I switch my stream to my phone as I head outside again. The sun has set and the city is recovering from rush hour, vibrating like a self-soothing cat.

"Jimpix, does an orthotist deal with people who have things stuck in their ears?"

> **jimpix:** like what
> **jimpix:** also no

"I swear I have a seed in there. Maybe a jalapeño seed or something."

> **racre001:** i heard of a guy who had an apple seed in his lungs and it sprouted

jackdaw2000: no way
racre001: yes way
jackdaw2000: no way
racre001: yes way

I return to the Latino supermarket. I wonder what the cashier will think of me, buying five habaneros and then another one. I wonder what he would think of me if I told him what I was going to do with this particular habanero, if I told him about excelsior404's indecent proposal. The basket of peppers in the produce aisle is as full as I left it earlier. It looks like no other shoppers today have such a refined palate.

My phone rings. My mom's name jumps out at me from the screen, covering up my stream chat. I don't want to talk to her, don't want to listen to what she has to say. But I know what happens next with these things. When I don't answer her for this long, she shows up at my place unannounced. And I don't want that to happen when I have my viewers in tow.

I reject her call and send a text: Sorry, grocery shopping. Everything ok? Call me.

Can we text? I'm tired.

Ok, she responds. Let's make plans soon?

Okay, I send.

Lunch? Tomorrow?

I'm working tomorrow.

What are your hours? she asks.

I take my viewers to the produce aisle and look for the smallest habanero I can find. I finally dig one out that's only about the size of a big toe. I rub its whorled skin against the inside of my wrist, my lips. It feels bumpy and clean. I tuck it into my pocket and leave without paying.

(!) You have a new private message
hot_pat_of_butter: so are you really going to do that dare tomorrow lol

mademoiselle_dell: hey

mademoiselle_dell: i just bought another habanero so ya i guess

hot_pat_of_butter: god

hot_pat_of_butter: thats hardcore

hot_pat_of_butter: some viewers are nuts

mademoiselle_dell: ya i think this one is

mademoiselle_dell: but he donates a lot

hot_pat_of_butter: yeah i tried to outbid him but damn

hot_pat_of_butter: be careful

mademoiselle_dell: thanks for that btw

mademoiselle_dell: i think it'll be easier than eating 5 habaneros tbh

hot_pat_of_butter: you did great

hot_pat_of_butter: also i just mean be careful in general

mademoiselle_dell: lol idk if i did great but thank u

hot_pat_of_butter: why not?

mademoiselle_dell: i was in the 8th circle of hell while i was eating and the 9th circle of hell on the toilet afterward

hot_pat_of_butter: its not about the suffering

hot_pat_of_butter: its about the mental

hot_pat_of_butter: the people who stay in the game get good at the mental

hot_pat_of_butter: theres enjoyment in that too

hot_pat_of_butter: were you proud of yourself after?

mademoiselle_dell: ya

mademoiselle_dell: the money helps lol

hot_pat_of_butter: you get addicted to the adrenaline over time

mademoiselle_dell: is that why u do it?

hot_pat_of_butter: yeah i love it

hot_pat_of_butter: i think its a fascinating and underrated world

mademoiselle_dell: thats cool

mademoiselle_dell: thanks for joining my stream today

mademoiselle_dell: though i think my viewers like u more than they like me

hot_pat_of_butter: nah, they're there for you

hot_pat_of_butter: btw if you are interested in watching or participating in the world record competition

hot_pat_of_butter: the grand prize is $20,000

mademoiselle_dell: wtf why so much money

mademoiselle_dell: idts lol

mademoiselle_dell: i dont have a death wish

hot_pat_of_butter: lol go watch at least. ill be there

hot_pat_of_butter: its an awesome event

mademoiselle_dell: maybe

hot_pat_of_butter: i think your stream is cool

hot_pat_of_butter: good luck with raising money for your sister

hot_pat_of_butter: with these kinds of things you really want to be driving the call to action home every time a new viewer joins. at least every 20-30 minutes if not more often

hot_pat_of_butter: talk about your sister, tell stories, all of it - its part of the pathos

mademoiselle_dell: thanks for the unsolicited advice

hot_pat_of_butter: sorry i cant help it

hot_pat_of_butter: ive been doing this for years

hot_pat_of_butter: let me know if you ever want to talk shop or collab

mademoiselle_dell: how would we collab?

hot_pat_of_butter: you're in nyc too right?

mademoiselle_dell: ya

hot_pat_of_butter: there are spicy food challenges i havent done here yet

hot_pat_of_butter: my viewers have been telling me to go eat the exxxtra hot fried chicken at Peaches Hothouse and something called a napalm burger in Hell's Kitchen

mademoiselle_dell: i live in hells kitchen

hot_pat_of_butter: lets do that then

hot_pat_of_butter: collab videos with other channels are fun

hot_pat_of_butter: great exposure

mademoiselle_dell: for me not u

hot_pat_of_butter: lol nah

hot_pat_of_butter: im happy to support a good cause

hot_pat_of_butter: and its a nice break from hearing the sound of my own voice all day

mademoiselle_dell: okay im in

Any buoyancy I'm feeling about my conversation with hot_pat_of_ butter is brought down to earth by a sudden and vertiginous change in weather. There's a temperature shift before my mom calls, like the drop of air pressure before a tornado. My phone rings and her name crashes onto my screen, loud as a curse word. I excuse myself from my stream and take the call out in the hallway, to the dismay of my viewers.

"Hello? Odelia?" she says, and I wince at my first name. All those singsongy vowels, the feminine flourish at the end.

"Hi," I say.

"Is this a good time?"

"What's up?"

"I wanted to know if this was a good time?" she asks.

"I picked up the phone," I say. My mom's voice is nasally, as if she's getting over a cold.

"I just want to make sure I'm not interrupting anything," she says.

"What's up?"

"You didn't answer my texts so I assumed you must be busy."

"What's up, Mom?"

"Nothing really. Did you do anything nice this weekend?"

"I guess so. It was a normal weekend. I had dinner with a friend tonight."

"What did you have?"

"Is this what you called to talk about?"

"I thought you said this was a good time to talk."

"It is a good time."

"Are you sure? You seem to be in a rush," she says.

"I'm good. I'm here," I say, rolling my eyes at my mom's circular searching, her seeking desire. She wants more from me than I can give her. This has always been true.

"When are you working tomorrow?"

"What?" I say. "Oh. Twelve to close."

"Do you want to have breakfast before your shift, then? I can come by around nine and pick you up?"

I look around. The hallway is empty. The navy carpeted floor is depressed in spots and exuberant in others, dancing floorboards jutting this way and that beneath the synthetic fiber.

"Are you sure? You'd have to drive in during rush hour and it would take you over an hour each way."

"I know how long it takes to come into the city. I'm offering. And we could visit your sister for a little if you have time after breakfast. I know it seems like a slog but it's just a thirty-minute drive without traffic if we take the West Side Highway."

"I don't know. I don't eat breakfast."

"You don't eat breakfast? Since when?"

"A while now."

"That's not true. When do you eat if you're at work until close? You really should eat breakfast."

"Why don't you come another day when I'm not working?" I say. "When?"

"When I'm at work tomorrow I'll talk to my manager and confirm my schedule for the week."

"I'd rather just figure something out while I have you on the phone. Maybe we'll just get coffee tomorrow since you don't eat breakfast. That'll give us more time to visit Daisy, anyway. Or you can switch shifts with someone and that'll give us more time."

"I can't switch shifts, Mom," I snap. "Not the night before. It doesn't work like that."

"Fine, forget I suggested it," she says. "Forget it. Coffee works. I'll meet you at your place?"

"Are you telling me or asking me?"

"This isn't a riddle, Odelia. I'm just trying to make plans with you."

"Right," I say. "I'll see you tomorrow."

"I'm sorry if my calls put you in a bad mood."

"I'm not in a bad mood."

"It's important that we talk even if it doesn't feel good."

"You saw it, too, right?" I ask. "We saw it, didn't we? Her hand moved?"

"Yes. I saw it, too."

I hang up, then wind up and kick the air in front of me. A tired, victimless motion. My mom is the only one who feels what I'm feeling, who is going through what I'm going through with Daisy. But that hasn't brought us closer. There's just too much there to parse through, too much to look at directly. Talking to my mom is like holding my breath underwater. I'm always trying to get out, to get some vital oxygen, and I'm attacked by this nagging feeling that I used to be able to breathe here. Wasn't I? I used to live here, too, under the ocean. But how? I mourn the loss of my gills, blame her for my rapid evolution. Even though it's my fault that we're different species altogether now. Some things can't be reversed.

WEDNESDAY

LiveCast Ranking: 350,322

Three in the morning. The cord that ties me to dawn is devious, taut, and the rest of the night occupies an unbridgeable distance ahead of me. Normally I masturbate when sleep slips away from me like this, but I can't do that with my viewers around. Even if it is too dark for them to see. They'll know. Excelsior404 will know.

My mom was thirty-four and single and wanted a child so badly it colonized her dreams: little dancing babies in a conga line. Night after night. So she used a sperm donor and had me, and it was just us for three years. My memories of the time are the cool exterior of a metal Betty Boop lunchbox, mud sticking to an inflatable green bouncy ball in the backyard, the faint lavender detergent smell of a yellow blanket with big-eyed giraffes on it.

I was her full-time job, in addition to her full-time job managing the pharmacy on Main Street, and she did both of her jobs well. But then she fell in love with Gary. He was balding and she was prone to depression. They met at the pharmacy when he was picking up his medication, made small talk about the confusing proliferation of cotton swab brands considering they have so little product differentiation. It took four run-ins before she finally asked him out. Their first date was to the pizza place right next door. They bonded over the price of bottled water at movie theaters. Gary and my mom dated for less than a year before she became pregnant with Daisy. An accident. A miracle. And then my mom had everything: not only a traditionally conceived child but a whole partner to go along with it.

They never married but Gary moved in with us in our small, rented home in northern New Jersey. We all lived together for about five years before he and my mom broke up. The things they loved about each other had become horrid. The shiny egg of his scalp, the slippery, self-indulgent brain cells of her depressed mind. For my part, I thought that Gary was perfectly fine. No better or worse than any other man of his species. Because Gary and my mom were never married, there was no custody battle. He had Daisy for a weekend now and then when we were growing up, but mostly she stayed with us. Sometimes Gary would come over for dinner, and when he did he brought Daisy a present, a doll or a new pair of sneakers, a twenty dollar bill. Once, on her eighth birthday, a bright green bicycle with streamers on the handles.

Daisy was younger than me and needed attention, and so my mom gave it to her. "You can't compete with a crying baby," she said to me once, so I stopped trying. I could toast bread by the time I was five, make an omelet by the time I was seven.

I remember one July, when Daisy was five and I was eight, our mom took us to an orchard in upstate New York to pick peaches. I remember that I wanted to sit on my mom's shoulders so that I could reach the tallest branches. She said no. I was too heavy and she couldn't hold me anymore. So I had to pick the rotten, overripe peaches from the low branches and the ground while she hoisted Daisy up in her arms.

The abandoned peaches on the ground were soft to the touch and irregularly bruised. In defiance I ate and ate, dusty skin and all, so that my basket was empty by the time we left and my stomach was full and gurgling, my skin pimpled and slick with sugar syrup. The butterflies were attracted to me: my hands, my lips. I vomited pinkish fluid all over myself on the ride home, making sure not to dirty the car's interior.

My mom pulled the car over and gave me her shirt to wear. It was big on me and smelled like her body odor: bitter lime. She drove the rest of the way home in her bra.

Another time, Daisy and I were playing tag in the backyard. I think we were eight and eleven. Our backyard was small and had few places to hide. The trunk of the red maple, the cystic hydrangea bush, a wooden children's playset, which had developed both a limp and a hunchback over the years. I was catching up to Daisy, about to tag her. She picked up a rock and threw it at my head. It was a small rock, but it met its target. I ran even faster. I was going to tackle her to the ground and—and then what? I didn't know. I just knew I had to catch her. She called for our mom and sprinted toward the back door. I had to reach her before she got through it. Tag would be over the second she got into the house, the safe zone. If Daisy was inside, under Mom's watch, she would be untouchable. I almost caught her, could almost reach the hem of her shirt and yank her back, and then she reached the door, and—

The sliding glass door shattered as Daisy ran headlong into it. She fell onto the kitchen floor surrounded by twinkling shards. Scratches bloomed slow on her forehead, her arms and legs. I stood right outside in the backyard, gaping at the hole in the door. It wasn't my fault. It wasn't my fault. It was my fault. When Mom came downstairs, I was the one she screamed at. Daisy cried in a relentless surge, like an open fire hydrant on a summer street. It wasn't my fault. We were playing tag. And then she threw a rock at me! A rock! The sliding glass door was too clean. She didn't see the glass.

Mom took Daisy to the hospital. Nothing was broken. She just needed a few stitches. I made an attempt to clean up the glass while they were gone, even though my mom told me to stay out of the kitchen. I pricked myself with a shard, right on the tip of my thumb. I could only see the shard when I looked at my thumb from a certain angle. It didn't hurt at all. But when I pulled it out, the spot bled.

I wasn't grounded or anything, but no one came to talk to me in my room, which felt worse. Later, when we went to get Daisy's stitches out, my mom asked me if I had anything to say. Sorry, I said. Mom asked Daisy if she accepted my apology and Daisy nodded. And that was that.

Daisy was mom's favorite. It was so clear I didn't even have to ask, and my mom didn't even have to answer. That's how I know that this "I forgive you" and "Do you forgive me?" business is a ruse.

As a kid I wondered if my mom would have had me in the first place if she knew that she would meet Gary and have Daisy a few years later. Bad seed.

So no, I'm not looking forward to coffee with her today, and I should probably give up on going to sleep, too.

• • •

(!) **You have a new private message**
excelsior404: youre awake
mademoiselle_dell: ya
excelsior404: did you like my dare lol
mademoiselle_dell: no
excelsior404: aw lol
excelsior404: dont be like that
excelsior404: you could have just agreed to meet up with me instead
mademoiselle_dell: no
excelsior404: yesterday you said i only donated $25
excelsior404: now ive donated over $300
excelsior404: surely that counts for something
mademoiselle_dell: thank u
excelsior404: can i send u a pic
mademoiselle_dell: no
excelsior404: youre being a bitch
excelsior404: why are you being a bitch
excelsior404: i cant sleep either and i figured you wouldnt be distracted by other viewers right now
excelsior404: but youre still giving me one word answers
mademoiselle_dell: i appreciate u showing an interest in my stream
mademoiselle_dell: but we're not friends

mademoiselle_dell: and i dont meet up with strangers
excelsior404: how can we be friends if we havent met yet
mademoiselle_dell: u want to be my friend?
mademoiselle_dell: why?
excelsior404: i think youre cool
excelsior404: we live in the same city
excelsior404: idk lol
mademoiselle_dell: im not interested
excelsior404: ok
excelsior404: maybe im not interested in giving you $500 either
mademoiselle_dell: u will find that i dont respond to this kind of pressure
mademoiselle_dell: im not going to meet up with u in person
excelsior404: so what do you respond to
mademoiselle_dell: literally
mademoiselle_dell: fuck off
excelsior404: why are you doing this mean act?
excelsior404: you dont have to do it over dm
excelsior404: i already told you that i know about daisy
excelsior404: idc if you lie to everyone but i know the truth
excelsior404: and i dont think youre a bad person but they will if they know
mademoiselle_dell: r u trying to date me or ruin my life
mademoiselle_dell: pls clarify
excelsior404: you are ruining your own life
excelsior404: im not going to protect you for much longer if you keep acting like this
excelsior404: idk why youre being so dismissive
excelsior404: when im supporting you more than everyone else
excelsior404: more than hot_pat_of_butter
excelsior404: i deserve better
mademoiselle_dell: shucks
mademoiselle_dell: listen
mademoiselle_dell: $500 is generous
mademoiselle_dell: even though ur a pervert
mademoiselle_dell: so thank u for that
excelsior404: thats a start
mademoiselle_dell: im going to try to go to sleep now
mademoiselle_dell: good talk
excelsior404: good night dell

* * *

A picture comes in. Pale upper thighs, pubic hair, flaccid male genitalia. The picture was taken in a dark room with flash. I close it and start to type out a vomit emoji in my chat with excelsior404, but my hand falters. I look through my viewer list and there he is, of course, my one viewer in the middle of the night, and I'm sure what he wants most from me is a reaction. So I just put my phone away and resist the urge to turn off my camera so he can no longer see me.

My first instinct is to text Lee about the situation, but they're sleeping. Besides, if I told them they'd tell me to end my stream, or worse: insist on joining it more. And that wouldn't work, not at all. They might even chastise me for encouraging excelsior404 or imply that it was my fault, like the Juice Body situation, which was but also wasn't. Why call your employees a family if you're just going to kick them out of the house like that?

Lee doesn't know about Daisy. And why would they? I moved into the building two months ago, out of a dorm where everyone knew about Daisy, where everyone talked about Daisy all the time, where everything was Daisy, Daisy, Daisy, and when I talk to my mom it's the same. My gold-star sister.

Daisy didn't want to go to NYU. She only visited me to appease my mom. She wanted to go somewhere small and artsy and gilded, like Vassar or Wesleyan. NYU was too campus-less, too community-less for her. The students too haughty, the professors too famous. Her happy place was always by the water, and even though Manhattan is technically an island, it is only technically so. The beaches are sparse and depressing, or else overcrowded and soaking with noise. But my mom said she might as well visit my school, that she might fall in love with it. My mom liked the idea of both of her girls being at the same place.

Daisy and I shared a bedroom until I was thirteen, when I moved into a spare room in the basement at my own insistence. It took a long time to convince my mom, but she finally acquiesced and hired someone to help move my twin bed down two flights of stairs. I never told her or Daisy this, but that first night was difficult. The basement was cold and scary, the nighttime music foreboding. I remember how badly I wanted to call it all off, go back up to the second floor, and sleep in my old room. But I didn't. I made a decision, a wrong decision, and I had to stick with it.

The last class I went to before I dropped out was Philosophy of Science. We talked about how all branches of science used to just be philosophy. We talked about paradigm changes: our accepted reality is now wrong, and nothing will be the same again. We talked about the existence of a cat in a box with a radioactive substance, unobserved. Schrödinger's seed in the brain: both there and not there at the same time. Kind of like Daisy.

I jolt out of bed when my phone rings, my mom's name smeared across the screen. It's five minutes after nine. I must have drifted off. I blink the sleep out of my eyes and send her a text. She's already sent me several this morning, starting with **Good morning!** two hours ago and **On my way!** an hour ago all the way to **Where are you???** a minute before she called.

Be out in a sec! I send. **Sorry!**

I change out of my sweatpants and put on jeans and sneakers, not bothering to change out of the oversized T-shirt I slept in. It's psychedelic with flower patterns. Almost girly. My mom might even like it.

There are no viewers in my stream right now. The number—a flatline, a zero—puckers up my insides. It's been three days straight of streaming and I'm used to a handful of people hanging out with me from the moment I get up to the moment I go to bed. This whole business of being unwitnessed makes me feel clammy, like an unshelled mollusk.

I brush my teeth and wash my face, then go have a piss at Lee's. I prop up my phone by the faucet and stare at my slack-jawed expression.

Streaming twenty-four hours a day is more work than I thought it would be. I'm almost tempted to boof one of Lee's Adderalls, chase it with a Xanax. I feel hungover today, greasy-limbed and loose after yesterday's habaneros. Aside from the associated gastrointestinal distress, I also sweated out about a pound of water, and bathed in more endorphins and dopamine than my body has ever flooded me with before. The potential for addiction is strong, I can see that now. Hot_pat_of_butter was right.

I look at my viewer history. Excelsior404 was in my stream until five in the morning. How horrible, to watch my dark screen like that, to listen for the sound of my breathing. If he's planning on narcing on me, surely he would have done so already, instead of throwing another challenge at my feet. He wants attention. And I'll give it to him, but only in the doses I prescribe.

I imagine him showing up at my door, presenting me with gifts: a gilded box full of dead doves, a swarm of bees mothered in his jaws.

"Come on, little moths. Come to my light," I whisper to no one. I don't want it to be just me out here, all alone with my mom. One viewer. That's not too much to ask for. And it's not just for my ego, either. If I have witnesses, I'll have to be on my best behavior.

I wonder if my viewers will notice any resemblance between us. I have my mom's caterpillar eyebrows in a slightly lighter shade of brown. A sharper chin. Wider hips. The overlaps in our personality are irritating, instructive. I see myself roll my eyes in my stream and there she is: her grimace directly behind mine, a shadow self. Being around my mom reminds me that I'm just a type A person pretending to be chill.

I grab a handful of nuts from Lee's pantry before I leave. Some cool ranch Doritos for good measure. A sip of organic strawberry lemonade straight from the bottle.

"What are you doing?" Lee asks. I turn around and they're standing in the apartment's doorway.

"How are you so quiet?" I close the fridge door and wipe my hands on my pants. "Sorry, I had to use your bathroom. I'm heading out now. No worries."

"Hey," they say. I stop. They're wearing bicycle shorts and a neon yellow top, holding a plastic drugstore bag. They take their shoes off slowly and sit on the kitchen stool across the island from me. "You can obviously use my bathroom whenever you want, but you can't just go through my shit. Especially if I'm not here."

"Fine. Fair. I get it."

"I don't know if you get it, Dell."

"I'm not an idiot." I say. I can't stand being told what to do, what not to do, or being lectured in any way. Especially by Lee, with all these square feet to spare and no student debt to speak of.

"I went out to run errands and when I came back you were neck-deep in my fridge."

"I'm sorry, okay? Is that what you want me to say?" My face is hot. I want to run out and slam the door behind me, but they just called me dramatic, and I don't feel like proving their point.

"Yeah, that works," they say.

"Really? That worked?"

"Yep," they say. I punch them on the shoulder and they slap the back of my head, not too hard. I leave and start down the stairwell. Zero viewers to overhear that interaction or hear mademoiselle_dell apologize, thankfully, though now I desperately need them to start filtering in. I take the steps one at a time with my hand on the railing, focusing on that glaring emptiness on my phone. I message a few of my viewers, letting them know I'm online: crabbybob, karnie_vibes, pklrik, and a couple others. Fourth floor, third floor, second floor, first floor, and I can see my mom waving from the other side of the glass door. I can't quite make out the expression on her face until I get closer: she's happy to see me. She's annoyed that I'm late. She's doing that twitchy thing she does where her mouth can't make up its mind: smile, frown, smile, frown. I reach for the door handle and step out into the morning air. Crisp and sobering.

> **trutherdare:** good morning
> **trutherdare:** going out like that?
> **trutherdare:** LOL

A viewer, thank god. A witness. I put my phone on mute and shove it in my back pocket with a view of the city behind me, sticky and sick with morning heat.

I can feel my mom clocking the looseness of my jeans, the circumference of my ankles, with a mix of concern and jealousy. I've been cut off from dining hall food, my prepaid nonrefundable meal plan, my Juice Body smoothies. And this ulcer has me completely unmotivated to put food anywhere near my mouth.

I give her a one-armed hug and we head to a coffee shop called Solid Ground on 53rd Street, about a seven-minute walk from my place. I time out the beat of my footsteps with the second hand of my thoughts. My mom goes on about her drive into the city, how our extended family is doing, what she bought at her local library's dollar book sale. She maintains a one-sided conversation with no issue, like I can when I'm on my stream and bullshitting the time away. Maybe I got that skill from her.

> **chillnessa:** hola turn ur audio on
> **chillnessa:** boring
> **trutherdare:** ^^^
> **burr9ty:** i dig it its like a stroll through the city
> **chillnessa** has signed off

Apart from its terrifically bad name, Solid Ground really is solid as far as coffee shops go. In the winter they dress up the entire store with twinkling lights. The front room is a grab-and-go situation, and they have a back room filled with low-lying couches and armchairs, mismatched coffee tables and bookshelves. The back room is dim and moody and was probably used as a storeroom at one point.

"What can I get you?" my mom asks.

"A black coffee."

"Milk? Sugar?"

"No, I'm good."

"You don't want a latte?"

"Black coffee is fine."

"Black coffee is fine." My mom shrugs, and heads back to the front room. The shop wasn't busy when we got here. I hope there are multiple people in line in front of her now. At least two. Ideally four. A latte. She wants me to have that extra substance in my drink if I'm not eating breakfast. I am hungry, truth be told. I just don't want to be doubled over with cramps while I'm trying to get through this, and I already risked that by scarfing down some snacks at Lee's. Stomach pain would be a handy excuse to leave if I'm down for the constant calls and texts afterward to make sure I'm okay. I could also use my current headache, which is probably from a lack of sleep but could also be the sprout intruding on my cerebellum.

I watch my mom in line. She isn't on her phone or anything, just reading the chalkboard behind the register, looking around. Her eyebrows tense together, her hands grippy and strange as they circulate in and around her pockets. She's nervous. I make her nervous. I hate that I make her nervous.

All the upright members of society are at work on a Wednesday morning and the back room is mostly empty. There's a dad reading *Gothamist* with an empty stroller beside him, drinking sour-smelling tea, and a teenage girl with a mullet gaming on a handheld device. I take my phone out of my back pocket. Six viewers. A beautiful, even number. I say good morning to trutherdare, burr9ty, pklrik, xinfected_ botx, and a couple new folks. And then I mute my phone again and prop it against an unlit candle on the coffee table.

My mom comes back with two ceramic mugs and a muffin.

"Blueberry oat," she says. "Want to split it?"

I shake my head and pick up my coffee.

"I can't eat a whole muffin by myself." She laughs.

"Then why did you get a whole muffin?"

"They don't sell half muffins."

"They should. That would be smart, wouldn't it? They wouldn't even have to charge half the price. If a muffin costs five dollars, people would definitely buy half a muffin for three."

"That's a smart business idea," my mom says. She's not being sarcastic, which pisses me off. "I think I'll eat half and then I can save the other half for later if you don't want it. I could have it for breakfast tomorrow. Or you could take it home with you. Maybe you'll want it later."

Other than the eyebrows, my mom doesn't look anything like me. She has long brown hair so dark it's almost black, thick and shiny as outer space. She's tall, too, and pale. She is very pretty, in a woodland way, like a handsome branch. I'm more like a toadstool. Today she's wearing wide-legged black slacks and a linen blouse. Far more dressed up than me. When she smiles, she shows a centimeter of gum above her top teeth. I avoid eye contact with my viewers.

"I'm glad we're doing this," she says. "It'll be good for you to visit Daisy. For both of us. I haven't been in a couple of days."

"I don't know, Mom. It's almost ten. I have work soon."

"We don't need to stop by for more than fifteen or twenty minutes," she says, then laughs. "God knows there's not much to do there."

"Maybe."

"I know that it's hard to visit. But you have to do it anyway."

Why? I want to scream. But I keep my mouth shut until I can bear to speak again. My head aches. The seed sprouts and wraps its roots around my limbic system. I have to be on my best behavior.

"I know," I say quietly. "I know. I just don't want to feel rushed. And today I would feel rushed."

"When was the last time you went to visit Daisy?" she asks.

"With you."

"That was a month ago, Odelia."

"I'm aware."

"Well, will you go on your own this week? And let me know?"

"Yes," I say, and I mean it. I watch my mom sweep muffin crumbs off her lap and onto a small napkin that she carefully folds and places under her plate. "How are you doing?" I ask.

"Terrible," she says, and I almost laugh out loud at the melodrama. "The traffic on the way in was awful," she said.

"I told you that you didn't have to come in."

"Right," my mom says into her latte. It's green. Some kind of matcha situation. After a moment she says: "I was thinking about you earlier. Do you think you'll go back to school in the fall?"

"To NYU? Absolutely not." I shake my head. "I told you, I'm not ready."

"But maybe you will be in a couple months, no? You have no way of knowing how you'll feel."

"I didn't take a leave of absence. I didn't even take my finals. I'd probably have to redo this whole past semester. It's not as easy as just letting them know I'm coming back. I dropped out. I would have to reapply."

"I'm sure they'll accept you again. It wouldn't be the same as someone applying with no background at the school."

"I'm not talking about this right now," I say.

"It never seems to be a good time to talk about anything lately."

"I've been busy. I've been working. I had more time when I was in school."

"I don't think that's it. Do you think that's it?" she asks. "Do you like our relationship right now?"

I roll my eyes. "Our relationship is fine, considering."

"Considering what?" she says. "Life is hard. And I'm your mom. You can use me as a resource. Call me to talk. Whatever you need. I'm not mad that you were late for breakfast. I'm not mad at you, no matter what you might think. We have to forgive each other."

I take a sip of my coffee, trying to keep my hand steady and my face from glowering red. I knew our meeting would go like this; I just didn't realize that it would turn so quickly. I take a deep breath, trying to untangle my nerves.

"Since when do you drink matcha?" I ask.

"What?"

I point toward her drink, which is green and foamy.

"Oh, this?" she asks. "I hate it."

I laugh, despite myself. "Is it what you ordered?"

"I'm not sure." She says, then takes another sip. "You're icing me out."

I look at her then, my eyes trembling in their sockets with restrained anger. I put down my coffee. "I'm not doing it on purpose."

"You won't even eat a muffin."

"That's your muffin. You got it for yourself," I say.

"No I didn't."

"You want to get into this right now? In here? With them?" I gesture at the man reading the paper. He pretends not to notice. To her benefit, the teenage girl playing video games genuinely doesn't notice.

"It seems like there's never a good time," she says. "I'm the only one who knows what you're going through. And you're the only one who knows what I'm going through. Doesn't that count for anything?"

"I get that," I say. How many viewers do I have now? Five? Seven? Thank god they can't hear us. I try to keep my arms quiet in my lap, my body language neutral. "I do get that."

"Well, I don't know what you expect me to do."

"Live your life."

"You are my life."

I raise my mug up to my mouth, but I don't drink. I could tell her about the stream. I could tell her about my ulcer. About Lee. The un-solicited photo that excelsior404 sent me. The opportunity I might have to collaborate with hot_pat_of_butter, how it could change everything. I could tell her how I got fired from Juice Body and I don't actually have work in an hour. I could tell her how rent is due in four days and I'm broke, broke, broke. How I never seem to be good enough for any of my homes, never good enough once people get to know me. Streaming is the first thing I've been genuinely good at in as long as I can remember.

I take a small sip of coffee and hold it, feeling it stain my teeth. Then I rip off a chunk of muffin and stuff it in my mouth.

My mom insists on dropping me off for the shift I don't have at the job I was fired from, even though it's only a twenty-minute walk from the cof-fee shop. For the suburbia-brained, a twenty-minute walk is untenable. Anything more than a block away calls for a trip in the Honda Odyssey. She deposits me by the entrance to Grand Central Terminal and honks goodbye. I step through the doors of the gargantuan building. Endless marble floors, heavenly ceiling done up in a flamboyant green. The shining beacon of the Apple store stationed on its gleaming moneyed pedestal, larger than life.

A terminal is the end of the line, as they say.

I lean back against a wall, out of the way of the roiling heat of foot traffic and consider whether or not to go home. If I am going home, I would want to wait a reasonable amount of time before I head back to make sure that I don't pass my mom on the way. It's not entirely rational, but driving through the city is slow, there are stoplights at every corner.

We weren't always this way. I remember certain intimacies. My mom would garden outside in the summer, wearing a big blue hat with a wide brim, and if I brought her out a glass of water she would down the entire glass in one go, which was a way of saying I love you. When she came back inside her fingers smelled like basil. I remember her as warm and tired and frizzy-haired, standing in front of the air conditioner with her eyes closed. I remember our hairs mixing in the shower drain. How our laundry would mix in the basket, too: my sweet, fragrant clothes with her slightly sour, earthier articles. Daisy's dirty laundry smelled like nothing.

I grip my stomach, anticipating a rumble of pain from the half muffin I ate. Nothing yet.

"You miss me, bitches?" I say to my viewers, smiling to show my canines. A dab of menace to get morale up. It's ten in the morning and I have sixteen viewers, many of them new. How do they find me? Animals drawn to the smell of death. I catch up on my chats from this morning.

> **xinfected_botx:** follow me on social media
> **xinfected_botx:** follow for follow
> **burr9ty:** whats ur handle
> **xinfected_botx:** guess lol
> **MSRN273:** hi
> **pklrik:** ummmmm
> **trutherdare:** I already had 3 cups of coffee today 0.0
> **trutherdare:** I usually don't drink any but i'm studying for a final
> **trutherdare:** hi MSRN273 ^_^
> **MSRN273:** hi from seattle
> **xinfected_botx:** good luck trutherdare
> **trutherdare:** thx

It seems that my viewers don't mind entertaining themselves while I'm busy, like well-trained children. They didn't comment much on my time with Mom. A bit of speculation about who the mystery woman was, how she's not as hot as Neighbor Lee, then the conversation changed to Beanie Babies, Shark Week, the Middle Eastern conflict.

I know it's been too long since I last visited Daisy. I know I have a blockage here. But can you blame me? Seeing my little sister hooked up to wires like that? It's classic body horror, right out of a scary movie. The image of her is an intrusive thought that I'd do nearly anything to keep out of my head.

"Quick, I need twenty dollars," I say to my eighteen viewers. "Oldest person in the room gives me twenty dollars."

> **chickenleggy:** 22
> **burr9ty:** i'm 38
> **chickenleggy:** I WIN
> **pklrik:** lol pwned
> **pklrik:** i turn 16 in january
> **MSRN273:** i'm 30
> **burr9ty:** is redtimepolice on
> **burr9ty:** i'm pretty sure they are older than me
> **trutherdare:** no
> **burr9ty:** ok fine
> **burr9ty** has donated $5

"Did I ask for five dollars? Are you trying to insult me? Do you want to get blocked?"

> **burr9ty:** no mademoiselle_dell
> **burr9ty** has donated $15

"That's better," I say. The parting of my hair is itchy. I scratch hard and get dandruff under my fingernails.

> **chickenleggy:** QUEEN DELL

"Now give chickenleggy a dollar, too, for her fealty."

chickenleggy: lol YAY
pklrik: what is feel tea
burr9ty: i don't think i can give money to another viewer on livecast
burr9ty: sorry chickenleggy
jimpix: all hail queen dell

• • •

Juice Body's hours are seven in the morning until eight o'clock at night, wide enough to accommodate the liquified produce needs of most commuters. It's Wednesday and if this week's schedule is the same as last week's, Krishell will be working the register. I speedwalk past the tourists and deke around a group of schoolchildren on a field trip. Mini yellow crossing-guard jackets to make sure they don't get lost in the shuffle, a battalion of little people holding on to the same teacher-fed rope. It's been a while since I visited this old castle, with its shimmery mural, vaulted stone. Marble floors so shiny you can nearly see yourself in them. It feels calm, despite the hubbub.

I hold my phone out in front of me as I navigate through the station, taking in the mess of bodies. The line at Juice Body is long. Around this time of day, it's not just commuters that grace the halls of Grand Central, there are also the local midtownies out for an early lunch or late breakfast, perusing the overpriced food market in the building's basement or grabbing a bagel with schmear at one of the fast casual joints on the ground level. The brand of human that gets a detox juice for a meal is a special one. You can intuit the hunger in their hands, the way they shove them in their pockets as they wait in line, grab their premade juice from the fridge with a white-knuckled fist and latch on to the bottle with unctuous urgency. I queue up behind these quivering hungers, fifth in line. And there's Krishell, flitting behind the counter, her hair held back by a very thick, very neon pink headband.

My stomach doesn't hurt yet. That's a good sign. A great one. Maybe today is a very special day.

When I'm third in line, I lean over and wave to get Krishell's attention. She's surprised to see me. I wonder if Nik is here. If Johnny is in I'll ask him about his mole removal. If it hurt. If they gave him his mole to keep afterward, in a little dime bag.

There's a new limited edition menu item called "BIG YE5 ENERGY" and I'm relieved that I don't have to memorize its contents. Plant-based collagen, mango, strawberry, broccoli, pitaya, flax fiber, stevia, almond milk.

Broccoli. Really.

It's a collaboration with Korean pop band YE5. I've never heard of them. Apparently they've sold out Madison Square Garden for an upcoming concert. New dates added. Buy your tickets with promo code "YE5JUICE."

"Anyone here a YE5 fan?" I ask my viewers. I have one headphone in and I'm holding my phone low, with a sublime view of my underchin.

chickenleggy: YES OMG
jackofnotrades1: my cousin is korean
jackofnotrades1: he sent me a link to a YE5 song last week ^__^
chickenleggy: COOL
jackofnotrades1: it was just ok
kirk_equivalent: r u korean
jackofnotrades1: no but my cousin is
kirk_equivalent: r u adopted
jackofnotrades1: no but my cousin is
jimpix: my cousin is in jail

"Not that I care, but these drinks aren't even healthy," I say to my viewers. The woman in front of me turns around and narrows her eyes. "They have so much sugar in them. Nut butters. Yogurt. Fruit. Sure, they're high in protein and have all these random macronutrients in them for you to pee out, but at the end of the day they're the same calories as two slices of pizza and enough sugar as a pint of ice cream."

The woman goes up to order her dandelion and celery detox juice ($13) and I step up to the register after her, leaning my elbows on the counter conspiratorially.

"Hey, champ," I say.

"Hey, Dell," Krishell says. "What can I get you?"

"Seems like you're busy today," I say. I turn around and lean against the register, giving an optical pat down to the line that's formed behind me, eight strong and buzzing with agitation.

"Yeah," she says. "You know how it is. But it goes pretty quick at lunch."

"How are you doing? Has Nik replaced me yet?"

"No. It's like no one wants to work these days," Krishell says.

"Do you really believe that?" I ask.

"No." She sighs.

I laugh, which startles Krishell. "Is mommy dearest here?"

"She— He stepped out."

"That scrooge never gave me my last paycheck, did you know that?"

She shrugs. "You left the store open with no one in it. That's, like, illegal."

"It's not even remotely illegal. There is literally no law about that. Whatever. I don't have time. I'm kind of also at work right now so I wanted to grab a quick power lunch." I waggle my phone in the air. "Want to say hi to my viewers?"

"Oh." She squints at my phone and gives a mechanical wave. "That's cool."

"Can I ask you a question?"

"Sure," she says, like she means the opposite. The line behind me is thrumming with desire, keen for kale.

"When you started working here, what T-shirt size did you ask Nik for?"

"What?"

"A small? Medium? Large?"

"I asked for a medium."

"And what size did he give you?"

"I don't remember. A small."

"Same. I had to go to the supply room and steal a couple medium shirts. It helps with tips or whatever, I get it, but the word 'Juicy' on the back of the shirt in big bubble letters always mega creeped me out."

"What's your point?" she says, voice neutral. She's not annoyed, not even listening. Her attention is on the nine, ten people in line behind me.

"The world is gross. And most work is inherently demeaning. Even at a place like this where everyone is nice and the pay is solid. That's my point. Listen, this streaming thing has been good, really good. I'm making more in an hour than I used to in an entire shift. If you ever want to leave this place, leave the 'Juice Body family,' let me know. I can help you out."

She shifts from foot to foot, staring at a spot between my eyes. That bovine neutrality, it gets to me, makes my fingers itch. If there was a tip jar on the counter, I'd swipe it. But all the tips are given electronically now, and there's nothing in arm's reach worth taking. Plastic cups, napkins, biodegradable straws.

"I'll have a BIG YE5 ENERGY smoothie," I say. "Seems like you have a lot of people to take care of, and I don't want to get you in trouble for socializing." I point to the security camera near the entrance of the store, glaring down at us. "You never know when mother is watching."

Krishell nods with relief and gets to work. I watch her shove a scoop of white powder into the blender, pink stuff, yellow stuff, green stuff. More white mystery powder. A hefty glug of almond milk. There tends to be leftover smoothie with these things. Measuring out ingredients is an art. Usually the smoothie-maker inherits the overflow and sets it aside for a snack, but Krishell fills up one and a quarter cups for me and hands them both over. She could get in trouble for that. I'm marginally impressed by her chutzpah.

"Thanks," I say.

"I'm doing a keto thing before Burning Man," she says. "No sugar." She rings me up and I even add a dollar tip ($17.75).

"Nik's not here, then?" I ask. "I'm going to leave a note on his desk."

"Wait," she says as I start walking past the register toward his office. "Dell." But she doesn't follow me. She can't. There are too many people in line. Nik's door is unlocked, like it always is, and I close it behind me with a smooth hush.

"Y'all," I say to my viewers. "I'm in my boss's office. The one who fired me without giving me my final paycheck. Thoughts?"

racre001: steal something

"Like what?" I ask, my brain buzzing. Nik could be back any minute. In fact, Krishell has probably texted him to let him know that I'm here. I could spill my smoothie on his computer. I could uproot his dying mandarin tree and smear its humid dirt on the walls. I could look for cash and pay myself out for my shifts last week, steal some allowance.

excelsior404: malicious compliance
excelsior404: he got mad at you for not locking up
excelsior404: so take his keys and lock him out of his office

"Maybe."

racre001: let me see

I turn the camera around so my viewers can see what I'm seeing. Then I sit at Nik's desk and open drawers. Pencils, pens, rubber bands, a calculator. "No sex toys. No hand gun. No bud," I say. "Yawn."

cindyrella: write ur name in sharpie under his desk
pklrik: ive done that

"Lame. So lame it hurts."

pklrik: poop on his desk
racre001: steal his wallet

I cross my legs and swivel in a circle in Nik's chair. He has a land-line, a desktop computer, a framed business school diploma on the wall. I could change the voicemail on his desk phone to something ridiculous, like the song "Pump Up the Jam" by Technotronic. I could send an email to the staff telling them they're all fired, that he's decided to close the store and pursue his real lifelong passion: ghost hunting.

I jolt to attention and open the internet on his computer, navigate to Juice Body's social media account. He had me go to his office and post from the Juice Body account a few times, mostly about changes to store hours, so I know his computer password (Juice123!) and his social media account password (Juice123!). I write out a message, publish it, and head out of the store without saying a word to Krishell, a smoothie in each hand and my viewers in my back pocket, complicit as ever.

We're putting the BODY in Juice BODY for #PRIDE!! Bottoms get a free Smooth Move Detox juice for the entire month of JUNE!!

My viewers adore me. I've never received so much positive reinforcement in my entire life for being an asshole. Fizzing with adrenaline, I chug the bonus smoothie and make quick work of the full cup. I like this expensive crap, it's a fatal flaw of mine. In terms of digestion, a liquid lunch goes down easier, meaning less stomach pain on the other side of things than the roughage of plants, the gassy sugars in legumes. This particular concoction is a shade of pink that reminds me of Pepto

Bismol. A salubrious pink hue found absolutely nowhere in nature. Is there anything more beautiful?

"Brain freeze," I say. This is dinner tonight: chugging down a hot pink smoothie in a minute and a half while a homeless man masturbates a few feet from me.

> **jackofnotrades1:** i hate that
> **wintrbrry:** i never get brain freeze
> **anomalous_donkey:** >:D
> **anomalous_donkey:** angry brain emoji
> **excelsior404:** press your tongue against the roof of your mouth

"Don't tell me what to do with my tongue," I say. This fucking guy. I close my eyes until the brain freeze goes away, and then take another hefty slurp. Maybe the cold will shock the seed in my brain, stunt its growth. Plants need a warm, wet environment to flourish, so I need to make my body as inhospitable as possible. That shouldn't be too hard.

Almost noon. So much time left in the day, so little time left in the day. I feel like I just woke up and now the hour hand is tick-tick-tocking toward five o'clock when I'll be providing this evening's entertainment. That stunt I just pulled seemed to pull in some word-of-mouth referrals. Conversations in the metaverse. Or maybe the LiveCast algorithm deigning to lift me up, place me higher in the rankings. An algorithm that seeks out people like me: hungry, wretched, raising money for a good cause.

Viewers have been trickling in since the morning: one, ten, twenty, forty. I'm hoping for sixty by the time I do my stream. I think we can get there. Sixty viewers, an average of five dollars each . . . we can definitely get there.

"Come, my little bees. Swarm to me."

> **jackdaw2000:** bzz bzz bzz

"What should we do today?"

anomalous_donkey: visit daisy

"You're obsessed. Everyone is obsessed."

cindyrella: oooooooooo
redtimepolice: i want to meet daisy
jackdaw2000: what if she woke up on camera
cindyrella: that would be amazing OMG

"I'm going to visit eventually. It's going to happen. Just don't bug me about it. You all sound like my mom."

I walk home and have instant coffee and a slice of bread. My mouth is dry and I have a hard time swallowing the bread. I shove it down my esophagus with over-hot coffee. The stomach pain hits soon after, stony and bitter. I need to get on health insurance. Get one of those jobs that takes pay out of your own salary to give you benefits that you still have to pay out of pocket for. According to the internet, my self-diagnosed ulcer is treatable with antibiotics and something called a proton pump inhibitor, neither of which I can get at the drugstore. Is there a black market for antibiotics? Would one of my viewers ship me some? I know that low-cost health insurance is out there, I'm just not sure how to get on it and I fear my network would be full of perverts with malpractice suits anyway.

I have a little less than five hundred dollars in my LiveCast account and almost double that in my bank account. Rent is due in four days. I can make rent and bills on time. But the very idea of fourteen thousand dollars was ill-conceived, impossible, cruel to everyone involved. A crackpot plan uttered by my one selfish remaining brain cell. I'd have to win the Carolina Reaper World Record Competition for that kind of money.

*　　*　　*

There are fifty-seven people in my stream, a pleasing number to humiliate myself in front of. As I've always said: if anyone is going to exploit me, it's me. Five hundred dollars for putting a habanero in my vagina. If I can get to sixty viewers, and they all give me between one and ten bucks, I could make a thousand dollars today. The number is insane. Both feasible and insane. Insane in its feasibility.

Lee isn't here, thankfully. I checked and double-checked a trillion times. The thought of Lee watching me do this makes me want to bury myself alive. They've met mademoiselle_dell, fine. But they don't need to get up close and personal with her. I never should have told them about my stream to begin with.

"Ladies and lads and everyone in between," I say. "The time is nigh."

crabbybob: nigh
kirk_equivalent: neigh
jimpix: woof

"I see some old friends and new enemies. If this is your first time in my stream, let me catch you up: this is a donate-a-thon. We're raising fourteen thousand dollars to put my little sister on private life support for a week. And I'm sorry to say we're doing a horrendous job. It's day three and we've raised less than a thousand dollars. Maybe we can turn that all around today, what do you think? Our generous benefactor excelsior404 has pledged five hundred dollars if I put a pepper in my vagina. My one request is: no perverts, no loiterers, no solicitors. If you're here, you're pledging to donate no less than five dollars, or you will be blocked."

chillnessa: vamooooos!
barbistani: i pledge $4
barbistani: jk jk jk jk jk

A handful of people drop off now that I've set the ante, but fewer than I expected. Four or five. "Now, I'm a simple girl, when it comes right down to it. Not to kink shame, there's just nothing sexual about this for me, and so I'm asking the same of you. This isn't Cinemax, this is *Fear Factor*."

> **kirk_equivalent:** its kind of hot though
> **chickenleggy:** lol pun

I get the habanero from my bag and hold it up to the camera, placing my palm behind it to help the lens focus. Baby grenade, gnarled and precious. "I guess I'm lucky habaneros are pretty small, and your kink isn't something like pineapples, excelsior404, or eggplants."

> **redtimepolice:** what if teh habanero explodes
> **redtimepolice:** or gets stuck

"If it gets stuck? I don't know," I say. The thought hadn't crossed my mind. Though the idea of having pepper seeds stuck in opposite ends of me has a sort of sick humor to it. Would I ask Lee to help me get it out? Go to the ER? I'd rather eat this habanero than stick it up myself right now. The sweaty adrenaline of a pepper high, the accompanying tunnel vision that blocks out all other thoughts and forces me to be present. But five hundred dollars is five hundred dollars. I stand and do a lap around my apartment, as big of a lap as I can manage within my meager square footage. Then I open one of my desk drawers and take out a condom. I have a handful of these rainbow foil-covered condoms from last year's Pride, when they were strewn off a parade float like so much angular confetti. I open the condom and slide the habanero inside, then tie a knot at the end and wiggle it around for the camera. "There. Stuck proof."

barbistani: lmfao
kirk_equivalent: thats konky
barbistani: protection is lame
kirk_equivalent: *kinky
pklrik: ^^^ LAME

I stand and angle the camera up so only the top half of my body is visible. The condom is wet, lubricated in my hand, the habanero inside like a deformed embryo that I'm about to suck back inside myself. I don't have to do this. No one is holding a gun to my head. But I'm going to. I can't let my viewers down as they pack the room with their non-bodies. I show the habanero to the camera one more time, little red nub of a thing, potent and firm, before reaching into my pants. I feel a slight pressure and give as I insert it inside myself, making sure that part of the condom remains outside of my body. The feeling is not entirely unpleasant. I hold my empty hands up to the camera.

"Ta-da."

People go off in the chat, encouraging me, exclaiming their support and fealty and unconditional love. It wasn't decided how long the habanero had to be inside of me, but it would feel like cheating to take it out right away. I sit down slowly, feeling the pepper shift and settle with a slight twinge of discomfort. If I wiggle in my seat in a certain way, it even feels good. "Who's going to write this piece for *Cosmo*? 'Ten Tips to Spice Up Your Sex Life.'"

I wipe my fingers on my shirt and catch up on the chats, which are going off. Everyone has something to say, most of it congratulatory, in awe of my bravery, my fearlessness. They're saying that I'm a vibe. Clap emojis abound, and the money starts coming in.

crabbybob has donated $10
jackdaw2000 has donated $5
pklrik has donated $8

"Chillnessa? Wintrbrry? I see some stragglers in my viewer list who haven't coughed it up yet. Don't mess with me here. I'm talking real, gold-backed United States dollars."

> **chillnessa** has donated $6
> **barbistani:** idt USD is backed by gold anymore
> **cindyrella** has donated $10
> **jackofnotrades1** has donated $5
> **karnie_vibes** has donated $10
> **karnie_vibes:** hi from vancouver

I love the sound of money coming in. I close my eyes and listen to it. With nearly sixty viewers, it lasts a while, like the scattered, buttery sounds of popcorn in the microwave. Nothing, and then a cacophonic concentration of dings, before they get fewer and further apart.

"Wintrbrry? Going once? Going twice?"

> **jackdaw2000:** maybe he's in the bathroom

"Don't care. Too late." High on cash, I press the "Block" button and wntrberry disappears from my viewer list. "Well," I say. "I thought that I was the star of the show, but it seems like our generous benefactor is trying to stir up the suspense."

> **excelsior404:** yo
> **barbistani:** ......
> **trutherdare:..**
> **jackofnotrades1:** ....
> **excelsior404** has donated $200

"What?" I say. "Are you fucking kidding?" I yank the habanero out of me and wave it in front of the camera before throwing it in the unlined trash bin under my desk. It misses and hits the wall hard before dropping to the floor. "We said five hundred dollars. You said five hundred dollars."

excelsior404: you cheated
chickenleggy: BLOCK HIM
jackofnotrades1: off with his head
excelsior404: she cheated
excelsior404: she didnt show it
excelsior404: i could only see her upper body
excelsior404: we don't even know if she did it
excelsior404: she could be a liar
excelsior404: she could be lying to all of us

I grip my desk until I can see the whites of my knuckles. "What do you think this is, a sleight-of-hand show? You think I'm some kind of magician? Who the fuck are you to call me a liar?"

barbistani: idt she cheated
crabbybob: i could tell she did it
crabbybob: her face twitched

"Fuck you, my face did not twitch."

excelsior404: it doesn't matter. the point is we don't know for sure
excelsior404: so $200
excelsior404: its generous

"You are an inch from being blocked, excelsior404. Blocked within an inch of your pathetic life."

excelsior404: ill dm u
excelsior404 has signed off

I want to shut off my stream and throw my laptop out the window, throw my plants out the window, throw myself out the window. But I don't have a window, so instead I get up and shuffle to the McDonald's at the end of the block, the one where the bathroom door perpetually has a fake "Out of Order" sign on it. My stomach is pulsating disagreeably, but I can still stand up straight, so I'm fine on the Dell pain scale. I order a Sausage McMuffin ($1.19) and hashbrowns ($1.09) from the dollar menu and a small caramel frappe ($2.39) because I crave sugar when I'm angry. I stand by the trash can and eat, grease staining my hands and face. In seconds I'm done, and my hands are empty, and my brain feels saggy and pendulous with salt. I use the end of a straw to dig into my left ear, trying to remove the budding sprout. I give up and drag myself back up the block to my apartment. The last place I want to be right now.

Two hundred dollars is a lot. I know that. And with my other viewers, I made another hundred or so. Nothing to scoff at. But he humiliated me, backing out like that at the last second. This is my dungeon, and if anyone's going to be a piece of shit, it's me.

I open Juice Body's social media. My post is gone. I try to log in to Juice Body's account, but the password has been changed. No text or calls from mother dearest, though I do have an email. It reads: **If you ever come into my store again I will call the police and have you sent to jail**

I type back a response, my fast-food fingers dirtying up the screen:

Directly to jail?

Do not pass go? do not collect $200?

How about $400?

I'm definitely not getting my paycheck now. I message Hot Pat, whose profile says he's online:

mademoiselle_dell: tell me about this napalm burger
hot_pat_of_butter: hey!
hot_pat_of_butter: it's not too bad. There's ghost pepper sauce on it and pickled habaneros. You could def handle it
mademosielle_dell: i dont think i've had ghost peppers

hot_pat_of_butter: ghost peppers do not equal ghost pepper sauce

hot_pat_of_butter: they remove the seeds before they turn peppers into sauces

hot_pat_of_butter: seeds are the spiciest part

hot_pat_of_butter: and then there's the cooking process and the other ingredients to temper it further

hot_pat_of_butter: you're looking at at least half the scoville of the raw pepper if not less

hot_pat_of_butter: and if you ever want to eat a raw ghost pepper, i recommend Pepper Prince at Union Square Farmers Market

mademoiselle_dell: woah expert

hot_pat_of_butter: its my livelihood lol

mademoiselle_dell: im down for burgers tomorrow

hot_pat_of_butter: nice, we can both stream it

hot_pat_of_butter: 6 PM? i'll send a message to my viewers

mademoiselle_dell: great

mademoiselle_dell: thanks dude

mademoiselle_dell: means a lot

hot_pat_of_butter: welcome to the community

mademoiselle_dell: lol thanks

hot_pat_of_butter: the hot sauce community is tight

hot_pat_of_butter: and there aren't a lot of female streamers / competitors

hot_pat_of_butter: what you're doing is great

mademoiselle_dell: ur giving me too much credit

hot_pat_of_butter: did you really do that thing today with the habanero pepper

mademoiselle_dell: ya

mademoiselle_dell: were u in my stream

hot_pat_of_butter: no i couldnt make it

hot_pat_of_butter: im sorry that you had to do that

hot_pat_of_butter: i hope it wasnt too bad

mademoiselle_dell: ???

mademoiselle_dell: i didnt have to do it

mademoiselle_dell: its not a big deal

mademoiselle_dell: ive done worse for less

hot_pat_of_butter: :(

mademoiselle_dell: dont need ur sad face

hot_pat_of_butter: sorry

hot_pat_of_butter: just seems extreme

mademoiselle_dell: its not

mademoiselle_dell: it took like 10 seconds
mademoiselle_dell: and i made more than i made eating 5 habaneros

I start to type another sentence, something about how hot_pat_of_butter doesn't know me, how he has no right to judge me, how he should get out of my fucking business. But I delete it. He's famous, after all. Successful. And he invited me to stream with him. I need to not fuck things up for once.

hot_pat_of_butter: i get it
hot_pat_of_butter: but you dont have to do everything your viewers say
hot_pat_of_butter: do what you want and the right viewers will come over time
hot_pat_of_butter: talk about your sister and share things and they'll donate
hot_pat_of_butter: you gotta control the conversation, build a culture
hot_pat_of_butter: if you just do what they want, all of a sudden you're stuck with the wrong type of audience
hot_pat_of_butter: know what im saying?
mademoiselle_dell: ya
mademoiselle_dell: i just dont rlly have time for that
mademoiselle_dell: this is like a life or death thing so
mademoiselle_dell: see u tomorrow

• • •

Somehow, without realizing it, I broke 300,000 today. Sometime during my habanero stream, my ranking jumped to 297,777. A sleek and tolerable number. What does collaborating with a top hundred streamer do to your ranking? I should expect to break 250,000 easily, maybe skyrocket to the low 200,000s. But for now, my daily dare is over and there are thirty or so people hanging out in my stream. I transfer it to my phone and swoop my camera across my plants, their many tentacled, entangled limbs reaching all the way up to the ceiling to form a queer canopy, a fecund jungle. It seems like the more I ignore these plants, the bigger they get, the more muscular. Some leaves are as broad as my face and serrated, war-hungry, their musty dirt-smell clogging my nostrils.

Lee knocks on the wall adjoining our apartments. I don't knock back.

I water the plant with the thick, bright green leaves last. Pretty thing but vengeful. Her name is crown of thorns, or Christ plant. Street value up to forty dollars if I play my cards right. I approach gingerly and try to water her from afar, but her too-soft leaves find me, as do the thorns beneath them. I pull my hand back and examine my palm, a pearl of blood emerging slowly from the shallow channel of my life line. And now she seems to lean, sweep her leaves toward me for an embrace. I put the watering can down and step back. Copper. Saliva.

Angry. They all are. Because they've been listening to my thoughts through the seed in my brain, and they know what I've done, what I'm up to. I need to sell them before they can organize their squirming undergrowth, razor leaves held against my throat in my sleep.

"That's it," I say. The condom-wrapped habanero is still on the floor beneath my desk, and my mom's comments about Daisy this morning still linger and take up space, pressing out against the walls. "Tomorrow, I'm getting rid of all of you."

THURSDAY

LiveCast Ranking: 299,839

"Good morning," I say to my viewers, even though it's closer to noon. Even though it's not a good morning. I slept in so much that my LiveCast ranking plummeted back to the 300,000s. Get up, clock in, entertain. Otherwise, people start to evacuate and the algorithm turns on you.

I look at my plants: "Not a good morning for you, either."

> **chillnessa:** buenos días
> **jimpix:** its not morning
> **jimpix:** its morning where i am but not where you are
> **kirk_equivalent:** its dinner time for me =D
> **redtimepolice:** i wish i could sleep in that late lmaoo
> **jimpix:** all hail queen dell

I switch my stream to my phone and tuck it into my back pocket so my viewers can pick up my audio and see what's behind me. Then I get an extra-large cardboard Home Depot box from under my bed, the one my succulents came in when I adopted them last week. I fill the box with as many plants as I can. My apartment looks emptier already. More floor space, more air. Still, it's not enough. I need all of them and their teeming, grubby hands gone. I drop the plants off on the ground floor and walk back up the five flights to my apartment to refill my cardboard box once more. I open the door with my hip and there's Lee, standing right outside.

"What's up?" they say.

"What's up with you?" I ask. My stream is on, my viewers undoubt-edly doing backflips to have Lee onstage. Their favorite supporting actor.

They look at the box of plants in my arms. "Are you going some-where?"

"I'm taking all my plants downstairs."

"For a time out?" They laugh. I miss that dumb laugh, like Pop Rocks. "Do you need help?" they ask, and I consider saying no, but I'm already winded from going up and down the stairs once, and I have at least three more trips ahead of me. They pick up my heaviest plant, a bamboo palm with thick woody stems and spry leaves. It sways as they walk, carefully, carefully, behind me down the stairs. My viewers have a great view of them, but I'm not about to tell Lee they're being broadcast. I know how uncomfortable it would make them, and I do need the help.

"Do you want to have lunch?" they ask. "I have leftover chili from last night."

"I'm going out."

"Oh. Cool. Where?" We put the plants down on the ground floor and head back upstairs to do another trip.

"I'm going to get rid of these parasites. Growing plants is a young man's game."

"Want some company?" they ask, no trace of exertion in their voice. That's what a three-hundred-dollar-a-month gym buys you.

"That's okay. I'm streaming. I'll be streaming."

"Right," they say.

I slip past them at the top of the landing, using two hands to shovel plants into my cardboard box for the last trip.

"How did yesterday go?" Lee asks.

"Can you get those?" I point toward a family of air plants hung from the ceiling by thin white ropes. They reach them with ease, and then everything is gone but the grow lamps, which I'll keep for now. They're solid lighting for my stream, and they're not as intense if I throw a T-shirt or a sweater over them.

We walk down the stairs one last time, my neck and shoulders buzzing with effort.

"You didn't do it, did you?" they ask. "I stayed out of your stream out of respect for the both of us."

"I did it." I grunt, putting down the box of plants. We stand feet from each other on the first floor, the area around us overrun by plants. If someone were to come in now, they'd have a near-impossible time navigating past all the foliage.

"You're a different breed," they say, shaking their head. "It's not sustainable, though, is it? This whole streaming thing?"

I take my phone out of my back pocket as casually as I can and press mute on my audio.

"I'm not trying to hate on you and what you're doing," they say. "I just want to make sure you have a plan for what you're going to do after."

"I've made a thousand dollars in the past three days. This is the plan."

Lee gives me a look but doesn't say anything. I'm thoroughly out of breath and they are decidedly not, which is infuriating.

"That's not really a plan, though, right? Streaming the rest of your life, twenty-four hours a day?"

"What do you want me to say?" I ask, tired of this conversation, tired of Lee and their constant need for things to make sense, to have a plot and a purpose. But that's not life, not really. "What about you? What's your plan?"

"What are you talking about?"

"You think you have your shit together? Really?"

"Don't turn this on me, Dell," Lee says, and I know I should back off, but I can't. Not with my viewers in my pocket and all these awful plants around me.

"You can give it, but you can't take it?" I say.

"Sorry," Lee says. "Fine, sorry. I shouldn't ask you questions about your life."

"Say what you want to say, but I'll ask you questions right back. I use your bathroom every day, Lee. I see how fast you go through your pills. I mean, how many psychiatrists do you have on speed dial?"

"Are you serious?"

"Because I doubt one doctor would prescribe you Adderall, Klonopin, and Xanax. You'd need to have a couple doctors on rotation. Two? Three? What do you tell them? Seriously, I'm curious."

"You don't know anything about me," they say. Not enough anger in their voice to escalate, not enough hurt to de-escalate. They head up the stairs at an even pace, neither stomping nor rushing, and I'm left in the fluorescent entryway surrounded by my furious undergrowth.

I hail a cab, and the elderly driver helps me load the plants carefully into his car. I lean over and strap in my ZZ plant carefully, as if it were an unruly toddler, and then we're ready to go, plants in the passenger seat, back seat, and trunk. I unmute my stream, apologizing to my viewers for the interruption in today's scheduled program. All forty of them. The cabbie stops abruptly at a light and I have to remind him that he doesn't want dirt spilled all over the interior of his car.

"That's it, kids," I whisper to the plants in my lap, by my side, crowding my feet. "It's time to say goodbye." My phone is in the mesh back of the seat in front of me, giving my viewers a spectacular view of my crotch. The driver doesn't notice me mumbling to myself. He has his headphones on and seems to be on an urgent ten-way call in a language I don't recognize.

kirk_equivalent: i'm carsick D:
jackdaw2000: where are we going

trutherdare: to the park
jackdaw2000: yawn
jackdaw2000: lets do something cool today
kirk_equivalent: scheming

Twenty minutes and about as many dollars later we arrive at Washington Square Park. I tip the cabbie and he helps me unload my plants onto the sidewalk. I've been thinking about setting up shop here for a while. The park is essentially one big arty marketplace. The locals are used to the unregulated peddling, and the cops don't mind. They're more focused on the drug deals at the outer fringes of the park, the public bathroom full of used needles. Weed smoke curls in avant-garde shapes and evaporates in the sun. Abandoned Frisbees sit in the empty fountain. I spy high-top Converse sneakers in every color of the rainbow. Purposefully ripped-up clothing that costs more than my rent. Hair any color but natural, any style but down. So many exposed navels. These are the weird-cool kids, the punks and the hippies. And now that it's summer, we're left with the rejects whose parents didn't want them to come home, or who had no home to go back to. Maybe I'd be hanging out here today if I hadn't dropped out.

My old dorm is a ten-minute walk away on Third Avenue. It's NYU's biggest and I lived on the seventh floor, in room 709. My mom thought the number was auspicious, odd on both ends, like me. I remember hanging out in the fifth floor lounge, with its whiteboards and flat-screen TVs. My roommates and I coordinated our hunger so we could eat together. We coordinated our sleep, our study schedules, our menstrual cramps. We coordinated everything so no one would ever have to be alone. Those girls, they're probably still coordinating to this day, without me.

I remember the dining hall on the first floor, the wormy rice and overcooked beans I had for lunch every day. No matter how much

Tabasco I added, those meals tasted like nothing after Daisy got sick. Isn't that bizarre, how grief can devour? How it can make everything it touches just like itself? Everything I ate, saw, said, heard, smelled was grief. I lost my coordination, in all senses of the word.

I remember coming to tour the NYU campus when I was in high school. I thought if I could fit in anywhere, it would be here. Look at all these unironic mullets. And for the most part, I was right. I could be myself among these deceptively smart misfits, and I made friends fast, and the edges of my depression started to soften. I felt accepted for who I was, which was snarky, and strange, and absolutely opposed to all types of goals.

I bring my plants one by one from the curb to a quiet patch of grass. The sun is high in the sky, halfway through its aria. Laughter splits the air, a boom box blasts old-school R & B and a competing boom box blares symphonic techno. People walk by and evaluate my wares. I can tell who the window-shoppers are in an instant. Buyer's intent is a scent I've become an expert at sniffing out. Ruddy-cheeked dopamine, the faintest whiff of yeast. My senses are awake to the subtleties of a glance, how the right foot roots itself in place to linger a moment longer. Most people browse for a minute and then depart with a quick nod or a smile or nothing at all. Others do a lap and come back, or stay a while, chatting idly while they run their internal mathematics: How much? How long? How far?

Some guy in a pristine Wilco T-shirt wants to buy a ficus. When I tell him that it's sixty dollars, he asks if I'll "gift" it to him, for "good karma." I snatch the plant out of his arms. Dramatics aside, I sell two plants in the first ten minutes: a succulent ($10) and a Swiss cheese plant ($35).

Another dude in low-rise jeans and futuristic rectangular sunglasses comes up to my makeshift shop front. I prop my phone up on the bench beside me so I can get up to greet him. He's looking for what everyone is looking for: low-light plants that are hardy and won't up and die on you one day. Something you can rely on.

"What you want is a snake plant. I have one over here. I can sell it to you for forty dollars," I say. "It's fully grown. Super healthy. Low maintenance like you're looking for, and I'll include the pot as part of the price."

He shifts his feet. He gets low and evaluates the plant, sniffing its long, waxy leaves. "Twenty-five," he says.

"You're wearing Burberry sunglasses."

"So?" he asks.

"What did you pay for those, three hundred dollars?"

"I thrifted them for a hundred fifty."

"Let's call it thirty, then," I say. "You can thrift this plant, too."

He puts the cash in my hand and hefts the plant up under his arm. Three children sold, too many more to go, and the day is draining away like liquid from a tin of fish, leaving behind salt and oily residue. I fear I'll have to load up the rest of my plants into another taxi in an hour and take them home, cannibalizing my profits with another cab ride.

"Cheap plants!" I yell. "Dirt-cheap plants! Pun intended! Everything must go!"

Another sale ($10). Another ($25).

Every couple of minutes I get up and shout around, then return to my bench to talk to my viewers. They're enamored with this up-close-and-personal account of my street hawking. Very urban. Very gritty. Very chic. I sell six more plants in the next hour ($132). At three o'clock, a guy offers to trade me a hand-rolled joint for a succulent, and I oblige, lighting up to help pass the time. I haven't eaten yet today, ulcer pain–averse as I am, and the weed reminds me that I'm hungry, starving actually.

excelsior404: i love WSP
jackdaw2000: wut

excelsior404: washington square park
anomolous_donkey has signed on
anomolous_donkey: hello beautiful people
jackdaw2000: I dare you to yell something
chickenleggy: HI
jackdaw2000: yell something crazy

"Plants that'll reverse your kid's vaccine-induced autism!"

racre001: lmao
jackdaw2000 has donated $1
racre001: another one
chickenleggy has donated $2

"Cheap plants that'll make your dick hard!"

racre001 has donated $1
jackdaw2000 has donated $1
racre001: mademosielle dell is literally a hustler
excelsior404: yes, she is
racre001: is weed legal in nyc
anomolous_donkey: mademoiselle_dell what is your foot size?

"Hey?" someone says. I whip my head around. There's a man coming toward me, his voice eager. "Dell? Oh my god, it is you. Hey, Dell!" My old classmate Lucas approaches, blowing his fucking bubbles.

Lucas is a bubble influencer on social media. Bubbles blown through the loop of his fingers, bubble caterpillars chasing their own tails. His best trick: a bubble inside of a bubble. He makes his own liquid with iridescent glitter. Makes watermelon- and hibiscus-scented bubbles, too. Sells his products on Etsy to music festival goers and elementary school teachers for mongo bucks.

It's just soap and water.

"I can't believe it's you," he says. I want to mute my audio so badly, but my phone is a few feet behind me on the bench, and Lucas keeps his hands on mine when he breaks away from a hug.

"Hey," I say, wondering if my eyes are red, if he can tell that I'm high. Not that he would care, but paranoia has worked its way deep into my marrow, nestled close to the seedling in my amygdala. I wish I were anywhere else in the world, even back at the coffee shop with my mom, or at the bottom of the Gowanus Canal.

"Did you change your number? I've called and texted you like a million times."

I blocked him is the truth. I didn't block everyone who texted me to see how I was doing after Daisy got sick, only the ones who kept bugging me even when I didn't answer. Admittedly, it wasn't very many people.

"Yeah," I say. "I lost my phone and had to get a new one." I need to snatch my hands away, walk five steps, and mute my audio before he says something that can't be unsaid. But he keeps smiling and talking and nodding.

"And you didn't transfer your number?" he asks. "That's insane not to transfer your number. Having to memorize a new phone number would, like, ruin my life right now. Can I get your new number? Can we catch up?" His earnestness catches something in my throat and makes me want to say yes, but the urge passes. "I miss you, Dell! We talk about you all the time. Like, where is she? Where has she been? It's like you fell off the face of the earth. Where have you been?"

"What?" I say. "It's fine. I'm fine."

"That night was awful. It's not just on you, you know. We were all there. We—"

"It's fine."

He looks at me, something like pity in his eyes that I can't abide. "It's not fine. Why the hell would it be fine?"

"What do you want me to say?"

"It would be great to know why you haven't been answering me or anyone else for the last few months."

"Yeah, I bet it would," I say. I dash over to the bench and grab my phone. If I weren't high, maybe I'd be able to handle this conversation. Maybe. But I can feel my heartbeat in my teeth, and if he keeps talking I'm either going to break down or bite his head off. "I'll see you later."

Lucas starts to say something but I'm not listening. I walk away from him, away from the rest of my horror-show plants. He doesn't follow me, and once I'm out of sight, I realize I'm running. I remember myself among the cloud of tourists, the fog of pedestrians, and slow back down to a walk. I feel like I could walk right through all these people, and they would only feel a passing breeze. My high has bottomed out into a dissociated state of sobriety, and by the time I get home, I'm shaking so hard I can barely unlock my door.

My apartment is a dark womb and my covers are a darker womb within that womb. I have no interest in moving or doing anything of value. At least my plants are gone. No one plotting to get me in my sleep.

I abandoned over three hundred dollars of plants at the park. Irresponsible. Mindless. But if I had to go back and do it again, I would do the same thing. Because I'm not a brave person, or even a particularly good one.

Lucas will probably tell anyone who cares to listen that he saw me, that I acted like a total maniac, that I ran off like I had something to hide. I wish I could erase myself right off the earth, blow away the shavings left behind. The closest I can get is deleting the listings for my plants.

trutherdare: who was that
MSRN273: mademoiselle_dell's boyfriend
burr9ty: NO that was not her boyfriend
burr9ty: no way

xinfected_botx: u all r so nosy
xinfected_botx: ffs

As long as I lay here in the dark with my screen brightness all the way down and my audio muted, they'll think I'm resting, and they'll entertain each other for a while. Not too long, but it'll buy me some time.

A direct message comes in from excelsior404. Instead of opening it, I toss my phone off my lofted bed. It hits the floor with an underwhelming thud. Jesus Christ. I climb down and pick it up. It's too hot in my apartment.

jackdaw2000: woah
jackdaw2000: that gave me motion sickness

I look at the time. Almost two in the afternoon. Four hours to get up, put clothes on, and walk a couple blocks west. I don't like my odds of success on that one. But hot_pat_of_butter has mega followers. He's a top 100 streamer. The mental math isn't hard to do. I need ten times the viewers to make ten times the money. I've made about one thousand dollars from my stream and I have another thousand dollars or so in my bank account. Today is Thursday. The end of the month is in three days, so I have four more days to meet my absurd goal of fourteen thousand dollars.

Besides, as far as I can trust my own judgment, hot_pat_of_butter seems like a normal, genuine person. If he weren't so successful he'd probably be utterly boring, forgettable, but here we are. I turn on the lights and squint against the glare of my childless grow lamps.

"Fine. I'm up. I'm up," I tell my viewers, and they bless my return and curse my absence. I can't give them a dark screen and nothing to root for and expect them to hang around. But I am somehow back to where I was last night: 299,792. One step forward, one step back.

"Are you down for another road trip?" I smirk at my camera, exuding energy I sincerely don't have.

I let myself into Lee's apartment. They're in their bedroom, deep into their workday, doing whatever it is they do behind that closed door. They won't hear me, they're listening to remixes of video game soundtracks on their noise-canceling headphones. Still, I tiptoe to the bathroom and close the door quietly behind me. The last thing I want to do is talk to them after our conversation this morning.

My face in the mirror is anemic, the bags under my eyes fat and yellow. Lee has all this fancy shit. There's nothing in their bathroom that I've seen in the aisles of a Duane Reade. Just all these little unisex pastel bottles. Camellia leaf water. Hemp oil. Cocoa butter. Ingredient lists so clean I could eat the products and not get sick.

Orange prescription bottles cozied up with all these organic, chemical-free lotions and potions—the irony isn't lost on me. I wonder if Lee would find it remotely funny. Probably not. Maybe I'll bring it up once I'm on their good side again. For now, I'm the reigning queen of asshole kingdom: Who am I to judge someone for how they get through the day? The truth is that anyone who seems like they have it together is getting some form of help or another.

I angle my camera toward the ceiling and chat with my viewers as I take a quick, cold shower. I keep the left side of my head tilted down so water doesn't get in there and water the seed, the budding plant. It's getting so big now that I can almost feel it if I stick my pinkie nail in deep. I turn the water off and stand on the mat in front of the sink without a towel, using one of Lee's cotton swabs to try to wrestle the plant out, but I fear I only succeed in pushing it in further. For a moment, I imagine Lee coming into the bathroom and wrapping me in a towel, laying me down on the bathroom floor and excavating my ear with their fingers. And then I get dressed and close the door behind me quietly. I'm starved. I try to remember the last thing I ate, but I can't. McDonald's.

I open the fridge and take out a glass container of chili. Lee makes great chili. Beans and meat and everything. It's too hot out for a warm meal so I'll just eat it cold. I don't mind. I fill up a bowl and top my chili with shredded cheese and a dollop of sour cream, grab a spoon from their utensil drawer.

"Dell, is that you?" Lee calls from their room, but I don't respond, just let myself out.

• • •

(!) You have a new message
excelsior404: did you get my pic
excelsior404: ???
mademoiselle_dell: fuck off
excelsior404: what
mademoiselle_dell: im going to block u
excelsior404: why are you so mad?
excelsior404: $200 is a lot of money
mademoiselle_dell: I'm always mad
excelsior404: why?
mademoiselle_dell: people, places, things
excelsior404: i've given you hundreds of dollars in the last few days
excelsior404: dont tell me to fuck off
excelsior404: ...
mademoiselle_dell: u made me look like an idiot
excelsior404: no i didnt
excelsior404: fair is fair
excelsior404: $500 is a lot so i would need to know im getting my moneys worth
mademoiselle_dell: listen dickhole
mademoiselle_dell: u pledged and gave me money of ur own free will
mademoiselle_dell: i will block u in an instant
excelsior404: i thought you were better than this
excelsior404: really when i followed you i thought you were special
excelsior404: but youre just a bitch
excelsior404: transfer me my money back
mademoiselle_dell: what
excelsior404: if you dont want to talk to me then i want my money back
mademoiselle_dell: no
excelsior404: are you serious?
excelsior404: transfer me my money
mademoiselle_dell: dont donate money u dont have

excelsior404: i have the money its just not for bitches like you
excelsior404: and i already told you
excelsior404: i know the truth
mademoiselle_dell: blocking u
excelsior404: ill make another livecast account and find your stream again
excelsior404: and ill tell everyone about Daisy
excelsior404: youre a liar
excelsior404: and a bitch
excelsior404: i know girls like you
excelsior404: i was just trying to help you because i thought we had a mutual respect for each other
excelsior404: and i felt bad for you with your sister and i know what it's like to feel the way that you feel and i thought
excelsior404: why not do this nice thing for someone
excelsior404: but you know what you don't deserve it
excelsior404: you never deserved it youre just as bad as all the other bitches out there
excelsior404: no youre worse because you lie and lie and lie and youre ungrateful for the people who actually care about you
excelsior404: and actually want to help you and get to know you for who you are
excelsior404: well good luck because I'm not protecting you any more
excelsior404: there are no more chances

He's still typing. I don't want to see what he has to say next. I click into his screen name, and find the "Block" button, press it before he manages to hit "Send."

I do something I haven't done in a long time, maybe ever. I get on my hands and knees and clean the floor of my apartment with a rag and hot water. From my low vantage point, I can see the dust under my radiator, see it gather like an army under my dresser. I work my way over in damp circles. Sneezing and reaching until all the dust is gone. My viewers can't possibly understand what this means to me, not having to replace my plants with new ones or spend time creating listings online. Reselling plants to gullible idiots was my way to buy groceries or pay Lee back for the shit they spotted me. But I don't need to do that anymore. And if there ever was a reason to keep streaming, it's this: no more vital screech of stretching spines, organic matter reaching upward and outward, this sickening natural intelligence. Monstera Deliciosa, String of Pearls, Dracaena. Plants taking up every inch of floor space and proliferating more quickly than I could name them, vines intertwined until I had nowhere to step, apical buds bloated with children, axillary buds yearning toward the grow lamp, or toward me, whatever burned the hottest. Taproots and lateral roots growing to impossible densities within their pots, threatening to explode like pipe bombs of ceramic and moist earth.

A text from my mom: **Did you go visit Daisy today?**

I'm glad to have my apartment to myself again. Even if I don't have my brain to myself. The seed, sprouting in my ear and suckling vital nutrients. I shake my head from side to side. I can't feel it. That doesn't mean it's not there.

I don't have my apartment to myself, either. My viewers lingering like a chorus, waiting to witness me. Some familiar names, but they're all just strangers. Excelsior404 isn't here, thank god. Lee isn't here. Just forty faceless names, or nameless faces. Sometimes just a string of letters, numbers, and symbols. My stomach pain railroads in from the chili and I try to slow it down with eight Gaviscon tablets.

"It's nearly time to hang out with Hot Pat!" I say to my viewers, smile screwed on tight. "Are we ready?"

chickenleggy: YAAAS

"I don't think we're ready! Are we ready?"

anomalous_donkey: napalm! napalm! napalm!
racre001: i can't wait!!
anomalous_donkey: :D

"That's more like it."

*　　*　　*

A pit stop before the big show. I chat with my viewers as I walk down to the Union Square farmers market. There's a viewer from Gothenburg, Sweden, and one from Baku, Azerbaijan, and a dozen more from a dozen other fake-sounding places. I read out loud from a Wikipedia page and we have a group discussion about the merits of spicy peppers, their various uses. "Hot peppers are native to Middle and South America. Their seeds were spread in the mouths of birds, who don't have heat receptors, through the continent. It wasn't until Columbus arrived in 1492 that these peppers were brought to Europe, Asia, and then Africa. Before then, all those cuisines had was black pepper to add a kick to their food. Totally dismal."

> **MSRN273:** black pepper is kinda spicy if you add a lot
> **kirk_equivalent:** no its not
> **MSRN273:** lmaooo ok

"Do you think seltzer is spicy, too, MSRN273?" I say. "Why people eat spicy food is another question. There's no section on the Wikipedia page about that."

> **kirk_equivalent:** adrenaline

Yes, I think: adrenaline. Dopamine. Endorphins. A controlled risk. Self-harm. I'm not going to go as corny as a "natural high," but you get my drift. The hormones are there and in the right quantities.

> **chillnessa:** jajaja i prefer rollercoasters
> **redtimepolice:** i like that one hot sauce
> **redtimepolice:** i can never spell it
> **cindyrella:** what OMG lol
> **redtimepolice:** seracha
> **MSRN273:** sriracha

redtimepolice: yes
redtimepolice: i like that one
kirk_equivalent: dumbass

"Did you know," I say to my viewers. "That habaneros are not even in the same league as ghost peppers? Habaneros are 100,000 to 350,000 on the Scoville scale. Ghost peppers are closer to 1,000,000. That's what's in the burger I'll be eating with Hot Pat in a couple of hours."

In retrospect, eating five habaneros was merely painful. But in the moment, it was unbearable. A custom, bespoke hell. At three times the potency, a ghost pepper could really wreck me. My throat could close up. I could insta-vomit. Not that I have to eat a ghost pepper. Just some ghost pepper sauce on a burger. Hot_pat_of_butter said it shouldn't be too spicy, shouldn't be an issue for me. Which is boring, when you get down to it: people don't tune in and donate to watch things go smoothly. The show must go wrong.

I clear my throat. "The ghost pepper is a hybrid chili cultivated in northeast India. From 2007 to 2011, it held the world record for the hottest pepper in the world. In 2011, it was superseded by the Trinidad Scorpion, which was then beat out by the Carolina Reaper in 2013."

kirk_equivalent: that's fire
crabbybob: literally

"Pepper spray grenades made with ghost peppers were used by the Indian army in 2015 to flush out a terrorist hiding in a cave."

barbistani: was it osama
pklrik: no obama killed osama
pklrik: with his bare hands
barbistani: with his barack hands
crabbybob: i didnt know pepper spray was made of peppers
kirk_equivalnet: its in the name rofl

The Pepper Prince stand is there at the farmers market, just like hot_pat_of_butter said it would be. It's sold out of a few things at this time of day but not ghost peppers. My viewers crawl around on top of each other like bugs, and all I have to do is walk around, do my thing, and let them do theirs. I hum a tune: "The Farmer in the Dell." It comes to mind once in a while, for obvious reasons. When I was a kid I thought it was called "The Farmer and the Dell," like I had a friend. Now I know that a dell is a small, secluded valley. A safe haven. Good for the farmer. How calm she must be knowing that the conspiring forces of gravity, wind, and water have worked together to hollow out a home for her.

Excelsior404 is gone. I blocked him. There's an intimacy to streaming, like inviting people not into your home but into your brain. Nestle and sprout, like a seed, growing in real time as I head back uptown with my loot in tow. I know that excelsior404 could rejoin my stream at any time, under a new screen name. In fact, he probably already has.

My mom calls. The phone rings eight times and then stops, and she doesn't leave a voicemail. The Gaviscon has worn off and my stomach aches in a way I can feel in my lower back. I'll take more when I get home, but in the meantime the seed in my brain throbs and makes my vision glow and blur, my jaw feels tight and cracks some. I open my mouth as wide as it can go until I hear it pop. Sometimes I get so angry I feel like I could set myself on fire, burn myself down to the wick.

Ping! Ping! Ping! Chats like tiny missiles as I head back to my apartment from the farmers market. With this many viewers the conversation is nonstop.

> **cindyrella:** peppa pig eats hot peppas
> **burr9ty:** dont go there
> **jackdaw2000:** how many peppas could a peppa pig peppa
> **burr9ty:** my niece loves that show

burr9ty: it is dogshit
trutherdare: say toy boat seven times fast

When I get home, I'm almost surprised that the plants haven't somehow returned to haunt the place. I chomp down twelve Gaviscon tablets and chug half a bottle of Pepto Bismol.

I remember one summer Daisy and I were at our grandma's house. It must have been right before I entered high school. Daisy and I shared a bedroom on the second story. There was a plant on the windowsill that was crawling with aphids, a monstrous portrait. Movement where there shouldn't be movement. We tried to ignore the dancing bugs and go to sleep but we were afraid they would crawl into our ears, our nostrils, our mouths and lay their eggs inside of us. Daisy was ten and I was fourteen. It was an airless summer night. I opened the window and she bumped the plant out with her hip as she spoke to me about her day, so smoothly I would've thought it was an accident if I hadn't known better. The plant didn't make a sound when it landed in the grass. We looked out the window and saw the dirt spilled in an arc on the back lawn, a murder of roots thrown in different directions.

I lay on the floor of my newly clean apartment and close my eyes, searching for the coolness between the wooden slats, the air-conditioning from the apartment beneath me that sometimes seeps its way up, and sometimes not at all, with no rhythm or pattern. The seed in my ear is driving me out of my mind. I can feel it if I lay on my side or if I talk too loudly. I stick my finger in my ear often to search around, which I know is only pushing the seed in deeper, impressing it into the soil of my brain. Soon it will sprout. Soon it will grow and repopulate my apartment with greenery and life again.

The evening is here and I have done nothing but wallow, talk to virtual people, and ignore the real people in my life. My mom texted me a couple more times and Lee shot me a **What are you doing today** and a **We should talk** that went unanswered. Since Lee and I met six weeks ago, we've basically been hanging out every evening, talking and laughing or just rotting on the couch together, scrolling on our phones. I miss them, but I'm tired. My stream takes the energy out of me, fills it with a foreign element, and sends it back into my veins cleaner and brighter and denser than it was before. And besides, Lee doesn't want to be on my stream, they've made that clear.

I look at my count and do a double take. There are seventy-three viewers in my stream. LiveCast ranking: 223,590. The last time I looked there were fewer than fifty viewers in here. Seventy-three is very high. Its abundance hits me like a potent drug, straight to the space behind my heart. My stomach pain is momentarily forgotten, as are Lee and excelsior404. Where did all these people come from? When did they join? What I feel is adrenaline, strange delight. Seventy-three viewers plus hot_pat_of_butter's audience, five dollars a viewer . . .

I plaster a smile on my face and turn the energy up to a ten.

"Ladies and gentlemonsters and everyone in between, we have some new viewers in the house today. For those of you who are new to my stream, let me break it down for you," I say, giving my spiel about the streamathon, my sister. "No drama. Just donations. And something you have to know about me is that I am, at my very core, a deeply antagonistic human. I love disagreeing for the heck of it. I love being a hater. And most of all, I love blocking people. And since this is a charity streamathon, there is one criterion for being blocked and one criterion only: not donating. Since a lot of you are new, I'll give you a second to get acclimated. There, second's over."

kidchaos125 has signed off
fluffybuffalo_: hi everyone
fluffybuffalo_: i'm here for the hot pat collab

That explains it. He mentions me once in his stream and my viewer count nearly doubles. How many new viewers will I have after tonight? Will I wake up with hundreds of little eyes watching me in the morning? Will it be glorious?

I would never have to be alone again. This idea nestles like a fact in my body. A crowd at the tip of my fingers, a generous flow of income. I try to imagine all of my viewers in the room with me. Seven laying on their stomachs under the bed. Five sitting hip-to-hip on my desk, braiding each other's hair. Eight squeezed like sardines on my lofted bed. You'd think that it would feel claustrophobic, but it doesn't. It feels amazing.

Hot_pat_of_butter can teach me how to build a brand. He can teach me the ins and outs, or I can teach myself. I could do this. I could really do this.

I'm due at Governor's Burger on Eleventh Avenue at 5:30 P.M. The time draws nearer and nearer but never quite makes it, the seconds dissected into infinitely smaller decimals. Finally, I put on my favorite non-ripped pair of jeans, the ones that actually have pockets I can fit my hands into, and a Dead Boys T-shirt, slip on my cleanest pair of Vans. My idea of looking presentable is dressing like a skater chick, which saddens me because I never did learn how to skate. I tried, but being three inches above the ground just doesn't agree with me. I brush my hair and put on under-eye concealer, and then I'm ready to go.

    xinfected_botx: show us ur OOTD
    MSRN273: leggggoooo
    xinfected_botx: drumroll
    cindyrella: OMG the pervs need to drink some water
    cindyrella: lets see hot pat :)))))

Governor's Burger: I've walked past this place before. The building's awning is beige, faded. A tired storefront, its logo a burger with a crown on it. Governors don't wear crowns, do they? The phone number on the side of the awning is 718-GUV-BURG. There are pictures of menu items stuck to the windows at slapdash intervals, casting erratic shadows on the black-and-white tiled floor inside. I find the picture of the napalm burger with ease. It's the biggest picture on the exterior of the building, and it's surrounded by flames. The buns are a bright, devilish red, hopefully just for photographic effect, and the patty itself seems to be four inches tall.

My stomach is still gnawing despite the Pepto Bismol I chugged earlier, so I dip into my stash. I'm not going to mess this up. I chew four Gaviscon and swallow the chalky dust without water. The aftertaste is chemical and sweet, like cherry candy. I linger outside for a moment to ground myself. Mademoiselle_dell is about to have her debut on hot_ pat_of_butter's channel. This is a big fucking deal. I pretend to catch up on my stream chats until my anxiety has partially faded into boredom, and then I head inside.

Hot_pat_of_butter looks exactly as I expected him to, but not. I've watched his stream. I knew he had red hair and clear skin, green eyes and a narrow face. A big waggy dog. But he looks older in person, in his thirties not his twenties, and he's taller than I expected. His hands are large enough to palm a basketball, but his wrists are dainty little things, misplaced on his body. He sees me come in and breaks into a smile, rips off his headphones.

"Yo!" He offers me a high five. Not a hug, I appreciate that. Other than us there are only one or two other tables occupied at Governor's Burger. They keep looking over at us. I wonder if they recognize hot_ pat_of_butter, or if they're just taking in all his equipment and wondering what the deal is. "Great to meet you," he says, and I can tell that he means it.

"Yo," I return, angling my phone toward him. "Wave to my viewers."

cindyrella: OMG HI!!!
jackofnotrades1: yo ^__^
anomalous_donkey: happy thirsty thursday everyone
crabbybob: ^^^^

It's been a while since I met someone new on purpose. Hot_pat_ of_butter and I have spoken before. He's watched my stream and I've watched his. But this is different. I'm giddy, alert to everything. I turn the camera around so that it's facing both of us. "I'm here with Hot Pat, you ghouls. Is that fucking wild or what?"

"Hey, dungeon crawlers!" hot_pat_of_butter says. "Hang tight because at six o'clock we're going to eat the spiciest burger in Gotham City."

He guides me to our table and starts to set up his equipment.

"Gotham City." I snort. "Where did you come from?"

"Delaware." He smiles. "Did you put a loading screen on your stream?"

"What?"

He takes my phone and I can hear it start to vibrate with enthusiastic chatter. My viewers never get that excited to see me. When he hands the phone back to me, my audio is muted and there's a black screen that reads: "Live stream resuming at 6 p.m. — Napalm Burger Challenge with @hot_pat_of_butter." He shows me where to click if I want to add music to the loading screen, where to click to adjust its length or to turn it off altogether. When he finishes setting up his ring light, camera tripod, and all the thick black cords connecting his video camera to his laptop, he goes into my stream settings again and links my stream to his from six to seven o'clock.

"That way, when I start my stream, it'll be mirrored to your viewers. Everyone will see the same feed."

"And it'll just stop doing that at seven?" I ask. I thought I knew Live-Cast's streaming mechanics, but this is a whole other level.

"Yeah, so you have to be ready for that, and we can extend it manually if we go longer."

"Sick," I say. "What do I call you, by the way?"

"Hm?"

"On your stream. Do you want me to call you Hot Pat or . . . "

"Patrick." He smiles. "That's fine."

"You can call me Dell." First-name basis. I try not to be too pleased about it. "'Dungeon crawlers'?"

"You refer to your stream as a dungeon sometimes. I thought it would fit."

It does fit. Everything fits. The interior of the restaurant is gunky and old, the corners of the floor unswept, but Patrick's smile is immaculate, and he's an expert at this: the equipment, the hype building. It suddenly strikes me as obvious that he'd have nearly a million subscribers. Not shocking at all but inevitable, part of the nature of things. The Gaviscon I downed outside has set in and I'm feeling better than I have all day.

We sit side by side at a four-person table, Patrick's camera angled so that we're both centered on-screen, black bean–sized microphones pinned to our shirts. Patrick's phone is propped up on the napkin dispenser on the table in front of us so we can see chats as they come in. He asks if I'm ready to go, then clicks a button on a remote control, and the video camera beeps red. His energy ramps up so violently, so immediately, that I almost jump out of my seat.

"Hey, everyone! Hey, hotties! What's up? Hot Pat here with one of my favorite new streamers, Mademoiselle Dell, for a super special, super awesome New York City collab! We're here at Governor's Burger in Hell's Kitchen. Fun fact: this place has been open since 1996. That's almost three decades of serving up fat stacks of meat to the city that never sleeps. They added the napalm burger to their menu three years ago. And I talked to their team—get this: only a quarter of the people who order the napalm burger actually finish it. That's right. If you can't handle the heat, get out of the kitchen. Can Dell and I withstand the fire? Are we up for the challenge? I think yes. What do you think?"

He doesn't usually seem this animated on his stream. I wonder if you have to really turn it up in order to come across as excited, over-emote for the people in the back row. If so, I probably come off as a complete slug. I stare at Patrick's phone propped up in front of us. Chats coming in a mile a minute, I can hardly read them before they disappear, and at the top of it all, his viewer count. It keeps changing, dilating by the hundreds with each second that passes. A thousand viewers. Two thousand viewers. Three. And then we've sold out Carnegie Hall, in this dinky little burger place. His LiveCast ranking climbs from 55 to 54 and stabilizes. Dollar signs blur at the corners of my vision, and all I can think is: Is excelsior404 here? He's blocked from my stream, but not Patrick's.

"What do you think, Dell? Are we ready?" he asks.

"Hell yeah. Let's fucking go!" I say, more verve in my voice than I meant to muster. I smile broadly and bare my sharp, sharp canines.

"You heard her. Let's f'ing go!"

Patrick waves over a waitress and orders us two napalm burgers. I hope the food doesn't take too long. This is a livestream. You can't edit out the waiting process through some crafty fast-forwarding or a "thirty minutes later" screen. What if it takes an hour? What if they're out of the burger altogether? I want to ask Patrick, but we're live, so all I can do is keep a sticky smile on my face and try to maintain eye contact with the camera and not the viewer count in front of me.

"So," Patrick says. "While we're waiting for our burgers, let's get to know our cohost for today." He turns to me. "I first found Dell on my discover page. I'm always on the lookout for talent in the hot-pepper-eating world. And she was good, let me tell you. Barely a wince when she chowed down on some habaneros on her channel. So when I found out that she lives in New York City, I thought we had to get together and do something fun. But the real clincher is that—unlike greedy me—her whole thing is that she's raising money for a good cause. Dell, do you want to introduce yourself to our viewers and tell them what you're all about?"

"Not really," I say. Patrick laughs. I clear my throat, hoping the sound isn't too loud on the microphone clipped to my shirt. If I look straight at the camera in front of me, I can't make out the chats or the viewer count in my peripheral vision. Can't think about how much I might make and if I'll meet my goal by the end of the night. If I'll . . .

If I look straight at the camera, I can only see the red light that means we're live, smell the faint sweat from Patrick beside me, or from me, there's no way to tell without giving myself a good sniff. But not now. Now I have to talk. I clear my throat again.

"I'm pumped to eat some burgers today. I'll be honest, I had no idea who Patrick was when he reached out to me. Like, what kind of weirdo tries to meet up with a stranger from the internet? But then I looked him up and found out that he was the kind of weirdo who is also very successful, so when he offered to buy me a burger a block away from my apartment, I happily obliged."

"Tell everyone what you're raising money for, Dell."

"I'm on day four of a streamathon right now, the point of which is to raise some cash. My little sister has been in a coma for nearly two months. She's shown signs of improvement—breathing on her own, some motor function—but the doctors held their monthly death panel and decided that they're tired of keeping her around. My goal is to raise fourteen thousand dollars to bring her home and put her on private life support where some angel of death doctor on hour eighty of his shift can't decide to pull the plug because he needs a nap. I think being home will be good for her. No one actually gets better in hospitals—that's a myth, and there's no evidence to support it. So, my mom and I are excited to have her home with us. Thanks, everyone."

"Wow," Patrick says. I want to roll my eyes, mostly at myself, but I keep still. "That's deep. What else can you share about your sister? Why is she in a coma?"

I shrug. "I'm better at talking with a full stomach."

"Ha. Can't argue with the guest of honor. So you heard it, hotties. We're here for a good cause. All donations we receive today are going directly to Dell to help her reach her goal and help out her sister. Now, let's eat some burgers!"

Almost as if it was coordinated—and maybe it was—a waitress brings out two burgers, two extra-large Cokes, and two glasses of milk. Milk? No way that wasn't coordinated. Also, this is a counter service place. The waitress hasn't gone to any other tables, and now that I actually think about it, she's the cashier. Patrick must have talked to the place in advance, had them time the burgers and drinks just so. There's also no one else here anymore. When did they leave? Did Governor's Burger close early for us?

> **pokelawls:** clap clap clap
> **uneasyzeez:** who dis
> **dolocolo:** meow for me hot pat
> **pokelawls:** meow for us hot pat
> **frograw201:** anyone else on the sober train
> **_paperbat_:** meow meow meow
> **uneasyzeez:** whos the new chick
> **mysti4n:** MEOW

Clearly I had no reason to worry. These are very professional hands I'm in. Hands attached to a person in the top hundred LiveCast rankings who has granted me an exclusive hour of donations from his audience.

Well, I do have some reason to worry, because the burger in front of me is massive. I can hardly fit my hands around it. I pick it up and show the camera. The buns are bright red, just like they were in the picture on the outside of the building, dyed an alarming hue of stoplight.

"You think the buns are spicy, too?" I ask Patrick.

He rips off a piece of bread and puts it in his mouth, then seizes his throat, opens his eyes wide. The veins on his neck pop.

"Are you okay?" I ask. "Is it spicy?"

He starts to laugh. "No. It's just bread."

"You scared me."

"No way I scared you," he says. "But I definitely scared them," he points at the camera. Patrick puts his burger down and addresses his viewers once more. "Let me tell you a little about the napalm burger. Red buns — nothing spicy there. Then we have a ten-ounce burger slathered in ghost pepper sauce and topped with pickled habaneros. Looks like we have some melted pepper jack cheese, a thick slice of tomato, and some relish." He picks up a bit of relish and puts it in his mouth. "Onion. A little spicy, maybe serrano peppers. It's good. I thought I'd miss having some actual pickles in there but it's good relish." He turns to me. "Now, Dell, you've never eaten a ghost pepper before, right?"

"No, never."

"How are you feeling about this?"

How am I feeling? I can sense excelsior404's presence. See his exposed thigh, bird's nest of pubic hair. I know he's here. I know he's watching, just like I know that my stomach pain is going to ratchet up to eleven the second I start eating. But if anyone is going to exploit me, it's me.

"I'm ready," I say. "I'm fucking ready."

I pick up the burger with two hands and try to squash it down so I can take a proper bite. But it's the size of my face. There's hardly any use in trying. I rip a bite off a corner and get some bun, meat, sauce, and relish. The burger isn't amazing, but I love any kind of food that I don't have to pay for. The meat is juicy and cooked medium-well, slightly pink in the center. The sauce is hot, real hot, but not nearly as bad as the habaneros I had the other day.

Patrick looks at me and says "Yum" with a full mouth. "Has the spice kicked in for you?"

"I think so," I respond with my mouth full, too. While I track the chat out of the corner of my eye, the modulating viewer count, Patrick talks to his audience about the burger, about the place, the history of it. It seems that Governor's Burger did close down at six o'clock for us after all. The cashier comes and sits in a chair off to the side, watching us, both bored and amused at the same time, as I'm sure I would be in her position. Considering the fact that about ten thousand people are watching his stream right now, I doubt Patrick had to pay for this meal or any other part of this experience. That's right, ten thousand. I shouldn't fixate on the viewer count, but I can't help it, squinting as I am to make out my least favorite viewer. A few donations have already started to come in. Small ones—one or two bucks a piece—but we're just getting started. If even a fifth of them donate . . . if they all gave a dollar . . . if even a tenth of them gave a dollar . . . and some might even give more than a dollar. Woozy-making numbers.

> **zimbilibmim:** im so hungry
> **pokelawls** has donated $1
> **angelasmirkle:** that burger looks like shit
> **frograw201** has donated $5
> **pokelawls:** clap clap
> **pokelawls:** wtf
> **mysti4n:** MEOW
> **craxwayon:** shes hot
> **zimbilibmim** has donated $1

Neither of us has touched our milk. It isn't needed. This burger is a novelty, a weak bid at virality. The truth is it isn't that spicy. I can recognize that it would be too spicy for the average eater, but I'm not an average eater, and neither is Patrick.

"Has the heat hit you yet?" I ask him.

"There's definitely some ghost pepper in there, but only in the flavor. There's a sweetness to it that really works for me. The heat has been mellowed out, though. I miss it."

I miss it, too. And I'm sure hot_pat_of_butter's viewers miss it. This isn't what they came for. They came to see us suffer, not chitchat and idle on a lazy afternoon. They came to see real human pain.

"We're talking maybe 100,000 to 200,000 on the Scoville scale for this burger," Patrick says. "But that just means that I can actually enjoy it, which is rare on our show, and a lucky day for our guest, right? We're not going to put her through the ringer today, are we? I guess we'll have to do that another day. Damn, though, look at her go."

Patrick is talking about me, about the fact that my burger is almost gone. I'm used to eating fast before my stomach pain sets in, and I forgot to turn off that reflex. I look over at his plate and he's taken maybe four bites in the time it's taken me to scarf down ninety percent of my food. And the sooner we finish, the sooner the stream will be over, and the donations will stop coming in. I put my burger down and wipe my hands on my pants.

"Don't stop on my behalf," he says.

"I wish it were spicier," I say.

He shrugs, unphased. This is just another day for him, just another stream. But for me, it could be everything. "It's spicier than the hari-kari tuna roll we ate on the stream a few months ago in Florida, but not by much. If an unsuspecting person came in here and ordered this, they might not be able to finish it, but I don't think they'd be in agony or anything."

He takes a bite, and then another. Soon our food will be gone and the show will be over. Ten thousand viewers slipping through my fingers. I can't go home with nothing to show for it.

"As we start to wrap it up here, and now that you have a full stomach, maybe you can tell our viewers a little bit more about your sister, Daisy," Patrick says. "I think they'd love to hear about what happened to her, and how you've been navigating everything. As her older sister, I know you've gone above and beyond to take care of her and make sure she has the best possible chance of waking up. I bet our viewers would love to hear about that process and how it's been for your family."

My inner ear throbs, the plant wiggling and tender. I take the two ghost peppers out of my bag and proffer them to the camera. "Before we get into that, shall we have a little more fun?"

Patrick looks the peppers over with a serious expression, takes them from me and weighs them in his hands. Then he gets up, and I think he must be mad at me, pissed that I changed the plan on him. He walks over to turn off his camera, but then he's standing in front of it, giving his viewers—our viewers—an up-close look at the peppers. I can see the chat moving a mile a minute. Message after message after message. So many exclamation points.

"It seems that Dell has brought us some ghost peppers," he says. "These are in the sauce that's on our burgers. The spice has been totally cooked out, though. Mixed with other ingredients and kicked down about a million notches. But she was thoughtful enough to bring some fresh peppers with her today. Pepper Prince?" he asks me. I nod. "Terrific. For those of you who came to my homemade hot sauce workshop last year, you might remember that we used ghost peppers to make our own barbecue sauce. Now, these two are very fresh, you can tell by the deep red color. And they're heavier than they look, which tells me we're in for it. But I never turn down a challenge."

Patrick sits down beside me again.

"Are we doing this?" I ask him. In lieu of a response, he picks up the bigger pepper and eats it whole, picking off the stem with his teeth. I was just going to take a bite, but I can hardly do that now. I have a moment of hesitation—what if I can't do this?—but there's no backing out now. I'm on camera, live in front of thousands, and Patrick is looking at me expectantly. So I do the same, trying not to overthink it.

We chew in silence for one, two, three seconds. Ghost peppers taste different from habaneros. Definitely sweeter. Less fruity. More smoky. The heat blooms in the back of my mouth, trickles up my nose and makes it leak. Patrick hands me a tissue and I blow, aware that the sound must be awful on the microphone. And then the heat intensifies beyond a threshold I thought possible. My head lights up like an alarm and I clutch at my chest, riding a wave of acute heartburn.

"Oh my god," I say, and it comes out like a question. This pepper is so hot it feels illegal. Like snorting wasabi. "Oh my fucking god," I say, a statement this time.

I look at the glass of milk on the table in front of me but don't move toward it. Not until Patrick does. But he doesn't seem to be in pain at all. He drinks some water to help swallow the pepper down and then shows off his empty mouth to the camera. Panic starts to set in. How is he not in pain? Is it actually pain that I'm feeling, or just the sensation of extreme heat? Capsaicin is just sending pain signals to my brain, that's all. Right?

One million Scoville units. One million drops of water to dilute one drop of ghost pepper concentrate. That's four times the heat of a habanero. Half the heat of a Carolina Reaper. I—

Fuck. It's getting worse. It's very much getting worse by the second. I feel hot and cold at the same time, and the thought that the heat hasn't peaked yet makes me regret everything that led up to this moment. An impossible squeezing pressure behind my eyes but I don't dare touch them, just press them shut and let my leaky tears squeeze their way out, watering my root-brain seedling. I could've just eaten a free burger and gone home. Why the hell did I have to pull this stunt?

Oh yes, that's why. I can see line after line of green donations in the chat, though my eyes are too watery to make out the amounts. Lots of green interspersed with black chats, coming in too fast to read. Ten thousand viewers, I think to myself as stomach acid climbs up my throat to strangle me. I may have even broken 200,000. I won't know until later, and I can't check my LiveCast ranking if I'm dead. I focus on breathing. Focus on counting the seconds, the imaginary dollars coming to scoop me up in their folded wings. Patrick makes his mouth into a tiny "O" shape and inhales sharply. "I'm cooling down my mouth," he says. "Try it out."

"I can't."

"No?"

"I'll look dumb."

He laughs. "The heat takes up to ten minutes to fully set in," he says.

"And then we die?"

"And then we defeat death," he says, with a wiggle of his eyebrows. "Aren't you happy you brought the peppers?" he asks.

"Never been happier," I say, and the acrid smell of the pepper makes its way out of my mouth to my eyes, forcing them shut again. Pepper spray ranges from 500,000 to 2,500,000 Scoville units. I basically just ate pepper spray in front of a packed theater. Patrick starts hiccuping. A wet burp slips in alongside one of his hiccups, and I wonder for a moment if he's going to vomit. He downs his glass of milk, and I do the same. It keeps getting worse. My throat is so hot. I'm having difficulty swallowing, and I consider how long it would take for an ambulance to get here. I blink and blink but I can't clear the rheum from my eyes. I can't see the green donation lines anymore. I can't see anything.

Did Daisy feel pain, before she fell unconscious? Would things have been different if I had called an ambulance right away?

My organs clench, and I can feel the edges of my ulcer flickering with heat. "I really don't want to shit my pants," I say, shuttering my mind against other thoughts, other panic attacks. Patrick laughs. This guy laughs a lot. Which was endearing before but now really pisses me off. I force my eyes open and focus on the bead of sweat working its way down the back of his neck, down the collar of his shirt.

"Am I allowed to curse on your show?" I ask.

"Go for it."

"Well then, fuck you," I say to Patrick, and then to the cashier watching us and cracking up: "Fuck you, too. Why don't you make yourself useful? Fill up a bucket and dump some ice water on us?"

She gets up.

"No," Patrick says, laughing and waving his hands. "Hold on. Not ice water. Do you have anything else? Like soft serve?" She nods and heads into the kitchen.

"Good idea," I say. "Great idea." My stomach starts to cramp, and I take two more Gaviscon tablets out of my pocket, chew them up quickly.

"What's that?" he asks.

"Antacids."

"Where did you get those?"

"My pants."

I can hardly talk. I hope my throat doesn't fully close up. This is so much worse than a habanero, the difference is unfathomable. I want to jump up and slam myself against the ceiling. I want to lift a car off a child. Anything to expend some of this excess adrenaline. Green lines keep coming in. Everyone loves to watch me suffer.

"You ate the pepper," Patrick mutters. "The pepper didn't eat you."

"What?"

"It's my mantra. I made this choice. I'm in control."

Patrick takes the top bun off his burger and chews it slowly, like a cow. I wish I had a bun, wish I hadn't gulped down my burger so fast. But soon the cashier is back with soft serve and I grab it out of her hands and shove it right down my gullet. French vanilla. Ultra sweet and tacky. It helps a little, but not much. I stand and reach for my toes and Patrick watches me, amused.

"Come stretch with me," I say. He gets up and tries to touch his toes, his hands landing on his lower thighs. "Now some jumping jacks," I say, and we do jumping jacks, the two of us, while the camera and the cashier watch, and somehow my throat doesn't close up even though I'm losing my breath. Patrick is red and sweaty and smiling. And that's the real difference between the habaneros and the ghost peppers: I ate the habaneros alone. I was in my own head, alone with my thoughts, trying to keep myself sane. Now, Patrick and I can keep each other sane. I can look at him and know if I'm going to be alright, like with a flight attendant on a plane.

Patrick asks the cashier if she wants to join us for some exercise and she politely declines. We eventually stop jumping and sit back down.

"Every orifice of my body is sweating," he says. "I've eaten every pepper on earth. I've eaten ghost peppers a dozen times. But it doesn't get easier."

He lets out a thick, noxious burp and then it's my turn to laugh. I look over at his viewer count: 11,224 viewers. I can't see the total amount of money we've raised but I can see green messages continue to come in, scattered in between the normal chats. Cheers, jeers, and greetings. We did it. I did it. We put on a great show. The hard part is over. Now I just ride out the wave of heat that's still crashing through my guts and hope I don't have to excuse myself to go to the bathroom while we're still on air.

*　　*　　*

Home. Stairs. Lee's bathroom. The most unforgiving diarrhea I've ever had. Light leaks out from Lee's closed bedroom door but I dare not knock. There are questions behind that door that I don't have the energy to answer. Dehydrated and shaky, I drink glass after glass of water from the bathroom sink, using Lee's toothbrush cup. My guts are squeegeed clean, my insides are sloshing, and I'm ready for bed. It's early but I'm wasted away, head pounding and muscles sore. The heat has abated for the most part, embers no longer shooting down the length of me. What I'm left with is a soggy brain, limbs loose in their sockets, and the surreal feeling that it wasn't me who ate the pepper but someone else, someone with more chutzpah.

Today mademoiselle_dell made $4,402 dollars. My LiveCast ranking is a shining, glimmering 189,739. I message Patrick to thank him.

> **hot_pat_of_butter:** thats awesome!!
> **hot_pat_of_butter:** it took me about a year to break 200,000
> **hot_pat_of_butter:** and then another year to break 100,000
> **hot_pat_of_butter:** and then another five years to break 100 lol
> **hot_pat_of_butter:** keep it up dell
> **hot_pat_of_butter:** once you get to 100,000 lets chat about what we can do together
> **hot_pat_of_butter:** should be soon if i know you :)

I fall asleep and dream of Daisy knocking a plant off a windowsill with her hips. "Oops." She giggles. "Don't tell Mom." The plant doesn't make a sound when it lands in the grass. I look out the window and my body is spilled out on the lawn, arms and legs twisted in improbable directions. Out of my cracked skull sprouts a thickened root, a bursting spiral of leaves.

FRIDAY

LiveCast Ranking: 190,341

I wake up on Friday morning with 112 viewers in my stream. The algorithm has blessed me with a bountiful harvest. My LiveCast balance is $5,356. My viewers talk to each other, yell at each other, no need for me to keep them company. I feel like I'm watching a play, and at this point in the action it's impossible to tell where things are going, when some forgotten character will enter from stage left with a knife in his hand.

All these strangers. It was different when it was just a couple dozen names that I could recognize. And I suppose there is glory in having this many people around me, but it's also dizzying. Mademoiselle_dell is the one who can handle all this, and I usually slip into her with ease. But I'm barely awake and my brain tubes are backed up, unmyelinated and sticky with phlegm.

"Top of the morning, ghouls and goblins."

chillnessa: buenos días
jimpix: its almost noon in EST
jimpix: how is ur sister
MSRN273: r we visiting daisy today
excelsior303: yeah are we?

The knife glints in a scrape of light. I scoot my chair back, roughly, scratching the floor. I click into his screen name—excelsior303—and press the "Block" button, and then I'm left breathing hard. I make my-self a cup of instant coffee and wash my face with water at the tiny metal sink in my apartment. The water tastes like pennies, blood. I fill up a cup and chug it down, then fill it up again. I knew he would rejoin. He said he would, anyway. Wishful thinking to believe that he would just move on with his life, go pester someone else with a dying sister.

The seedling in my brain throbs and aches. Growing pains. I chat with my viewers on autopilot, getting to know the new ones, greeting the OGs. They talk about how sickening I am, in a good way. How ill I am, in the best way. How I slay. How I kill it. How they're gagged. How I'm so great it makes them want to unalive themselves. All the slang that dances around the language of death, trying to control it.

I should do something epic today, but I still feel wobbly from yester-day, and I'm so focused on my list of viewers that my eyes nearly cross. Each new screen name is a flinch, is excelsior404 in disguise. Have I seen casabianca here before? Pokimane2k? One screen name—snack_sparrow—reminds me of *Pirates of the Caribbean*, which reminds me of Johnny Depp, which creeps me out, so I go ahead and block him just in case. I feel like Scarface, slanting my eyes at friends and strangers alike, trying to protect something as fiddly and fickle as this minute of online success. There are eyes everywhere. Between the floorboards. Beneath the popcorn ceiling. The only way to defeat them is to meet their gaze headlong, but each time I do, six more sets of eyes pop up in their place. It's the plants all over again.

During the worst days of my depression in high school, I felt a bit how I do now. Stagnant, immovable. But I know I'm not back there, in that submersible space, because I have all this money now, all these supposed people in my corner.

I wonder if the support team at LiveCast would let me block an IP address.

jimpix: yea lets visit Daisy!!

"Why are you all obsessed with Daisy? What about me? Is anyone worried about me?"

xinfected_botx: ur a good sister

"Enough of that, yeah?"

jackdaw2000: how is your ulcer
cindyrella: idt a seed can grow in your brain btw OMG
cindyrella: it needs soil water sunlight
fluffybuffalo_: ew!!!!

"I've stopped trying to get it out. It's growing on me." I do an exaggerated drum sting.

fluffybuffalo_: barf!!!!
xinfected_botx: ily mademoiselle_dell
fluffybuffalo_: mother

"Mademoiselle Dell loves you back," I say. "Every single one of you."

New Voice Message, 9:31 AM
Hey, Dell, it's Mom. I know we only met for breakfast a couple of days ago—was it Thursday? No, Thursday was yesterday. I saw you on Wednesday, so that was two days ago, but it feels like much longer already because I can't seem to get ahold of you. Are you ignoring me? I feel like you're ignoring me. We didn't even have breakfast on Wednesday. Just coffee. Call me when you get this.

• • •

New Voice Message, 9:39 AM

When I was your age, I only talked to my mom once every other week. She lived across the country, though, and talking on the phone was more expensive back then. I only live an hour away. I understand needing your space and not wanting to talk to your mom all the time. That's probably normal for someone your age. But right now? I want to talk to you. I want us to talk. And it doesn't have to be all the time. So maybe there's something we can do about that, some kind of middle ground. What do you think? Are you okay? I'm certainly not. Not at all. I fell apart after talking to our neighbor Sharon the other day. She reminded me of how you and Daisy used to play in the driveway when it rained. You both loved the rain so much. I don't know where you got it from. You couldn't pay me to go out there with you. The second it started raining you two would scream and run outside in whatever clothes you were wearing. And I always had to lay a trail of towels for you by the door because I knew you'd get everything muddy when you came back in. But you two were so delighted, there was nothing I could do about it. Do you still like the rain? Anyway. Let's find time to talk today.

•   •   •

New Voice Message, 9:43 AM

You can just send me a text if you don't feel like talking. A sign of life every other day isn't too much to ask. Some of my friends talk to their kids every day. I don't need us to be like that. I think that's too much, sometimes, and I don't want to put that kind of pressure on you, though of course I wouldn't mind. Some of my friends, their kids call them to ask what they should wear or what they should have for dinner. I wouldn't mind that, but maybe it's too much. I don't need that, I really don't. I know how independent you are. I love how independent you are. I'm sorry if it feels like I need that kind of relationship, but I really don't. I have a life of my own. I work all day and I'm tired and the last thing I want to do at the end of the day is get on the phone with someone, so I get it. At the very least I remember being your age and it never crossed my mind that I should talk to my parents more. But things are different now, with Daisy. And I know you don't like when I talk about that but I'm trying to be realistic and honest about how I feel. It's better for both of us that way, so nothing goes unsaid. So visit her, okay? Or don't. I don't want to pressure you. But you really should. I don't want you to regret not visiting her enough. I know you said you would do it on your own time. And it's almost Sunday anyway, so we can go together, just like we planned, which is fine by me. I can pick you up on Sunday. We don't have to plan it out now, we can talk tomorrow, or whenever you want. No pressure.

•   •   •

New Voice Message, 9:50 AM
I was planning on going to see Daisy around noon on Sunday so maybe I can pick you up at nine or ten and we can actually have breakfast. Not at that coffee place but somewhere we can sit down and order some eggs or potatoes or bacon or something. Unless you really liked that muffin. If so we can go back to the coffee place, that's fine, if it's easiest for you, although I'm sure there are other muffins elsewhere. I thought the muffin was only okay. But whatever you want, I'm flexible. So why don't you pick a place for Sunday and text me to confirm and we can go together before we visit Daisy? No hurry, no pressure. Okay? Bye.

•   •   •

I am met with a sudden and unbearable craving for chili. I don't want to check in with Lee, but I'm hungry, and not in the mood to get dressed, be a human, spend money.

"The plan is to sneak in as quietly as I can," I tell my viewers. "Lee hates when I go through their shit. But it's a workday so hopefully they're in their bedroom in a meeting or something."

redtimepolice: OoooOooOOoooh
xinfected_botx: day 5 of streamathon and its time to sleuth
karnie_vibes: no one asked for the play by play
xinfected_botx: go back to vancouver
karnie_vibes: i never left
MSRN273: fight

"Jesus shitting hell, I'm just going to steal some soup."

anomalous_donkey: >:D

I close my door behind me and tiptoe over to Lee's, my phone in my hand in front of me so my viewers can see what I'm seeing. I listen at their door: nothing. I open it slowly and peek my head around. Shit. Lee is on the couch eating salad out of a plastic yellow mixing bowl. They turn and catch my eye before I can retreat, their face unreadable. Not excited to see me, that much is clear. I click the "Mute" button on my stream and pull my jean jacket around me like a straitjacket.

"Hey," I say, coming inside. "What's up?"

My phone is at my side, seeing the room upside down. I can imagine my viewers booing, demanding I turn the audio back on, fleeing in droves. I can feel my LiveCast ranking plummeting down, down, down. I have to make this fast.

"What's up yourself?" Lee says.

"Are you taking a lunch break?" I ask. "Isn't it early for you to eat lunch?"

They shrug.

"Do you mind if I grab some of that chili you told me about?"

"Didn't you already?"

"Oh, yeah. Sorry about that. I was starving."

"Did you come to apologize for yesterday?" they ask, inspecting their cuticles. "Are you going to bring my bowl back?"

"I'm going to bring your bowl back. Why would I keep your bowl?"

"I don't know," they say. "I just wanted to know if you were going to bring my bowl back."

I look at them but they don't say anything else, just pick up their fork and continue going at their salad, piercing their fork over and over into the tumble of finely chopped kale and pecorino cheese. It smells lemony and fresh. They scoop up a crouton and chomp it loudly. Eating fast like they need to keep their anger down. I cross my arms and look around. They keep it brisk in the summer, AC on full blast. I'm so hungry I start to feel lightheaded.

"I'm going to bring your bowl back," I say. "Obviously."

They put down their salad and turn to me. "No apology, then?"

"Listen, I—"

"Are your viewers here? Are you streaming right now?"

"No," I say, my phone gripped tightly in my hand. My viewers can't hear anything, can't see Lee, so what's the difference?

"I got a direct message from one of them this morning."

"What?" I say. Lee takes out their phone and hands it to me. Excelsior404. I blocked him, but Lee—l-nino9—did not. And why would they? They'd have no reason unless I told them to, which I should have. I absolutely should have. But then excelsior404 could have just messaged them with a new screen name. A reptilian hydra with too many heads to keep track of. I focus on Lee's phone, forcing myself to open the message. It's a link to a PDF. Some kind of legal document. At the top it says "The City of New York: Certificate of Death."

"What is this crap?" I whisper, putting Lee's phone down.

"I don't know," they say. "What is it? Why would he send it to me?"

"He's harassing me," I say. "That's the guy who told me to put a habanero up my vag. He even sent me a fucking nude. He's been harassing me since I started streaming. I blocked him and then he rejoined my stream under a different name. He knows you're my neighbor. Clearly, he's trying to start shit."

"But why would he send me that? What is that?"

"Do me a favor, just block him? Seriously. He's creepy. He's a creep."

"This certificate, are you related to this person?" they ask, their gaze astringent.

"My last name is really common."

"Isn't that your mom's name at the bottom? And that date? A couple months ago?"

I lean over and look. At the bottom of the document there's a date and a line for a legal relative of the deceased: Kimberly Danvers.

"I'm confused, too," I say, trying to keep my voice steady even though I'm desperate to get out of here. "Why did he send this to you? I don't know why. I couldn't tell you. Just block him and forget about it."

Lee gets up and goes to the kitchen. I watch them from the couch, trying to read their body language. The tattoo on the back of their left ankle is visible in their bare feet, a bumblebee the size of a dime. They cover the salad bowl and put it in the fridge, then open a can of mandarin orange seltzer. To my left on a bookshelf is their middle school spelling bee trophy. It was one of the first things I asked about when we met. They won on the word "albumen," the white of an egg. The trophy is legit, and way heavier than it has any right to be, featuring a winged bee wearing a crown and standing with its hands on its hips. I've fantasized about that trophy before. Not stealing it. Just gumming the marble between my molars for a little while, rubbing its wings for good luck.

"I finished the chili last night," they finally say. "There's none left."

"You're going to block him, right?" I say.

"Why have you been ignoring me?"

"What?"

"Lately, you're either ignoring me or being dickish. There is no in-between. Usually there is an in-between."

"I haven't been ignoring you. I've been streaming. I've been working. I made over five thousand dollars in four days. This isn't a hobby. You don't want to be on my stream and I'm streaming twenty-four hours a day, so."

"You're not streaming right now."

"I step away sometimes."

"You can step away to take a half-hour shit in my bathroom, but you can't step away to say hi to me?"

"I—"

"It's fine. You're doing your own thing. I get that."

"It's not that—"

"I joined your stream last night," they say, which shuts me up. I feel faint. I need to eat something. I need to get out of here. "I know you said not to, but you weren't answering my texts or your door, and I just wanted to see where you were. Like, in the world. I was worried about you. I wasn't trying to spy on you. I only joined for a second. I saw that you were eating a burger with someone. Probably someone important, if you're making that much. It looked important, so good for you. Congratulations. But when I joined, I saw some chats. They were talking about someone named Daisy. Donating money for someone named Daisy. And then I get this link sent to me. I'm not trying to spy on you or get in your business. Just explain this to me. Please."

"You joined my stream? Because you needed to know where I was?" A smile crawls onto my face. More of a smirk, really.

"Stop."

"It's just kind of clingy, that's all."

"Alright, Dell."

I stand up too quickly and get lightheaded, steady myself on the back of the couch. I feel seasick. How many viewers have left my stream in the last few minutes? How much has my LiveCast ranking dropped? Hunger makes my guts snake together tightly, rippling with pain. I head for the door, but Lee stops me.

"This streaming thing—it seems like a lot. Like it's tiring you out. You know you can talk to me about anything, right?"

"That doesn't mean I want to."

"So you just want to come to my place whenever you want and not talk to me?"

"You gave me your key before we were friends. We didn't have, like, a stop-and-chat clause in our nonexistent key contract. Am I supposed to come give you a hug whenever I need to use the bathroom?"

I roll my eyes and try to move past them, but they don't budge. I don't want to push them, but I need to go. I step forward, so close that our faces nearly touch. They inhale sharply and something changes in their eyes. Then I reach for the doorknob behind their back and turn it, letting myself out.

LiveCast ranking: 202,071.

redtimepolice: mission failed
MSRN273: fight fight fight

What a malevolent, malignant little tumor. I've never wanted to punch someone in the face more than I do excelsior404, and I've never even seen his stupid face. He probably has a baby face. Squashable. He probably has zero muscle mass, from sitting in his black-and-red gamer chair all day and night watching streams and rotting. Sending that to Lee. What the hell was that?

burr9ty: why did you mute???
Trutherdare: oh no -__-
redtimepolice: weres the chili

Eyes on my viewer list. One hundred some-odd names. I scan them quickly and then slowly and then quickly again. Where are you hiding?

I try to put myself in his shoes, and it's not as hard as it should be. If the roles were reversed—if I found out that Nik had a stream, let's say—I could see myself harassing that motherfucker. I could see the obsession developing. Minus the obvious misogyny. The other difference is that Nik actually owes me money for labor done under contract. Excelsior404 only thinks I owe him money. That's not how the internet works.

Jexxy458? Austrinroolz? Wesam1997?

I click into profile after profile, trying to find ones that were created during the last day. Nothing. But that's not foolproof, because he could have other accounts, ones he created years ago for other reasons. He could have logged in to a friend's account. He could be anyone.

But he's not just anyone. He's right there: excelsior202. I should just block him, I know that, but I can't help myself. My incisors are sharpened by anger, my claws extended from their nail beds.

> **mademoiselle_dell:** hey dumbass
> **excelsior202:** hello
> **mademoiselle_dell:** what the absolute fuck do you think you're doing
> **excelsior202:** exactly what i said i would
> **excelsior202:** exposing you
> **mademoiselle_dell:** im ending this
> **mademoiselle_dell:** whatever this bs is, its over
> **mademoiselle_dell:** this was cute when i had like 3 followers
> **mademoiselle_dell:** but i streamed with hot pat yesterday
> **mademoiselle_dell:** im a fucking top 200,000 streamer
> **mademoiselle_dell:** im actually doing things with my life
> **mademoiselle_dell:** maybe u should do the same
> **excelsior202:** u need to pay everyone back
> **mademoiselle_dell:** lol ask fucking nicely
> **excelsior202:** youre a whore
> **excelsior202:** and a liar

Blocked. I screenshot our conversation and show it to my viewers. "Look: this happened about a second ago. Our old friend excelsior404—we're done with him. He's been stalking and harassing me and my friends in real life. He might start reaching out to you as well. So if he does, if you see his name pop up in my stream in any form, or if you see someone with a different name that you think might be him, just report him. Okay? And let me know so I can block him."

> **jimpix:** yes queen dell
> **jackdaw2000:** aye aye
> **chickenleggy:** OMG noooo ofc
> **burr9ty:** reach out to livecast

"Yes, burr9ty. Yes." I click through LiveCast's support options and open a ticket to block someone's IP address. Let me think. Worst-case scenario, he turns everyone against me. I could just stop streaming. Close up shop. I have over six thousand dollars between my LiveCast balance and my savings—enough to pay all of this month's bills and the next, enough to tide me over until I find another part-time, menial, benefit-less job. But fuck that. I'm good at this. Patrick said so. And it won't take me years to break the top 100,000 like it took him—I can do that in weeks, I know I can. I'm just getting started.

It's not like I have to keep this streamathon going forever. Once I build up my viewer count, I can just stream for a couple hours a day, even take time off if I wanted to. Once I break the top 100,000, I can start putting ads on my stream, link up with affiliate programs.

Patrick probably used to work a desk job. I bet his friends and family pressured him to go back to it when he first started streaming. Thought he was pathetic, wide-eyed in his optimism. Now look at him. He could buy and sell his friends and family for fun. He could retire tomorrow and rip up small bills to feed the birds at the park.

I've been on air for a little over a hundred hours. If I break down my profits, that's over fifty dollars an hour. I don't want to give that up. I can't. But what excelsior404 did, messaging Lee, that was violence. Pure and simple violence. He warned me, to his credit, but how was I to know that he wasn't all talk? I doubt he's going to stop here, stop with Lee. People like him, once they set their sights on taking someone down, they're relentless. Not having a life will do that to you. And that isn't the type of energy I can afford to have directed my way right now.

My viewers want to chat with me. They want to entertain me, and they want me to entertain them back. But I'm too vigilant, hunting my viewer list for warning signs, storm clouds. I stick an absentminded finger in my ear, scratching, digging. I feel the edge of a petal, something pliable and lush. I scratch too hard and cut myself. The tiniest drop of blood trickles out of my ear and dries to rust in its folds. The plant is too deep, I can't uproot it on my own. I need some sort of specialized instrument, like a scalpel, or a chainsaw.

• • •

(!) You have a new private message
hot_pat_of_butter: heyyyyyy
hot_pat_of_butter: yesterday was sick
hot_pat_of_butter: i can't believe you brought ghost peppers
hot_pat_of_butter: so awesome
hot_pat_of_butter: how are you feeling
mademoiselle_dell: hey
mademoiselle_dell: yes im a shining star a beacon of health and wellbeing
mademoiselle_dell: jk
hot_pat_of_butter: lol same
hot_pat_of_butter: my stomach is always off the day after i eat a pepper like that
mademoiselle_dell: my stomach is always off so
hot_pat_of_butter: lol
hot_pat_of_butter: congrats on making bank too
hot_pat_of_butter: im glad my viewers were able to help

I don't know what to say. I want to say thank you, but I don't know how, and so I say the opposite.

mademoiselle_dell: its whatever
mademoiselle_dell: im not going to meet my goal though
mademoiselle_dell: and my ranking dropped a little today
hot_pat_of_butter: that's normal. itll rise a ton after a big stream and then restabilize
hot_pat_of_butter: how off are you
mademoiselle_dell: off
mademoiselle_dell: i need to double what I've made by sunday
mademoiselle_dell: and its friday so
hot_pat_of_butter: :(
hot_pat_of_butter: sorry to hear that
hot_pat_of_butter: that sucks
hot_pat_of_butter: whatre you going to do

mademoiselle_dell: idk

mademoiselle_dell: i could eat a scorpion pepper today

mademoiselle_dell: prob not enough

mademoiselle_dell: whatever

hot_pat_of_butter: youve got tricks up your sleeve

hot_pat_of_butter: just be yourself and have fun with it

mademoiselle_dell: ok lol

hot_pat_of_butter: be spontaneous

hot_pat_of_butter: if something is exciting to you itll be exciting to your followers

hot_pat_of_butter: and livecast will see that engagement and reward it

mademoiselle_dell: ok

mademoiselle_dell: ill try

mademoiselle_dell: to be spontaneous lol

hot_pat_of_butter: worst case scenario

hot_pat_of_butter: let me know what you need, okay? maybe i can match your donations on the last day or something

I'm not going to accept Patrick's pity, and I'm not going to cry. I can still fix everything, I just need to figure out a plan. Because if a problem is my fault to begin with, I should be able to fix it, shouldn't I? That's only fair, to be able to reverse things, get a second chance. Other people get second chances all the time.

hot_pat_of_butter: you could do the world record competition

mademoiselle_dell: lol what

hot_pat_of_butter: im serious

mademoiselle_dell: ya ok

Patrick sends me a link. Last year's winner—a man built like a linebacker with a severe case of baby face—announced that he wasn't going to the world record competition tomorrow because of a personal conflict. This man not only holds the world record but absolutely demolishes everyone year over year. Last year he ate 122 grams of Carolina Reaper in one minute. Each pepper weighs four to five grams, so that's essentially 30 peppers in a single minute. One every two seconds. The person in second place ate less than half of that.

> **hot_pat_of_butter:** the world record holder won't be there...!!!
> **mademoiselle_dell:** so what
> **hot_pat_of_butter:** so
> **hot_pat_of_butter:** you dont have to beat the world record
> **hot_pat_of_butter:** just whoever else signs up that day
> **hot_pat_of_butter:** thats massive
> **hot_pat_of_butter:** you could actually win
> **mademoiselle_dell:** lol i ate one ghost pepper and died
> **mademoiselle_dell:** carolina reapers are 2x so
> **hot_pat_of_butter:** but you didn't die
> **hot_pat_of_butter:** you also didn't have a thousand people cheering for you in person
> **hot_pat_of_butter:** and you weren't surrounded by live TV cameras
> **mademoiselle_dell:** ur saying i should sign up
> **hot_pat_of_butter:** i'm saying you should win
> **hot_pat_of_butter:** prize is $20,000

He sends me a sign-up link. I open it briefly and then close it again.

> **mademoiselle_dell:** u think highly of me
> **mademoiselle_dell:** idk why
> **hot_pat_of_butter:** i think youre cool, thats all
> **hot_pat_of_butter:** anyway you don't even have to win
> **hot_pat_of_butter:** you could just stream yourself competing and make some bank anyway
> **hot_pat_of_butter:** ¯_(ツ)_/¯
> **hot_pat_of_butter:** its an idea

Another text from my mom. If she weren't my blood relative, I would have blocked her a long time ago. Baffled, curdled love. I have to see her on Sunday, and she's going to ask if I've visited Daisy. My viewers have been asking, too, and I'm running out of excuses. They want to know where their money is going.

MSRN273: leggoooooo
MSRN273: but wait
MSRN273: anomalous_donkey wanted to go too and hes not here right now

"I don't see how that's my problem."

raven96: wtf hospital why

"New people: I'm not doing this for my professional and personal development. We're raising money to put my sister on private life support. And we're not doing a good job of it. We've raised a little over five thousand dollars so far and we need to more than double that by Sunday. So for today's activity, today's grand mistake, we're going on a field trip to Mount Babel Hospital."

jimpix: how much to see daisy
theflawless1: im not donating to go to a hospital

My fingers shoot to the "Block" button before I can fully process the message. I am defensive of my right to be ruthless, especially when it comes to Daisy. If this were a hot pepper eating challenge, I might've hesitated for a moment, given theflawless1 a chance to grovel. But this is my little sister. This is different.

I switch my stream to my phone and head out the door, holding my phone in front of me to give my viewers a tour of the city. My heart is beating out of my chest with the effort to keep my voice even as I chat. Some pledge a dollar, five, ten. It doesn't matter. A numbness has spread from the tips of my hair and taken root just beneath my skin, a force field of agita around me.

It takes about twenty minutes on the train ($2.90) to get to Mount Babel, a fraction of how long it takes my mom to do the trip and yet she was back and forth every day for a while. The white awning, the floor-to-ceiling glass facade. This is a fancy hospital for expensive illnesses and only the most exotic cases. Daisy fell into the former category until Dr. Dole the pineapple man decided to give her the boot.

"In terms of watching me suffer, would you fuckheads get more satisfaction from watching me visit my comatose sister in the hospital today or take part in the world record competition tomorrow?"

MSRN273: both
chickenleggy: both!!!
kirk_equivalent: definitely both

"Damn," I say. "Well, if I'm doing both, you better make it worth my while."

I've only been eating hot peppers for a couple days. I'm not at a competitive level. It wouldn't be ambitious of me to sign up, or brave, it would be a suicide wish. Pure and simple hubris. It would, however, be a great way to break 100,000. And Patrick thinks I can do it.

Would the pain get worse after, say, Reaper number five? Or is it a matter of tempo, of learning to swallow raw, unchewed bolts of fire?

Outside the hospital's front entrance I whisper to my viewers. "I haven't visited the hospital in a while. Don't ask me how long. But people have been asking for this on the daily, so we're doing it. I just ask that you be respectful and grant me some privacy, whatever that means. I'm not sure how legal it is for me to livestream in a hospital."

crabbybob: field trip!
kirk_equivalent: =D

I need to steel my nerves: if I were a smoker, this would be an ideal interlude for a cigarette break. Instead, I lean against the side of the building for the time I imagine it would take to smoke a cigarette. Then

I put my headphones in and my phone in my back pocket, a view of the world behind me. Whenever I visited Daisy in the past, I had to check in with the front desk and get a visitor badge. Have my picture taken. Sanitize my hands. Get buzzed in. There's a time limit, too, and visiting hours, and maximum visitors per room, etcetera. But there's a queue at the front desk eight-strong, and the door to enter Daisy's wing is directly on my right, and . . .

It swings open as someone exits and I slip in with ease. And then I'm on autopilot, the map of trauma downloaded to the soles of my sneakers.

"Okay, we're in," I whisper.

xinfected_botx: special ops hospital
trutherdare: ill be ur lookout LOL

My heart rate is betraying me. At this moment, I'd rather be anywhere but here, anyone but me. But my feet keep moving: I make a left and then another left, then take the elevator to the third floor, crossing my arms and wrapping my denim jacket around myself to hold in my discomfort and hide my absence of a security badge. No one stops me to ask where I'm going, or if I need help. They might even recognize my face, my aura. I have that family-of-a-patient scent about me.

"Seriously, though, if y'all could keep lookout, that would be great. I'm not exactly supposed to be here."

redtimepolice: 0.0
trutherdare: YES
racre001: lookout for what
racre001: you should steal something
barbistani: ill keep lookout too =D

I stop at room 3218. I hear the beeping of machines inside, but not much else. The briefest moment of hesitation and then I crack the door open slightly and stick a toe in. No doctors or nurses, no other patients. A wave of jamais vu crashes into me. I've been here before and yet I haven't. The room is divided into four curtained-off bays. Daisy's curtain is closed but the rest are open, the beds empty. I prop my phone near the door, on a table that has a view of the hallway.

"I guess we're doing this," I tell my viewers. "I'm in here with no visitor badge, nothing, so I'm enlisting you all to help me out: I'm going to close the curtain and hang out with Daisy for a little while, and if anyone looks like they're going to come in I want to hear some sound effects. I don't care which ones, just send me something quick and dirty so I know to leg it out of here."

> **MSRN273:** we dont get to see Daisy?
> **racre001:** im on lookout

I walk over to Daisy's curtain and open it, and there she is, exactly where I left her. Cheeks pink. Hair less greasy than my own. Fast asleep. I pick up my phone and turn it to show the bump of her feet under the covers, then whip it back around just as fast.

"That's it, okay? Now, keep your eyes open. I'm serious. It wouldn't be good if I got caught here, and I need you all on this. Can I trust you?"

> **redtimepolice:** yes 0.0
> **jackdaw2000:** prob not
> **racre001:** yeah!!!

I put my phone back down and return to Daisy's bed, close the curtain behind me so it's just us. I sit beside her feet and count her toes through the scratchy, time-stained covers.

One, two, three, four, five.

Six, seven, eight, nine, ten.

Wiggle your toes. Move your hand.

Please.

I turn on the TV in the corner of the room. Is *Jeopardy* always on in every hospital room around the world? It's an old episode with Alex Trebek. I hear footsteps in the hallway, but my phone doesn't erupt with noises. I hear the distant whoosh of privacy curtains in other rooms. At intervals the machines around the bed beep in a consistent and soothing manner.

Daisy was always so much prettier asleep than when she was squawking, clomping around the house. Loud, wonderful girl, always singing off-key. I want to lay down and wrap my arms around her bird bones. I want to pick up her hand and use her smaller, daintier pinkie nail to try to excavate the plant from my brain. I want to talk to her, tell her how things have been, how I can't bear to talk to Mom anymore, the way she looks at me. How I'm going to pieces in this very particular and uninteresting way. But in reality I just sit on the edge of the bed with my head between my knees.

How did you do it, I think. How did you get everyone to love you?

Even the neighbors all loved Daisy. When she was fifteen and wanted some cash, she knocked on the door of every pet-owning house in our area and asked if she could walk their dogs. She got a whole business going overnight. Bought one of those hands-free dog walking belts and everything. Mr. Grant, an elderly man who lived at the end of the block, had a blind, deaf chihuahua that she would carry in her arms as she walked, and place on plots of grass so it could relieve itself. I thought it was just one of her weird phases, a fleeting interest, but she continued to walk these dogs all throughout high school, even when she had track practice or homework. I wonder who walks them now.

"This term describes a bird's migration back to its birthplace," Trebek says. And then comes the answer: What is homing?

I get up and escort my viewers out of the room.

barbistani: are u okay D:
MSRN273: lookout successful?

"Yeah, I—"

My tears retreat when I spy Dr. Dole down the hall. Head neurologist, a redundant title. He won't recognize me, will he? He has too many patients, families of patients. I'm so sure he won't recognize me that I don't bother to look down or turn in the other direction.

"Odelia," he says, and the sound of my name out of his mouth is so strange I don't recognize it at first. "Odelia," he says again. "How are you?"

Dr. Dole clocks my lack of a visitor badge instantly. He could sic security on me, have me escorted out, banned from visiting Mount Babel ever again. My viewers set off their sound effects—cannonballs and farts and Wilhelm screams—but it's too late.

Run. You always run. That's how it works. A moving target doesn't get hit.

But he says he wants to talk to me, just for a few minutes, and despite my better judgment I follow him to his office in the hospital's basement. Which they don't call the basement, of course: the elevator button is labeled "LL" for "lower level." I wipe my nose on my sleeve. A bald spot swirls clockwise on the back of his head. My phone vibrates with incoming messages in my pocket.

Bzz. Bzz. Bzz.

Bees begging to be let out.

Dr. Dole. Pineapple chunks, pineapple slices, crushed pineapples in a can. Sharp green leaves growing out of his shoulders. Prickles all over his skin. If he were a pineapple I would roll him down the hallway on his side. He'd bump and roll, bump and roll, until finally, an errant scalpel would find him and he would leak golden syrup everywhere.

Dr. Dole isn't a pineapple. He's long-faced and slim and his spikes are safely hidden beneath his lab coat. He opens a door with his name on it: Dr. Samuel Gregory Dole. It looks more like another hospital room than an office, the same floors and walls and anodyne floral curtains on the windows betraying a devotion to sterility. The only difference is that they've put a desk in this room instead of a bed. He sits down and gestures for me to sit across from him.

"Are you visiting someone?" he asks. "What room were you in?"

I roll my eyes. "Yeah. I know. I didn't check in. That was a dumb thing to do—a dumb thing to not do—and I was just about to leave when you saw me. I swear."

"You know, your mom stays in touch with me," he says. "She's a good woman, a good person. Not all my patients' families are like that. Some patients have no one to visit them at all. And your stepfather—"

"Gary? He's not my stepfather." I take out my phone in a show of boredom, and swiftly mute my stream's audio. "Why are you telling me this?"

"I just wanted to ask you how you're doing. How you're feeling about things," he says, making eye contact with a spot on the bridge of my nose. Probably a trick he learned in bedside manner class in medical school. "I am surprised to see you here."

"Is this conversation part of your job description?"

"Sometimes," he says.

I cross my arms tightly over my chest. "You didn't want to talk when we told you that Daisy's hand moved. Or when she was breathing on her own."

"Your sister showed signs of a persistent vegetative state," he says, and I don't like his use of the past tense, not at all. "Unfortunately, the improvements we wanted to see just weren't happening when we wanted them to, which tells us that there is permanent, severe brain damage. We told all this to you and your mother. Several times."

"Daisy only went into a coma two months ago," I say, narrowing my eyes. "One woman was in a coma for thirty-seven years."

He laughs. "Not in my hospital."

"Have you heard of Munira Abdullah? She woke up from a coma after nearly thirty years."

"I am not familiar with the case you're referring to."

"And Annie Shapiro. She woke up, too."

He shakes his head and shrugs, as if to say: not my problem.

"I know," I say, and I have to put in effort to unclench my jaw so I can get the words out. "I get it. I know how these things work. I don't have a brain for systems, but I know that they're not built to work in my favor. And you need to clear up the bed space, I get that. But this is my sister we're talking about. My family."

"Odelia, we're not the enemy," he says. "We make the best suggestions that we can with the information that we have. And in this case, the information said that your sister was not getting better."

"I swear to god, she practically gave me the middle finger the last time I was here."

"Private life support—"

"Is for rich people," I spit. "The hospital doesn't want to foot the bill anymore. You decide who lives and who dies, and it's not on your conscience because you can give people fake options for care that would put them in medical debt for the rest of their lives. It just is what it is, right?"

"We look at all the evidence: brain activity, movement and reflexes, response to stimuli, breathing patterns, pupil size, I could go on. Your sister could have been at any other hospital and you would have gotten the same prognosis. This is one of the best hospitals in the world, Odelia. We did our best, we always do our best."

"You keep saying 'we,'" I say. "Why do you keep saying 'we?' You're the head of the unit. It's not 'we'—it's you."

"Did you come to the hospital today to talk to me about your griev-
ances?"

"No, I didn't come to the hospital today to talk to you about anything."

"Your sister—"

"Daisy. Her name is Daisy."

"Daisy," he says. "We called every other hospital in the city on her
behalf. No one wanted to take her, given her state and her prognosis.
We gave your mother the rest of her options, and we made a decision
together. Your mother was at peace with that decision. I think it would
be best if you came to peace with it, too."

"Is it easy for you?" I ask.

"Is what easy for me?" he says. And then: "No. It's not easy for me."

The seedling in my brain batters against my skull, searching for
a way out. I look at the painting on the wall. A generic watercolor of
a choppy lake surrounded by windswept trees. Just a landscape at first
glance, except there's someone there, out on the water on a small boat,
barely visible.

"I think I have an ulcer," I say. "It's really bad, and it's getting worse
every day."

He looks at the painting as well. "I should escort you out," he says,
and stands up. He starts to walk me toward the elevator but I speedwalk
ahead and he doesn't try to catch up. I get there first and slam the "Close
Door" button over and over, but it doesn't close in time, and he gets on
with me. Dr. Dole walks me to the nearest exit and I expel myself out of
the hospital, somewhere entirely different from where I entered.

•   •   •

LiveCast ranking 185,853. I turn my audio back on and glance at my
balance. Two hundred and one dollars richer. That's nice. One hundred
thirty-one viewers, an average of sixty-five cents each. But not everyone

donated, of course, it was mostly my tenured viewers, and their donations ranged from a dollar to twenty bucks each. It's more than I expected to make, to be honest, considering that my audio was off toward the end there, and I didn't even let them see Daisy. A week ago, that number would have made me scream in delight. But right now I just feel numb. Strange messages drift into the chat and float without context, hieroglyphs.

> **wolfgang070:** probably flinstones chewables
> **austinroolz:** heck
> **therealshrimp160:** we got sinners in the chat fam

I've gotten to the viewer count where there are too many chats to catch up on. Which is a helpful distraction to keep me from thinking about that nothing, nonsense conversation I just had with Dr. Dole. If I were to scroll back and try to read through all of the messages that came in during the last hour, there would be a hundred more to go through once I caught up. Like eating my own tail.

What's increasingly clear is that my viewers don't need me anymore. They haven't for a while now. They can keep each other company. I'm just the vessel for their doing so, the holder of this uneasy space. Some of them know about Daisy, why I was at the hospital. The ones who have been with me since the beginning understand the gravity of today's visit, why I would keep the camera angled away from her hospital bed in order to protect her privacy, why they should pay me for the privilege of this mediated access. But my newer viewers aren't so generous.

> **talamaine:** id fuck you
> **jexxy458:** why is the audio muted??? im leaving
> **jexxy458:** this sucks

"I will block all of you. Try me."
Instead of thinking about Daisy, I think about excelsior404. No sign

of him in my viewer list, which I read through over and over again as I walk. If he's here, he's using a very different screen name. In my inbox is an email from LiveCast support. Yes, I can block an IP address. Wondrous news. But then I see how many fields I have to fill out and my mouth goes sour: *Why do you want to block an IP address. Tell us more about your request. Attach evidence to support your request. Is there anything else you'd like us to know.*

How many days does the LiveCast moderation team take to approve requests, anyway? The internet doesn't have an answer for me. But it's Friday. So not tomorrow, and not the day after. Monday at the earliest. Let's say my request gets approved at nine o'clock in the morning on Monday. It's Friday afternoon now. That's about sixty-five more hours of this low-grade terror, at minimum.

A *ping* goes off, signaling a new viewer. Hello, zspacey1989. I click into their profile. Picture: a dog in a baseball cap. The account was created four years ago. It has twelve followers and is following seventy-three other streamers.

Not excelsior404. No blocking needed.

Right?

I close my eyes and lean my skull against the wall behind me. The air is warm, my upper lip moist. I shimmy off my jacket and tie it around my waist. People walk past me in a blur of brackish water. I could fall asleep here, standing up like this. But I would only dream of Daisy, of root structures so deep and ancient that they hold the entire planet together.

I text my mom to let her know that I visited Daisy and then I stuff my phone in my back pocket. Most of my viewers don't mind being carried in that way, with a view of the street behind me, the sounds of the cityscape pouring in. I could have an entire stream where I just let viewers from around the world see and hear the city as I walk around, and I bet it would be moderately successful.

I shouldn't have gone to the hospital. My head is pounding, my teeth are throbbing in their gums. I feel useless and vile, and the only counteroffensive is to make myself feel even more useless and vile. I go to a food truck and order a cheesy chicken burrito ($5.99) and a fruit punch Gatorade ($3.29), then walk toward Stuyvesant Town, a private residential complex above the East Village and the primordial chaos of Alphabet City: A for assault, B for battery, C for coma, D for death.

Just like at the hospital, I'm not technically allowed to be here. But people don't actually get in trouble for sneaking into Stuyvesant Town like they do at Gramercy Park. A former classmate of mine lived here freshman year. She was a wealthy international student from Kazakhstan and her parents didn't want her to dorm with the normals, so they put her up in a four thousand dollar studio apartment. But she transferred to Harvard, last time I heard, and none of my other NYU friends could afford this area so there's a low risk of running into anyone I used to know.

I settle onto a bench by the fountain and watch the unemployed moms ferry their kids around the playground, the nannies chitchatting with one another. Private security patrols on discontinued Segways. I close my eyes and eat, focusing on cheese, meat, and carbs. This burrito is a surefire stomachache, but there's a certain psychic emptiness that only fast food can fill. And after all the spicy food I've had lately, it tastes decadently bland.

chickenleggy: YUM
chickenleggy: I WANT THAT

"Stop yelling."

My stomach starts to contort and cramp before I'm even halfway done with my food. When the pain gets bad and I don't have my usual armaments within reach, I roll into a ball and die, like a bug. I bring my knees to my chest and close my eyes, pretending that I'm floating in space. Knives having a party in my gut, sprinkling needles across the thin tissue at the bottoms of my lungs.

If I had money like the people who live here, everything would have gone differently.

I remember when we used to go to Wendy's on Wednesdays. I was eleven and Daisy was seven. We never got the kid's meal, out of self-respect. I'd get a spicy chicken sandwich and Daisy would get chicken nuggets and fries. My mom, a vanilla Frosty. For birthdays we went to Applebee's, and that was nice. The bright marquee, rotund apple, red as a slapped cheek. I remember thinking it was so fancy to do that, to sit in a booth and order from a menu with pictures in it. Mozzarella sticks with marinara sauce, no matter where you order them, are fire. It's impossible to mess up a mozzarella stick. If you do, you're basically a terrorist.

Sophomore year of high school there was an overnight field trip to Philadelphia to see the Liberty Bell and I couldn't go because it cost too much money. They put me in the school library for two days and told me to read and do my homework. Daisy would walk past the library doors between classes and make funny faces at me. During gym, she got permission to study in the library instead. She didn't have to do that. No one asked her to do that.

I have almost seven thousand dollars combined in my bank and LiveCast account but I don't feel rich, not at all. If I'm going to be worth anything to anyone, I need to double that number in the next two days, break 100,000 in the rankings.

One more week. One more week. One more week.

Belief alone can't keep Daisy alive. I understand that. But that doesn't mean I have to accept it.

There's some kind of memorial by the park's fountain. When my stomach feels a bit better, I get up and waddle over. A ten-year-old girl got hit by a car and died while riding her bike on First Avenue. The bike is here: orange with streamers. Pictures of her, candles, the whole thing. Very maudlin.

"How much would you give me if I lit my burrito on fire and smoked it like a joint?"

> **jackofnotrades1:** lol $2
> **fluffybuffalo_:** omg smoked burrito
> **jimpix:** $1
> **fluffybuffalo_:** smoked meat
> **therealshrimpshady:** you cant smoke a burrito

"Can't or shouldn't?" I say. My burrito is wrapped in tinfoil, but within that foil is a layer of greasy newspaper, slick with oil. "One dollar each if I light it on fire?"

I show my digital audience my real audience: people reading, walking their dogs, sunbathing, watching over children, pushing their walkers, absorbed on their phones. There are a hundred and forty-one viewers in my stream, more than the people in the world around me. So, which audience is more real?

> **racre001:** ok $1
> **jexxy458:** yes
> **barbistani:** $0.50

"Barbistani . . . you hurt me."

> **barbistani:** $1 :)

"I'm doing this out of laziness, you know. I don't want to eat the other half of my burrito and the trash can is all the way over there."

I squat and inspect the memorial. The candles are intense. Not the usual votives or tea lights but red, heart-shaped lanterns with an inch of kerosene in each, wicks flickering above them. I suppose the purpose is to allow the candles to burn continuously, but to me it just seems like a fire hazard. More plausible deniability on my end, I suppose.

I bring the end of my burrito up to the closest lantern and angle my camera just so for my viewers. The greasy newspaper lights slowly and then falters when it reaches the fatty, cheesy center. I try again and the result is the same: a moment of light and then nothing. I fling the burrito into the nearby fountain. People look at me, neutral. It's too hard to startle people these days. I walk over to the fountain and show my viewers the carnage. The burrito sinks to the bottom of the fountain and pieces of lettuce, bell pepper, and black beans float to the surface like dirty bubbles. The water is tinged a faint hue of cumin and paprika. The stringy cheese tries to float but ends up wafting through imaginary waves, dispersing to other corners. No one is even looking anymore. No one cares.

> **chickenleggy:** GROSS
> **jackdaw2000** has donated $1
> **chickenleggy:** looks like barf
> **MSRN273:** lol
> **trutherdare** has donated $1
> **trutherdare:** even though you didnt smoke the burrito

A few other donations come. Crumbs. LiveCast ranking a stagnant 185,639. Why did I do that? I could've just walked another ten feet to the trash can.

I'm about to leave the park when another message comes in:

> **literallyjustgod:** why dont you light yourself on fire

Excelsior404? I click into his profile. I don't think so.

karnie_vibes: omg no dont do that
jackofnotrades1: id give $10 ^__^

"Ten dollars? To light myself on fire? That's a joke."

jackofnotrades1: lololol
anomalous_donkey: don't do that
therealshrimpshady: I'd give $20
literallyjustgod: $25
raven96: woaaah
crabbybob: stop
raven96: okay $25
karnie_vibes: $0
karnie_vibes: pls dont this is my favorite stream

"Karnie.Vibes. Sweet, sweet Karnie Vibes. Pretending that you care about me. You've only donated twenty-five dollars in total, you know. So I don't actually care about your opinion."

karnie_vibes: :(

"Should I block Karnie Vibes? What does everyone think?" I laugh, or rather, mademoiselle_dell laughs. Because she can't help it. There is no pause in the show, even as the smarter part of my brain is running through the decision tree. I can't actually light myself on fire. But there is a fountain right there, full of water.

karnie_vibes has donated $1
karnie_vibes: pls dont block me
literallyjustgod: fire fire fire
raven96: ya lets go
chickenleggy: NO
raven96: do it
chickenleggy: NO NO
chickenleggy: im logging off
karnie_vibes: same

200 | LIOR TORENBERG

But no one logs off. They would if they wanted to, but they don't. In fact, more people have joined my stream. LiveCast saw the uptick in my chat engagement and bumped my ranking up to 177,321. With that came twenty new viewers. One hundred and sixty-three people, some egging me on, others begging me to stop, but no one leaving the chat. How could they? It's not every day you get to see someone light themselves on fire.

"If everyone pledges twenty-five dollars," I say, "I'll consider it. And I mean it, no less than twenty-five dollars a person. This is a serious dare so I'm going to be serious about it. If you give less than twenty-five, you're blocked. And if I die, you're all going to be charged with encouraging self-harm behavior online, which is illegal. I read. I know the laws."

raven96: do it
MSRN273: ok $25
therealshrimpshady: $30
redtimepolice: $25

Even some of my OGs, the ones who have been with me since day one, are pledging money. It's what I asked for, but it still makes me feel some type of way. They don't care whether I live or die, so long as I provide entertainment. And if they don't care about me, how could they possibly care about Daisy? Most of my newer viewers haven't even heard the full spiel.

One hundred and sixty viewers, twenty-five dollars each. Best-case scenario: I pull this off and I'm four thousand dollars richer. Worst-case scenario: my outsides match my insides for once.

I position my camera on a nearby bench facing both me and the memorial. Then I blow out one of the kerosene lamps and unscrew its top. I pour the kerosene along the sleeve of my left forearm, my non-dominant arm. I'm wearing two layers, and one of them is denim. I should be okay. And I've done this before, in a way. The experience of spice is just the physiological sensation of heat in the mouth, the throat, the body. This is similar, isn't it? I've dealt with unbearable heat before. I can do this. The fountain is right there.

I can just barely make out my chats from where I'm standing. My viewers are begging me to continue, to stop, to continue. Some donations have already started coming in. Green line after green line, buying their tickets for the show.

The fountain is right there.

Before I can overthink it, I bring my soaked sleeve to one of the lit candles. My arm lights up so instantly, and then all I see is fire from my elbow to my wrist. I feel the glow of the heat, and then I feel the heat itself. It's burning through my jacket quickly, too quickly. And I know this was a vile, heinous idea but there's no turning back now.

> **chickenleggy:** STOP
> **hot_pat_of_butter:** what is going on??
> **wolfgang070:** holy shit
> **wolfgang070** has donated $25

"I'm not jumping in the fountain until I break 100,000," I yell at my viewers. I watch my ranking tick up, too slow. 173,000. 172,500. 172,000.

> **hot_pat_of_butter:** does anyone know where she is?
> **hot_pat_of_butter:** ???
> **anomalous_donkey** has donated $25
> **hot_pat_of_butter:** can someone call 911?

There are so many people around me in the park. I am vaguely aware of them screaming, running, mostly away, but some toward, phones aloft, recording me. My skin is burning. I can feel it starting to burn. And yet, I feel distanced, dissociated. I hold my arm out and stare at it. The fire is so bright. People gather around me, both real and virtual, but I'm all on my own. The fire begins to spread from my forearm toward my shoulder. It's only been a couple of seconds but it feels like hours that I'm standing there, watching my LiveCast ranking rise.

And then I don't care about my ranking anymore. Some kind of animal instinct shoots me into the fountain and under the water. I sputter and splash, my sleeve black, soot floating in the water. Bystanders gather around the fountain. Finally, someone stops filming and pulls me out of the water.

"Thanks," I say, then point at the memorial. "That's a fire hazard."

I am sopping wet. My left arm is throbbing. I pick up my phone and start walking home with my now five hundred viewers and another $3,200 in my LiveCast account.

Ranking: 99,730.

(!) You have a new message
hot_pat_of_butter: what the hell was that??
mademoiselle_dell: I broke 100,000 :)
hot_pat_of_butter: are you okay?
hot_pat_of_butter: did you do that on purpose?
hot_pat_of_butter: please say you didnt do that on purpose
mademoiselle_dell: im okay
mademoiselle_dell: it was only like eight seconds total
hot_pat_of_butter: are you going to the hospital?
mademoiselle_dell: no
hot_pat_of_butter: how bad is it?
mademoiselle_dell: its not bad
mademoiselle_dell: I ruined my jean jacket but im good
mademoiselle_dell: my arm hurts a little
mademoiselle_dell: maybe first-degree burns
hot_pat_of_butter: are you sure?
mademoiselle_dell: i broke 100,000
hot_pat_of_butter: when i said that we should talk when you break 100,000
hot_pat_of_butter: that is not what i meant
hot_pat_of_butter: that is the opposite of what i meant
hot_pat_of_butter: you cant stream if youre dead

mademoiselle_dell: cant i though
hot_pat_of_butter: what does that even mean
mademoiselle_dell: ¯\(ツ)/¯

I used to believe in all kinds of things when I was a child. To call me naive would be an understatement. I believed for many years that Mount Rushmore was a naturally occurring phenomenon, carved out by the journey of rivers to reinforce the primacy of America. I believed that evil witches existed but also good witches. That aliens could slip underneath our skin, warm themselves inside our bones. I was afraid of the tooth fairy, the way she would sneak into my room and steal my teeth. In my mind she wielded a sword of interlocking canines, wore a crown of thick molar white. So when I lost teeth, I wouldn't put them under my pillow, or even tell my mom. I found new hiding places: in the toilet tank, between the DVD cases, behind the teacups. Some I flushed. I imagined them rushed out to the ocean, mingling with the coral, finally resting with discarded shark teeth at the deep dark bottom of the sea.

On the way back to my apartment, a homeless woman gestures to me from the side of the street. She's disarmingly attractive, with hair down to her waist and large, clear eyes. She asks me for money and I surprise myself by taking a soggy dollar out of my wallet and giving it to her.

"That's it?" she asks.

"Sorry," I mumble.

"Whatever," she says, crumpling it into her pocket. I keep walking.

• • •

Patrick didn't take the news how I thought he would. I broke 100,000 in the rankings and I have nearly ten thousand dollars in my account. Yes, I know what I did was fucking crazy, but so was the outcome: I might be the fastest person to break 100,000 in the history of LiveCast rankings. And if I'm not the fastest, I'm certainly up there. It took Patrick years to do what I did in less than a week, so clearly I'm doing something right. I'm filled with a feverish mess of adrenaline and I want to celebrate with someone who actually knows me, cares about me, but I can't get into Lee's apartment. My key doesn't work. Knock, knock, knock. No answer. Are they home? Did they latch the top lock? They never do that.

I stand on the landing, still dripping from the fountain, and try my key again with no luck. No, they didn't latch the top lock, because then the door would at least open a little bit, a centimeter, before the chain caught it in place. I try my key again. And again.

> **barbistani:** hows ur arm
> **anomalous_donkey:** wut is happening :O
> **chickenleggy:** did hot pat leave
> **anomalous_donkey:** wtf
> **chickenleggy:** are you okay queen??
> **racre001:** im bricked up

I knock once more, louder. Did Lee change their locks?

I call their phone. It rings three times before going to voicemail. They cut off my call mid-ring. I call again and this time it cuts off after only two rings.

I send them a text: Did you change your locks?

Did you seriously pay hundreds of dollars to change your locks???
You're that pissed at me??
Lee? Are you being serious right now?

Three dots. They're typing. But then the dots go away. Reappear. Go away. I wait for them to reappear once more but they don't.

Say what you want to say, I send, but the dots don't come back.
You're not better than me, I write.

This has happened so many times in my head: Lee getting sick of me. But in my imagination they just ask for their key back, they don't go

and change their locks altogether. The drama of it, the indulgent avoid-
ance. I've imagined them cussing me out, their congenial outer shell
cracking and splintering. Stop using my bathroom! Stop eating my food!
I need my privacy! But it never went down like this in my head, flightless
and limp. Silence on the other end of the door.

If Lee's mad at me, it's excelsior404's fault. That ball sack. Let's assume I deserve it. I could've told Lee the truth, but I didn't. Well, fine.
No one has a right to my inner life. No amount of money or free food
or bathrooms gives someone that right. If they don't want to talk to me,
I can just talk to my other friends. My five hundred and thirty-two other
friends. After I find a place to use the bathroom, that is.

I look around my apartment for a jar, a bottle, any kind of receptacle,
but there's nothing. I've tried squatting over the sink before but the basin
is too shallow, pee ricochets everywhere.

"This is bad," I say to my viewers, my guts churning and bucking
with effort to hold in my bladder, spasming with pain from the ill-advised
burrito I had earlier, the only thing I ate today. "My cash-to-bathroom
ratio is bad. I've never been richer and had fewer bathrooms in my life."

> **barbistani:** rofl
> **fluffybuffalo_:** is ur bathroom broken
> **barbistani:** mademoiselle_dell doesn't have a bathroom
> **racre001:** ????
> **fluffybuffalo_:** how
> **trutherdare:** she uses her neighbors bathroom
> **crabbybob:** sheeeeeesh

First I have to go to the bathroom, then I have to shower. I smell
like fountain burrito. Chlorine and sweet onions. I slip on a pair of flip
flops and walk downstairs to the twenty-four-hour gym on the ground
floor. Going back there after all these months feels like defeat, but my
spirits are buoyed when I walk in and there's no one at the front desk. I

go straight to the women's locker room and rush to a stall, not bothering to mute my audio.

"Oh my god," I say, as I empty my bladder. "Best feeling ever."

barbistani has donated $1
barbistani: cuz i loled
pklrik: ^_^

"Go away, pklrik. You're too young to watch this."

pklrik: -_-
kirk_equivalent has donated $1

The showers here have shampoo, conditioner, and body wash in dispensers attached to the walls. Three different dispensers of identical nameless blue liquid. Not the good stuff that Lee has, but it is what it is. I put my phone and clothes in an open locker and shower until I'm as wrinkly and red as a pepper, the steam feeding my brain plant. I dislike the pepper analogy but it fits. The hot water makes my left arm sting, but it feels like a truly terrible sunburn, nothing more. My denim jacket did a good job of retarding my death for the eight whole seconds I was on fire. I don't have a towel so I stand in the shower until I feel dry enough to get dressed again. In the entire time since I arrived, no one has come in or out of the locker room. It's a Friday night, after all. Why would anyone go to the gym?

Too tired for the five-story climb, I lay down on a locker room bench and chat with my viewers into the night. After five days of streaming, I don't have to think before I speak anymore, the syllables expelled forward in a barrage of simper and snark. At some point, I jolt awake with no idea what time it is. The fluorescent lights are still on. My phone is on the floor. It must have woken me up when it fell. Two in the morning. Did anyone come in during that time and see me? Witness me, hair dripping, legs akimbo, splayed so uncomfortably on the metal bench?

I gather my things and leave. The night-shift employee is back at the front desk and looks up only briefly as I walk out. I jog up the first three flights of stairs to my apartment and then lose pace for the last two, suddenly out of breath and perspiring again even though I just showered. The upstairs neighbors are playing some kind of synth music. I don't hate it, but it makes everything feel subterranean, like I'm in a cave deep undersea. I knock on Lee's door, hard and relentless, until a text comes in:

ITS LATE GO TO SLEEP

Answer, I reply

WE CAN TALK TOMORROW DELL

When?

I wait thirty seconds but they don't respond. I raise my fist to resume banging, but something stops me. Exhaustion, regret, a slimy sense of shame. I let myself into my apartment. The windowless space is pitch-black in a way that snatches the breath out of my chest. A void filled to the brim with things I didn't know but should have. Like how fentanyl is fifty times more potent than heroin and a hundred times more potent than morphine, fatal at a two-milligram dose. How opioids interact with the brain's receptors to slow down cell activity, reactiveness, motor function, and autonomic functions like breathing and heart rate. Without enough oxygen, brain damage can occur, and organs begin to shut down. How the triad of symptoms for opioid poisoning are pinpoint pupils, respiratory depression, and coma.

Here's what I'm trying to say: it's unlike me to want to go to a fancy private university, let alone actually enroll in one. And if I were to enroll in one, it certainly wouldn't be one so close to home that my mom could visit me whenever she wanted. And if I did go to one of those fancy schools, I absolutely wouldn't study something inane like communications because I didn't know what I actually wanted to do. I wouldn't take out upward of sixty thousand dollars a year in loans for a random and general degree like that.

And if I did, I wouldn't subject myself to living in a dorm room the size of a thimble with two preppy, waxed girls named Michelle from New England. I wouldn't become friends with them over time, or go out with them on weekends. And if it turned out that Michelle and Michelle liked to binge drink or have a bump of coke while they were out dancing, pop an Adderall before they hit the library, I wouldn't feel pressured to do the same, that's not me at all. And I definitely wouldn't enjoy it, wouldn't love the way the substances smoothed my brain out like an iron. I wouldn't pregame every weekend with premium vodka at an anonymous international student's high-rise luxury apartment, the building so tall I felt myself sway along with it in the wind. That doesn't sound like me at all.

And even if I was someone who did all that, I wouldn't willingly elect to live with the Michelles again my sophomore year. I wouldn't continue on that way. And if I did, if I wasted my time in college on an unfulfilling degree and unfulfilling friends, I certainly wouldn't invite my seventeen-year-old sister to come visit me during spring break, my sister who was three years younger than me and starting to think about colleges herself. And if my sister did visit, I would take her to museums and Broadway shows and wholesome things like that, and I would hold her hand as we walked through the city to anchor her to me. I wouldn't take her out clubbing. Never. But if I did take her out with me on a weekend, it would only be to impress her, so that she thought I was cool and had friends, that I was doing better than I had in high school, that she and Mom didn't have to worry about me anymore.

Either way, I absolutely wouldn't let her accept any drugs or alcohol, or offer her any myself. If we went out dancing, we would keep it clean and be back by a reasonable hour. And if my little sister were to do coke for the first time, it wouldn't be coke from a random guy in the pee-stained unisex bathroom of some trendy nightclub that I snuck her into with my roommate's fake ID. But if we were to do that, I would make sure the coke was clean, and that she didn't do too much of it in that basement of heartbeats, and I would do some first to make sure that it was good quality. Even if I had a cold and wasn't feeling that well to begin with. If I had forced this outing on the both of us for the sake of fun, I wouldn't let her do coke alone. And if I did, I would make sure to keep her in my sights for the rest of the night so I would know that she was okay and having a good time. I wouldn't lose her in the crowd and keep dancing on my own.

And if I did lose sight of her, I would look for her right away, not a half hour later. And if I found her passed out in a lounge chair on the perimeter of the room, I wouldn't merely ask security to help me get her in a cab so I could take her home—I would take her to the hospital immediately, even if it got me in trouble.

And if she didn't wake up in the cab, or when we got home, I would surely call an ambulance then, not just have my roommates help me get her into pajamas and into bed next to me so she could sleep it off.

But if I did do that, I would stay up all night and monitor her breathing, her heart rate, not just fall asleep myself. And when I woke up in the morning beside my little sister and she was still unwakeable, I would finally do the right thing and call an ambulance, even though it was too late.

SATURDAY

LiveCast Ranking: 99,898

(!) You have a new private message

hot_pat_of_butter: how are you? hows your arm?

mademoiselle_dell: hi

mademoiselle_dell: fine

mademoiselle_dell: i am a golden god

hot_pat_of_butter: lol

hot_pat_of_butter: so

hot_pat_of_butter: . . .

hot_pat_of_butter: you there?

hot_pat_of_butter: 0_0

mademoiselle_dell: its 8 am on a saturday

mademoiselle_dell: im half asleep

mademoiselle_dell: what

hot_pat_of_butter: hear me out

hot_pat_of_butter: I really think you should register for the competition today

mademoiselle_dell: ????

hot_pat_of_butter: you dont have to show up

hot_pat_of_butter: theres no issue if you dont show up

hot_pat_of_butter: but i think you should get your name down in case you change your mind and they hit their participant limit or something

mademoiselle_dell: u r kidding

hot_pat_of_butter: no

hot_pat_of_butter: i think you should go and stream it and win and get the $20,000 prize

hot_pat_of_butter: obviously you dont have to

hot_pat_of_butter: but if you go we can collab again and link our streams no problem hot_pat_of_butter: the viewers will love it

mademoiselle_dell: why

hot_pat_of_butter: why what

hot_pat_of_butter: im going to stream the competition for my viewers anyway

hot_pat_of_butter: itll be sick

mademoiselle_dell: why do u care about me so much

hot_pat_of_butter: lol sorry

hot_pat_of_butter: idk

mademoiselle_dell: ????

hot_pat_of_butter: my little brother passed a couple years ago

hot_pat_of_butter: so i guess i get it

mademoiselle_dell: ur not into me right

hot_pat_of_butter: no . . .

hot_pat_of_butter: no offense

hot_pat_of_butter: youre over a decade younger than me

hot_pat_of_butter: i dont think of you that way

hot_pat_of_butter: sorry if i gave you the wrong impression

mademoiselle_dell: u didnt give me the wrong impression

mademoiselle_dell: im sorry about ur brother

mademoiselle_dell: how old was he

hot_pat_of_butter: 27. he slipped on an icy sidewalk and broke his neck on a mailbox

mademoiselle_dell: r u serious

hot_pat_of_butter: yeah

hot_pat_of_butter: the mailbox was shaped like a boat

mademoiselle_dell: thats fucked

hot_pat_of_butter: he loved sailing

hot_pat_of_butter: i'm sorry about your sister too

hot_pat_of_butter: i hope she wakes up

hot_pat_of_butter: shes lucky to have you

mademoiselle_dell: u think i should sign up for the competition

hot_pat_of_butter: its not until 2 pm so you have time

hot_pat_of_butter: but let me know if youre going so i can build some hype

mademoiselle_dell: u think i can do it

hot_pat_of_butter: yeah

hot_pat_of_butter: like i said before, its all mental

hot_pat_of_butter: and youre strong

hot_pat_of_butter: i mean - what you did yesterday is way crazier

mademoiselle_dell: yes i know

hot_pat_of_butter: lol

JUST WATCH ME | 215

hot_pat_of_butter: im not just being selfless btw
hot_pat_of_butter: my viewers like you
hot_pat_of_butter: youre a top 100,000 streamer
hot_pat_of_butter: and even when you werent, our collab outperformed all of my past ones by a lot
hot_pat_of_butter: you bring something edgy to my stream
hot_pat_of_butter: if this goes well we can figure out like a weekly show or something
mademoiselle_dell: ok
mademoiselle_dell: im in
mademoiselle_dell: just signed up
hot_pat_of_butter: YES!
hot_pat_of_butter: its going to be dope
hot_pat_of_butter: ill meet you at the expo hall at 1 PM?

I try to go back to sleep but I'm too full of adrenaline. I keep thinking about the hospital, how everyone was cheering me on, begging me to burn. I keep thinking about excelsior404, about that death certificate. About Lee changing their locks. The look on their face, striking in its arrangement of confusion, the line of their brows, the deep dent between them. Lee is not an emotive person in general. It takes some guesswork, some experience, to discern the nuance of their body language. But yesterday, everything was right there on their face.

When do you want to talk? I text them, then groan and hoist myself out of bed, climbing down the ladder carefully. The plantling in my brain rattles with each rung. I'm awash in the dopamine sickness that comes with a growing viewer count, a growing bank account, the fact that I could pay my rent and bills with ease tomorrow on the last day of the month. The comedown that finds me in between exclamation points, the empty space on the page that fills itself with marginalia. It's not enough. The money isn't enough. The time isn't enough. Nothing I do is enough, not even lighting myself on fire. Daisy has been haunting the space behind my heart for months, and I don't know what to do with all of this leftover love.

I texted my mom yesterday after I went to the hospital to let her know that I visited Daisy. Her answer came back hours later, a curt *okay*. Does she not believe me? Is she mad at me, too? And why wouldn't she be? I've taken everything from her, everything except me, and I'm a sorry consolation prize. There's an iceberg wedged in my throat, sharp and irregular. Nik gave up on me. Lee gave up on me. Dr. Dole gave up on me. My mom, eventually, has to do the same.

Sending Lee that document wasn't the end, it was the beginning. But if anyone is going to exploit me, it's me. And if I'm going to go down in flames, the least I can do is put on a good show.

"I had the most fucked-up dream last night," I say to my viewers. So many of them now, an unbroken chain of chatter. "I went to the bathroom in the middle of the night and turned on the sink tap and there was a vine sticking out of it, dangling in the flow of the water. So I tried to grab it but it kept shrinking back into the faucet. And I couldn't see that well because the lights were off. But I felt this terror, like I didn't want to turn the lights on. So eventually I got ahold of this thing through the water. It took a while because it kept slipping out of my hands and back up into the sink. But eventually I was able to grab hold of it and pull. I pulled harder and harder and the sink was groaning and I thought: shit, I'm going to break Lee's sink. They'll be so pissed. But I kept going and eventually this thing started coming out of the sink. But it wasn't a vine anymore. It was . . . insides. I don't know. An umbilical cord, maybe. Intestines."

infinememe: nasty
yousefxd: ew i hate ur dream
jackdaw2000: same
FAODR3AMZ: i have a recurring nightmare that the monopoly man is my boss and i have to give him a foot massage every day at the end of stock market trading hours

gotcha60: horrible
redtimepolice: what if Megara from Hercules was my girlfriend
redtimepolice: that would be the best dream

"Idiots. All of you. This is why I never tell you anything." I yawn and swipe through tabs on my computer, pointer finger groping around in my ear. "Carolina Reapers are named after their scythe-shaped tails," I read from Wikipedia, removing my finger and crooking it into a sharpened arch. "Redrum. Redrum."

hot_pat_of_butter: 2,500,000 scoville units
gotcha60: redrum
chickenleggy: OMG its hot pat
chickenleggy: HI HOT PAT
gotcha60: redrum = murder backward
MSRN273: spoiler
yousefxd: how is that a spoiler?? The Shining came out 45 years ago
gotcha60: iykyk

"Shut up. I have news. Someone give me a drumroll."

supkaitlyn: drumroll
gotcha60: all work and no play makes jack a dull boy
flabatr0n: tktktktktktktktk
MSRN273: its more like badabadabadabada

"You thought yesterday was crazy. But today I'm competing in the world record Carolina Reaper competition. In just a few hours, mademoiselle_dell is going to stand on a stage and eat the hottest pepper in the entire world, in front of the entire world. And you all should tune in because there is a high likelihood I'm going to shit my pants onstage."

hot_pat_of_butter: woohoo!
chickenleggy: OMG
chickenleggy: is hot pat competing too

flabatr0n: dont shit your pants on stage
hot_pat_of_butter: mademoiselle_dell and I are doing a joint stream tonight. I'll be there live to record the competition
infinememe: that's nuts :O

"To be clear, I don't want to do it. I'm not at world record level. I could hardly eat one ghost pepper the other day, let alone a record-beating amount of a pepper more than twice as hot. The thing about peppers is that the pain is not linear. It's exponential. If I've learned anything this past week, it's that there's no room for confidence. You have to respect the peppers. And me, competing today, that's downright disrespectful. But Patrick peer-pressured me into signing up and I have nothing to lose and nothing better to do. So if you love me, tune in and donate and support. And if you hate me, pledge some money to make sure I go through with it and make a complete ass of myself."

hot_pat_of_butter: tickets to the expo/competition are $10 if any locals want to come

"Oh god. No. Don't come."

chickenleggy: IM COMING
chickenleggy: to see hot pat
jackdaw2000: i can stop by
supkaitlyn: i cant come
jackdaw2000: where what time

Patrick posts the ticket link in the chat, and I hate him for it. I don't know the vast majority of my viewers anymore. New names hurtling in and out every second like comets. I won't recognize any of them, but they'll recognize me. Will they come up, ask me questions, talk to me as if they know me? A foul proposition, almost as frightening as the competition itself. But there's no turning back now.

. . .

Nearly ten thousand dollars in my bank account. I like how large the number is, how silvery and cool. A big fish with rainbow scales. So pretty and fine I can neither eat it nor let it go. But I'll have to do one or the other soon, I know that. Because there is no solid state in nature. The only thing I can rely on is change, and I want to enjoy having this particular change in my bank account for as long as I can.

The burrito yesterday really wrecked me, but I'm starving, and there's no food in my house. "Who wants to order me a pre-competition meal?" I ask my five hundred and fifty-six viewers, and they all clamber to attention.

kirk_equivalent: (.)(.)

"Is everyone disgusting or do they just become disgusting online?"

kirk_equivalent: yes
gotcha60: rofl whats for lunch

"I haven't decided yet. Ideally something that won't mess me up, stomach-wise. But all I can think about right now is fried chicken."

FAODR3AMZ: boobs
chickenleggy: fried chickenleggy
infinememe has donated $5

"You know I live in pretty much the most expensive city on the planet, right?"

hiccuptruck has donated $5
karnie_vibes: its expensive where i am too

"Just say it."

karnie_vibes: i live in vancouver
jackofnotrades1: get bbq wings
jackofnotrades1: they're the best
raven96: has anyone had korean wings?
kirk_equivalent: jackofnotrades1 isnt ur cousin korean

I order a ten-piece chicken wing combo with ranch dipping sauce, french fries, and a Diet Coke from WingStop ($28.84). No water for me, no nutrients for my brain plant. I show the receipt to my viewers and manage to get another ten dollars out of them. "I told you," I say. "That's how much shit costs." Not just food but fast food, which, in addition to being unhealthy, is supposed to be cheap. That's the whole point of it. Normally, I'd balk at spending nearly thirty dollars on a meal for myself, but this is a big day. Besides, it's probably my last meal on earth, considering that I'm going to meet the Reaper.

Before the wings come, I chew up six Gaviscon tablets and down half a bottle of Pepto Bismol. I put the rest of the bottle in my bag for later, to ingest right before I get onstage. All I've been eating is trash lately and my body is feeling it. Crackling nails. Sharpened elbows. For all I can say about working at Juice Body, I ate well. Bougie shit like spirulina and pea protein that kept me regular. Lots of vegetables and fruits, too. I could just gulp them down without knowing I was eating six stalks of celery and two entire mangoes. And no one minded if I took a banana or two home at the end of my shift. Well, maybe they did.

When my wings arrive, I set them out one by one on the desk in front of my laptop like little soldiers, waiting to be ripped apart. The timer at the top of my stream says that I've been streaming for six days, nearly to the minute. This time on Monday, I started broadcasting myself across the cosmos. One hundred and forty-four hours of me, me, me.

FAODR3AMZ: show us your tits

What if I win the competition today? What if I'm actually really good at this? What if I win and get twenty thousand dollars and I can try to make things right? If I win, I'll have enough money to end my streamathon and just go live whenever I feel like it. Build my audience over time. Get some ads going. Schedule weekly streams with Patrick and find out who else is on the hot pepper scene, too. There's a path forward that I could get excited about if I let myself. But it depends on how today goes, how far away excelsior404 stays from me and my viewers. He's been quiet since reaching out to Lee. Maybe he found some other woman to harass online. It's unlikely, but it's possible.

"Did this really all start because I happened to have a jalapeño plant in my apartment?"

yousefxd: yolo
jackdaw2000: good ol days lolol

I take a ripping bite out of a chicken wing, and then another, and then another, until they all bear the imprint of my teeth. Chiming chats come in, hazy nobodies interacting with one another in the murky swamp of the internet. Hundreds and hundreds of people. How many of them are also eating right now? Sleeping? Shitting? And among the horde, some old friends, familiar names. The only thing more pathetic than me streaming this long is the people who've been with me the entire time. My precious monsters.

• • •

I manage to eat half of my wings before the pain starts. A shimmy of lightning down my intestines, a bright red warning, strobing and hot to the touch. I gag and chuck the rest away. It's almost noon. The expo hall is about an hour away, and I told Patrick I'd meet him at one o'clock. I chomp down a handful of Gaviscon and put on a pair of jeans and a white T-shirt with my LiveCast handle written on the front and back in permanent marker. My handwriting has always been neat. I'll give myself that. I look in the mirror and the text is legible and large enough.

"How do I look?" I ask my viewers.

chillnessa: guapa
avomecado: im bored

I text Lee again. They haven't answered me all morning. I need hype. I need capital letters. I need exclamation points. Mademoiselle_dell needs to be fronting by the time I get to the expo. I manage to muster the right energy for my viewers as I walk to the train station, and they give it back to me in multiples. Every smile nets me five smiles back. Every joke nets me a sycophantic coo of virtual laughter. I take the train ($2.90) deep into Brooklyn, exiting across from Green-Wood Cemetery at five minutes to the hour. I was running late but all of my trains were eerily and irritatingly on time, as if the universe was conspiring to get me here. I arrive at the entrance to Industry City's expo hall a minute before one, and there's Patrick, waiting for me by the door. I see him before he sees me. I could still turn around. Take the train home. The New York Harbor is right over there. I could cannonball in, sink or swim. There are so many ways to have a mental breakdown, the options are nearly paralyzing. But if I'm going to fall completely and entirely apart, I might as well do it in front of an audience.

Patrick gives me a fist bump when I approach, no fuss, and I remember that I like him off camera. He's chilled out, like a normal human. He links our feeds together so that they're streaming the same content to our over ten thousand combined viewers. He's going to be my eyes for the next couple hours, showing my viewers around.

Together we head inside and walk the floor of the expo hall, a massive indoor space with about three dozen rows of booths. I didn't know this ecosystem existed, not like this, not in such excess. A sensorium of spice. Hot sauce purveyors, a beer and wine bar, merchandise, and all the spicy products one could imagine: chocolate with a kick, throat-searing ice cream, hot honey, habanero peanut butter, picante ramen that makes my eyes water just smelling its steam. A fountain of Frank's RedHot sauce that people can dip hors d'oeuvres into. We have to wade through a thick crowd to get around, but Patrick manages it expertly. He's comfortable here, in his zone. He offers to buy me a beer and I say no on account of my stomach, still rumbling and surly from the wings.

Patrick seems to know everyone. He stops to say hello to his friends at the Heatonist booth, which is conveniently located right next to his other friends at the PuckerButt Pepper Co. booth. There's a man at the latter that I recognize as Smokin' Ed Currie. The legend himself, the master trickster who first bred the Carolina Reaper in 2012. Behind him is a full-sized cutout of himself with a speech bubble that reads: "I'm betting on the powers of capsaicin to kill cancer cells in the long term—and you should, too!"

I consider what I might say to him if I were to go up and introduce myself. This is all his fault, after all. A literal man-made hell. Instead, I hang back, eyes glued to the stage by the far wall of the large, high-ceilinged room. The stage is empty now but soon I'll be called up to stand on it, soon the crowd will condense around me, pulled in by the gravity of the occasion. Who can eat the most Carolina Reapers in a minute? Who can willingly swallow the most pepper spray? It's like the Olympics for people who hate themselves. My mom, Daisy, Lee—none of them are here to cheer me on, and I have to be okay with that, because it's all my fault.

"Okay, you spooky dancing skeletons." I wink at Patrick's camera, which he aims at me while he continues to chitchat. "This. This is what we're here for." I take his arm and re-aim the camera at a row of four tables covered entirely in dairy products. Cartons of milk big and small, everything from nonfat to whole, chocolate to strawberry, milk-fed organic to mucousy conventional. Whipped cream. Flavored yogurt. String cheese in swirls of cheddar and mozzarella. "This platform is going to be my best friend today."

Patrick points at a tower of gilded sticks of butter and I laugh, but he insists that I take one, that I do my best to eat it before the competition. I consider tossing the stick of butter straight in the trash but the second he turns around, some chick waves and catches my attention. She comes up and introduces herself as Dorothy, aka Didi, aka chickenleggy.

Apparently chickenleggy is the type of chick that wears a knitted beanie in the dead of summer. I unwrap the stick of butter and take a hefty bite so I can't respond to her greetings, just smile and nod, then I drag her over to Patrick because I know it's him that she really wants to meet. She's said so herself on multiple occasions. And I'm not wrong, she gloms on to him like ringworm.

But jackdaw2000, he's here, too, and he's here for me. He's able to find me in the crowd using Patrick's video feed. An Australian guy, a barista, he has big cartoon eyes and a mop of wavy black hair. This grown man gets on one knee and kisses the top of my hand. I snatch it away and snarl, and he's delighted. He came here for mademoiselle_ dell, and here she is, scowling at her thrall.

Who else is here, I wonder.

The sound of feedback from the stage. A few people are up there tapping the microphone, setting up. I look at the time. Five minutes to two. This is all happening too fast. Patrick is looking at me. I can see him out of the corner of my eye, but I don't meet his gaze, just keep looking at the stage as I take another bite out of the stick of butter, and then another. The taste is oily but not unpleasant, might even taste great with some salt, and I feel like a kid, unwrapping the little gold butter pats at Applebee's to help Daisy with her toast. We would weld the slick gold foil into rings, one for each of us, one for Mom, too, and wear our rings for days until they fell off.

"Good luck," Patrick says, and I jump. The butter slides slick down my throat and settles heavy in my sternum.

"Why do you look nervous?" I ask him.

"I look nervous?" he asks. "Me?"

"Yeah. You look totally nervous."

He flips his phone camera toward himself and assesses his appearance in front of our viewers. "Do I look nervous, everyone?"

"You shouldn't be nervous," I say. "I should be nervous. Unless you're nervous for me, on my behalf. Are you? Are you nervous for me?"

"You ate that whole stick of butter already," he says. "I didn't even notice. Impressive."

"You don't think I can do this," I say.

"What? Of course I think you can do it. I'm the one who told you to sign up. And besides, aren't you a golden god or something?"

I nod. "Yes. Yes, I am." A crowd starts to form around the stage. The crew brings out Carolina Reapers in a bowl and a rolling whoop goes out. A guy in all black starts dividing the Reapers up into five smaller bowls, one for each competitor. One of those bowls is for me.

"Hey," Patrick says. "I do think you can do it. And so do they." He points at his phone. "Remember who you're doing this for."

Remember who I'm doing this for. As if I could forget. An announcer steps up to the microphone and announces that the annual world record Carolina Reaper eating competition is about to get started. He invites the competitors to gather offstage. So much clapping, little shockwaves through my smallest bones. I chug the rest of my Pepto.

"And when this is over, we can start planning for the future. Talk about what comes next for Mademoiselle Dell," Patrick says.

I walk away from him, begin my critical path toward the stage. "I'll be in the front row," he yells after me, and I nod without turning around. Today there is no fountain, no escape from the god of fire and brimstone. Which is just as well. That's who I'm doing this all for, anyway.

"Welcome to the tenth annual world record Carolina Reaper eating competition," the announcer booms into the microphone. "We have a representative from the Guinness World Records here with us today." He gestures toward a man in a dinky suit with a bright blue tie and a clipboard in his hands. "And we have five competitors ready to get fired up with us today and summon the devil together!"

I'm standing offstage with the other competitors. There's only one other woman. She's slim, tall, older than I would expect. Severe looking in a tight-necked T-shirt and jeans. Then a lanky kid around my age wearing a fedora, ponytail trailing out of his hat. A guy with a long gray beard in a sweat-stained wifebeater, reeking of testosterone. A skateboarder who looks like Shaggy from *Scooby Doo* whose shirt reads: "Lost in the Sauce."

I appraise them briefly and notice that, yes, the world record holder, the big baby face who sweeps the floor with everyone year over year, isn't here. Other than that, all I can take in is the deafening sound of screaming and clapping and cheering. Everywhere I look are camera crews. People recording on their phones. Kids sitting on their parents' shoulders. I see chickenleggy. I see jackdaw2000. I see Patrick up front, right where he said he would be.

On the stage is a long table with five bowls of Reapers on it, one for each of us, alongside pitchers of milk and water. The announcer calls us up and introduces each of us by our name and where we live. Three of us are from New York City, but the skateboarder came all the way from

Colorado, and the wifebeater is from Philadelphia. Then we're asked
to exit the stage once more and wait single file by the stairs. The other
competitors don't chat with me or with each other. We're silent as we
wait. Not patient, not calm, just silent.

"Here are the rules," the announcer says. "Each contestant will
have their turn onstage. They'll have sixty seconds to eat as many Carolina Reapers as they can. Their plate will be measured before and after
that minute is over. Because the peppers vary in size, we're going by
grams. When the buzzer goes off, you have to spit what you don't swallow back onto the plate. Set your stems aside, we will deduct those from
the final weight. Contestants can use competition time to drink water or
milk, but after their minute is done, each contestant will have to stand
onstage for another sixty seconds before they can eat or drink anything.
If they step offstage they will be disqualified. The person who eats the
most grams of Carolina Reaper and can wait out that one lousy, terrible,
no-good minute will be today's winner. And if you want a tip: you're
going to have to pace about a pepper every five seconds to beat the world
record."

"We're going to get started with Yevgenia 'Gene' Makarov of Brighton Beach. Step right up, Gene!" The other female competitor clears
her throat as she walks onto the stage. Gracefully, as if approaching the
guillotine, she perches directly behind the table with her hands folded
in front of her. The announcer counts her down from three, the "go"
loud as a gunshot. And then she begins to eat, grabbing peppers with
each hand and stuffing them in her mouth with uncanny speed.

"Shit," says the guy behind me. Shaggy. I notice that he's holding a
stick of butter down by his hips. He hasn't eaten any of it, and it's starting to leak onto the floor from the warmth of his hands. "Shit," he says
again. His eyes are wide as he watches Gene kick ass in her respectable
shoes and modest hairdo. Wifebeater pats him on the shoulder gruffly,
whether in encouragement or reproach it's hard to tell. The smell of

the peppers reaches my nose from the stage, fruity and potent. The timer goes off and Gene puts her hands in the air above her head like a criminal in police headlights, her body twitching. The crowd cheers, an absolute roar. She jumps around onstage like she's performing a ritual, shaking out her arms, and I understand the urge to move—to do something, anything at all, to distract from the inferno.

The announcer starts to count down the sixty seconds until she can leave and the Guinness World Record guy weighs her plate of peppers and scribbles something down on his clipboard. It looks like she ate about half the plate, maybe six or seven peppers. My heart beats out of my chest watching her do her dance onstage, grim and interpretive. A groan comes out of her, not so loud as to be heard over the cheering audience, but I'm only a few feet away and I feel it, low and ugly. It took multiple minutes for the heat from the ghost pepper to climax. How long does a Reaper take to reach its peak? I should've asked Patrick when I had the chance.

Thirty seconds left. Gene's jittering slows into a shuffle, and then she's completely still. Her eyes closed, her chest rising and falling rapidly. No, I want to say. Keep moving. Don't ever stop moving.

Gene stands like that for a while, still as a statue. I can't see her eyes from where I'm standing but I'd bet they're all pupil. And then she starts shaking her head, very slowly, almost indiscernibly, and next thing I know she is running offstage. I step aside and let her through. She dashes around the corner and out of sight, presumably to the women's bathroom.

Disqualified with ten seconds left on the clock.

I should check on her, but I won't, and neither will anyone else. No one wants to witness what she is going through right now. The transfiguration process as the pepper tries to exit the body any way it can. Gene has clearly gotten to Shaggy. The announcer calls him up next but he doesn't move. Wifebeater gives him a shove, but it can't be helped.

The announcer comes over for a quick sidebar and then confirms the news with the audience: contestant number two has dropped out. Boos. Hisses. Shaggy slinks off and disappears, and it's just me and wifebeater and fedora kid, who gets called up next.

Now, this kid has been preparing for his moment of fame. He does audience work with his hat and approaches the table with glee, with relish. I wonder what it takes to get to that mental state when faced with certain ruination. The announcer counts down and then fedora picks up a pepper too slowly, chews it too slowly, doesn't get to the swallowing part fast enough. A fatal flaw. That's why this kid was so excited: he's never done this before. This was probably a dare. Something dumb to make his friends laugh. But it isn't funny anymore. He looks like he's going to die up there, tears and snot everywhere. The heat hits him faster than it hit Gene, and even before his time ends it's clear that he's not built for this. He only eats one Reaper, but to his credit, he waits out the clock, and when his sixty seconds are up he picks up the pitcher of milk and pours it directly into his mouth, onto his clothes, onto the floor. No one bothers to clean it up. Guinness man finishes weighing his plate and scribbling his notes. The crowd whoops. And then fedora exits the stage with one hand up for high fives and the other wrapped around his intestines like he's keeping them in place. He walks over to a trash can and throws up.

Over his shoulder, near the edge of the crowd, I see Casper.

His name is Casper, right? I take out my phone to check and make sure. Yes, it's him. It's one hundred percent him. The guy who picked up a plant from me in the middle of the night on Monday. The guy who made me uncomfortable, who knows where I live, who isn't here coincidentally. No. Because he knows exactly where to find me at all times of the day and night. And yes, I recall a screen name now. A viewer that's been in and out over the last few days, observing but never messaging. Fr13ndlygh0st, aka Casper, aka excelsior404.

It's him. I know it's him. Excelsior404, who took my online details when I shared that dumb plant listing link on my first day of streaming and ran with them. Of course he'd pretend to buy a plant to scope me out. It makes perfect, stupid sense.

I'm about to check my stream, my viewer history to see if fr13ndly-gh0st is in my stream now, when the announcer calls my name.

"Next up we have Dell Danvers from New York City! Give it up for Dell!"

I step onstage, keeping my sights on Casper. The crowd is insane, raging and roaring, jumping up and down to get a better look at me. Except excelsior404. I mean Casper. He's just standing there, glaring. I refuse to meet his gaze. Refuse to do anything but focus on the task ahead. Most people go their entire lives without even thinking about eating the hottest pepper on earth, let alone actually eating it. There's a reason for that. Self-preservation. Self-respect. These peppers also aren't easy to find. It's not like a ghost pepper or a Trinidad scorpion pepper where you just have to know where to go. It's more like procuring an exotic pet. A Komodo dragon or Burmese python. You have to know who to talk to, know who will understand your very specific and sadistic desires.

Time moves slowly as I approach the table, willing mademoiselle_dell to move my feet for me. On the table are eight pimply brains dangling from their own individual brain stems, skin dappled and warped and veering off in wild directions. I think of collapsed lungs. Burst livers. These Frankenstein monstrosities never wanted to exist. This fact is very clear from looking at their barbaric geometry. I can feel the crowd's cheering as a quickening in my bones. My heart is beating so fast it's like one continuous droning thump, a sinister beat.

Fight or flight.

Casper née excelsior404 is on my left, only a handful of rows back from the stage. The fucking nerve to show up here. I'm not surprised, but I am furious. And the fury plants me where I stand, the seed in my brain sprouting roots that travel deep down my spine until they reach the thin wood of the stage itself, burrow through that until they find the molten core of the earth and wrap its throbbing heart tightly. I am a powerful tree, grounded in place. I am stuck but limitlessly kinetic. My anger is not a cage. It's as expansive as a forest.

I can do this.

Patrick, a friend, is mere feet from me. I look directly into his camera and flash my most wicked, unhinged grin. Teeth and gums and flicking devil's tongue. And then the announcer starts to count me down. I lean over and interrupt him, speaking directly into his microphone.

"Find me on LiveCast at mademoiselle-underscore-dell," I say, pointing at my shirt. "I'm live streaming right now with Hot Pat of Butter — donate to a good cause!"

"Anything else you want to add?" the announcer jokes, rolling his eyes.

"Yeah," I say, grabbing the microphone again. "That guy right there, the one in the gray hoodie? Yeah, you." Casper looks at me, then looks around. The audience stills for a moment. The announcer's hand twitches on the microphone, unsure what is going to come out of my mouth next on live television. "Someone keep an eye on that guy," I say. "There's a lot of children here and he's a known sex offender."

I give the microphone back to the announcer and it takes him a moment to regain his composure. But then he resumes his countdown and the crowd chants with him.

Five. Four. Three. Two. One.

A flurry of hands and peppers and chewing and swallowing. A minute goes by so quickly. The initial taste of the pepper is surprisingly sweet and fruity. The sweetness catches me off guard — a trick, the way Daisy's laugh could cover for something she didn't want to say. But even she

232 | LIOR TORENBERG

would have warned me that there's always a catch. The skin contact clings bitter to the corners of my mouth, the backs of my teeth. I don't know how many peppers I've eaten, only that I don't stop picking them up and shoveling them in my mouth until the announcer calls time, and then I step back with my hands above my head and open my battery acid–filled mouth wide to show that it's empty.

Sixty seconds until I can drink milk or water, or exit the stage.

Hot mouth. My hot mouth is so hot. So fucking hot. The capsaicin is beginning to do its dirty work, its murderous work. Motherfucker. Saliva dribbles out of my mouth in thick threads. I look at Patrick and his smile is wide, so wide I want to kick him in the teeth. It's not him up here, it's me, and I know that the spice has not even begun its ascent, let alone peaked, and it's already far worse than the ghost pepper was a couple days ago. Molten fire. Crackling magma. I want to vomit. I need to vomit everything in my body, organs included. Cold saliva fills my mouth and my stomach shudders. When I had a stomach virus as a child, my mom bought me red Gatorade and cherry Popsicles, and my vomit was a deep and ruinous red. I'm not going to throw up now in front of all these cheering people. I'm not. I wring my hands until they're white at the knuckles. I'm a ball of sensation and will, just trying to keep my airways open as the heat multiplies exponentially by the second.

Fifty seconds left.

My mom and Daisy and Lee might not be here but thankfully mademoiselle_dell is. Pure id, snarling at the audience and baring her canines. My brain goes fuzzy and aches in time with my heart. The crowd sways to the left and I go along with it, grabbing the table to keep myself from toppling. Claps like cannonballs as the announcer counts me down.

Forty seconds left.

The vapors coming out of my mouth make my eyes stream. Or

maybe I'm crying. It's hard to tell. I press my T-shirt against my eyes. Touching them with my hands would be certain death. All of my organs are trembling. My soul is trembling. The heat creeps down my throat and pulls it shut like a coin purse. I wheeze in a breath, and then another, and I think of Daisy, how it must have felt to overdose—if she felt pain, or if she just went to sleep. I'm not getting enough oxygen, I'm sure of it. I could die, I think. On this stage. In front of all these people. Right now. It would make sense. It would make perfect sense.

Thirty seconds left.

The heartburn, when it comes, is excruciating. I clench my chest, digging my nails into my skin in a furious red circle. I look up at the bright lights pointed at me from the ceiling, trying to keep myself upright. What I wouldn't give for some milk, some ice cream, a piece of bread to soak up this poison, scrounged and stolen from Lee's kitchen. Of course they hate me. Of course they've given up on me. I've given them no recourse. The heat gets worse with each breath. Unbearable is an understatement. I have no thoughts, only exclamation points. And I deserve all of it.

Twenty seconds left.

I'm not a good sister. I'm not. But I don't want to die. I want to live. I want to apologize to my mom. The pain makes me bargain. Just one more week. Just one more week. I'm so sorry. I am not a golden god. I fall to my knees on the stage, keeping my eyes on the ceiling, on those bright, bright lights. Heartburn so potent I'll drown in my own stomach acid. My vision narrows into a fuzzy black tunnel. Every time I think it can't get worse, it does. How many peppers did I eat? I didn't even look. My brain is a flimsy thing, a deflated balloon, and my stomach is a blimp about to burst.

Ten seconds left.

A noise through the tunnel. Patrick yelling my name. He's still smiling that fucked-up smile, that smile that's trying to convince me that everything is okay when it's not. It's not. Ten more seconds is an unbridgeable distance. The milk is right there in front of me. I crawl over to the table and drag myself up. The plate of Reapers is gone. The Guinness guy is weighing it off to the side in his dumb blue tie. I bite my fist to hold down vomit.

Five seconds left.

I don't want to die, not like this, maybe not even in general. I reach for the milk but my hands stay put. I'm shaking, cold and hot sweat mingling like opposing pressure systems. My white T-shirt is entirely soaked through, my screen name smudging and imprinting onto the skin beneath.

Four seconds left.

I wipe my mouth and a smear of blood appears on the back of my hand. I am deep, deep in my body, painfully present and way up in space at the same time. My consciousness is a bright ball of hurt below my rib cage, a spasm in my gut warning of impending doom.

Three seconds left.

A trillion ghost peppers. I imagine the pain scale of faces that doctors show you. The sensation in my body is somewhere far beyond it. Not so much a face anymore as a gaseous, angry mass.

Two seconds left.

Icy-hot tears mix with my sweat and land in my open mouth. My bowels squirm with a fierceness. I gasp for air.

One second left.

I realize that I've been crying this entire time, since the countdown began, maybe even before. Maybe since the moment I stepped onstage.

A bell goes off. Time's up. I don't go for the milk. I don't go for the water. I don't stop when the event's paramedic asks me if I need assistance. I ignore the applause, ignore everything. I sprint on soggy legs to the women's room, gripping my stomach. I reach the toilet just in time.

✻   ✻   ✻

That other competitor, the chick, is in the stall next to me. I can hear her bilious, bad-tempered sounds. It feels like she was onstage a million years ago. But it was fewer than ten minutes. Contestant number two, he was right to run away. I feel like I've done something horribly indecent and also illegal. The way I feel—if I were a cartoon there would be steam coming out of my ears, a whole lot of it.

The heartburn is unrelenting, like I've branded my insides. It peaks and peaks and peaks again, impossibly, and I have to remind myself to breathe. Every time that I think the heat has peaked, it somersaults onto a higher rung. The pepper is a heart attack, a stake shoved through my ribs. I want to lie down on the cold bathroom floor and rot. The only thing that keeps me grounded is tuning in to Patrick's feed on my phone—which is my feed—as he films the final contestant and chats with our viewers.

elite1441: we are the chumpion s
vexmafiza: yeeeeeee
racre001: queen dell
chickenleggy: SAY HI TO HOT PAT EVERYONE
karnie_vibes: where did mademoiselle_dell go
teejayoon: massive cope
jimpix: all hail queen dell

The next contestant is on, and he is an absolute beast. Wifebeater is composed onstage as he shovels pepper after pepper into his black hole of a mouth. Eyes beady and focused in his ultra-round face, he stands with his hands on his hips during the final countdown and then exits the stage with the same heavy, bearded swagger that he stepped onto it with. Makes it look easy, that bastard.

This wasn't worth it. The most excruciating moment of my life and I'm stuck in it with nowhere to go, no way to turn back time. It was disrespectful of me to think I could do this, prideful and obnoxious. No one does this. The universe does not condone it.

There are chats to read, a potential way to distract myself. I do a quick scroll, faster and faster, entranced by all that green. So many exclamations and expletives. So much shock and awe. Over twenty thousand people are on this stream right now, my stream with Patrick, twenty thousand floating dollar signs. It's all I can do to scroll with one finger as I climb up onto the closed toilet seat and bring my knees to my chest.

Five minutes pass since I ate the pepper, six, seven, eight, and the heat starts to abate. My nose is running like a fountain and my heart is on fire, but I'm alive and I'm going to be okay. No longer a bonfire in my lungs but a guttering candle. I ate the hottest pepper in the world and I'm going to be okay.

Once I'm squarely back in the confines of the pain scale, I notice the extraordinary pangs in my stomach, the cramping and gnawing. It's gruesome, but I'm used to stomach pain at this point. Greater than that is the euphoria, the rapturous sense of clarity at the top of this particular mountaintop. I check my LiveCast balance.

I just made over ten thousand dollars.

I take it back. It was worth it. On the other side of the pain, with this figure in front of me, I can say that it was more than worth it. Ten. Thousand. Dollars. $10,402, to be exact.

That brings the total across my accounts to just over twenty thousand dollars.

My LiveCast ranking is 89,029.

I did it. I met my goal. I exceeded my goal. And now I'm invincible and wild, stupid, crazy rich. I have everything I've ever wanted. If I can do this then I can do anything, even reverse time: call my mom, call Dr. Dole, call one of the million private care companies my mom got quotes from and hire someone and set up transportation for Daisy to get her from the hospital to my mom's place in New Jersey and help my mom set up a room for her and . . .

Her hand moved. It did. It was a good sign. We knew it. It was too perfect, too Daisy, to be a coincidence.

I feel giddy and carbonated. I get up and wash my face in the sink, the water cold and wonderful for my brain plant. I make faces at myself, wondering at my ability to stay alive, my ability to jump from the worst moment of my life to the best in a matter of seconds.

I step outside the bathroom, expecting to see Patrick and my viewers waiting for me, expecting to curtsy and twirl and high kick for the cameras.

"Hey," Casper says instead. "I've been waiting for you."

I feel like a cornered animal, analyzing my escape routes, eyes narrowed into arrow slits. I could blow my pepper spray breath in his face. I could go back into the bathroom and look for a window. I could knee him in the balls and yell for help.

"Good job," he says. I scan his face for something—anger, sarcasm, bile—but find nothing but a blank stare, black shark eyes that I can see myself in. "So, I'm a sex offender?"

I shrug, my stomach coiling into an angry knot. "I don't know what you do in your free time. Excelsior404, right?"

Casper nods. "How are you feeling?" he asks. "You looked awful up there."

"Yeah. Fine." I cross my arms over my chest to keep my guts from falling out, a mess of sharpened knives. My mind immediately goes to the phone in my pocket, but I know my viewers aren't there. They're on Patrick's phone. Our streams are linked and he's the one broadcasting. My viewers aren't thousands of miles away but right down the hallway. And yet, I've never felt less safe. They're all just strangers. And right now, I'm on my own.

"You blocked me," Casper says. "Instead of paying me back, you blocked me."

"You're a fucking stalker," I spit.

His face darkens. "I'm not stalking you, are you kidding? I'm . . . " He takes a deep breath, composing himself. "You're not even hot. Maybe on-screen, but not in person."

"Good, then. I'm not hot and you're not stalking me. We can move on with our lives."

"I have a responsibility to people. And when I find scammers like you, I get really pissed off."

"So this has nothing to do with the fact that your dick pic didn't do it for me?" I say, savoring the way his face twists.

"I may have liked you initially, thought you were interesting, but I quickly realized that you're just like everyone else."

"All other women, you mean."

The distance between us tightens, a slingshot pulled to its maximum point of tension.

"What do you want?" I ask.

"Come clean. Give everyone their money back," he hisses. "Give me my money back. You could've just done that instead of blocking me. We could've avoided all of this if you would have just given me my money back."

"You want your money back?" I ask, taking out my phone. "Fine. I'll give you your money back."

"Not just me. You have to pay everyone back," he says slowly. "I want you to do it. Now. Or I'll send that death certificate to everyone, not just your neighbor."

"You're doing great, by the way. I can tell you rehearsed this a lot, and I want you to know you're doing great."

"I hate bitches like you," he says. "You just steal and lie and take advantage of people's kindness. I've seen it too many times, and I can't let it go. Especially because you're so bad at it. I mean, anyone with access to the internet could figure you out in a second. It's almost like you wanted to get caught, like your viewers want to be fooled so they can feel better about themselves. But I can't let you do that."

"Listen, internet warrior. I'm not the one. I'm not the issue. Go kidnap a billionaire and have them give a million to charity or something. Use this anger and energy for something better. I believe in you."

Behind him, toward the main stage, I can hear the announcer on the microphone. The deliberations are over. He's ready to announce the winner of today's world record competition. He invites all the contestants back to take the stage in his booming, metallized voice.

"I have to go," I say to Casper.

He grabs my arm where it burns. I look at his hairless knuckles, his damp grip. He's stronger than I gave him credit for. The way he's holding on to me, I wouldn't be able to tear my arm away if I tried. The theatrics of it all make me dissociate a little, make me a bit shitty in a way I know I'll regret later. I wish my viewers were here to see this, for more reasons than one.

"What are you going to do?" I laugh in his face. "Strangle me? Beat me up? Knock me out? With all these people a couple feet away?"

"I don't want to do anything," he says. "You're the one who needs to do something. And I know you're smart enough to recognize this, but I'll say it anyway: it's not just the death certificate I can share. I have your address, your phone number, all of it."

"You're going to dox me?" I ask, and I know he's done this before. I know this isn't about the money. He wants me on my knees, humiliated, ruined—and he wants to be the martyr. I remember looking at his profile last week, when he first DMed me, looking at the streams he followed: all about uncovering the truth, untangling the conspiracy theories and the plots against him and others like him. And I know he's done this before, ruined someone's life with a click.

A week ago, I wouldn't have cared. What was there to ruin? But things are different now. I have money. I have a successful stream.

Maybe I can even make things right. Unless, of course, there's no way to make things right.

I can grovel, but mademoiselle_dell can't.

"Fine. Give me a fucking second," I say. He lets go and I return to my phone, click into fr13ndlygh0st's profile, and send him one dollar with the memo: *tiny peepee party funds.*

He clocks the notification on his phone. For a moment, he says nothing. His eyes are stony and even. Then he presses a few buttons and puts his phone back in his pocket with a definitive motion.

"Go ahead," he says. "They're calling for you."

A wave of nausea as I jog back to the main stage. The peppers, my gnawing stomach pain, that goddamn Casper. I lied. So what? People lie all the time. And it wasn't 100 percent a lie. Maybe 50 percent. I'd accept 50 percent. It's true that money would have saved Daisy, or at least bought us time when Dr. Dole called a couple months ago and said there were no other options, that they were going to turn her off.

My mom and I just wanted one more week. She was fighting in there. We knew she was. But we couldn't prove it, and we didn't have the money for private care, and no other hospital would take her. So that was it.

I didn't go to the hospital with my mom the day they turned Daisy off. I couldn't. I just couldn't accept that after all that time, all that hoping, all that waiting—it was over. Maybe I should've. Maybe it would've brought me closure, something. My mom said she put on Daisy's favorite song—"When the Party's Over" by Billie Eilish—and played her out. She told me that when she pulled the plug, it only took a minute for Daisy to stop breathing, another minute for her heart to stop. Just a single song, and then she was gone.

Besides, my viewers don't know Daisy. They don't love Daisy. They weren't there by her bedside every day for two months. They weren't at her funeral, watching all her classmates and teachers and her entire goddamn soccer team wail and sniffle at her closed casket. She was gone and it was all my fault. No. My viewers tuned in for entertainment. Like Casper said, they wanted to feel like they were doing something good with their wasted time, something productive. But saying "aw" and giving me five dollars isn't morality. Paying for live charity porn isn't more estimable than paying for anything else. If I tricked a few people, fine, but they were tricking themselves, too, if they thought they were actually watching my stream out of the kindness of their hearts. I lit myself on fire for christ's sake.

I step back onstage with the rest of the competitors. Even Gene, who disqualified herself because she couldn't wait out the clock, is up here. A genuine trouper. But if she's out, and number two never competed, and fedora guy only ate one pepper, then it's really just me and wifebeater. In a few seconds, I could be twenty thousand dollars richer. That's double what I currently have. That's way more than "just one more week." I could do it. I could actually win this thing.

I look over at my competitor as we stand shoulder-to-shoulder on the stage. He's too tall to stand shoulder-to-shoulder with, it's more like shoulder-to-belly-button. He smells faintly vinegary, like buttermilk. Probably two hundred and fifty pounds, but not fat at all, just massive, like a box truck, like any truck.

"Thank you for your patience, everyone, as we've finished tallying up today's scores," the announcer says. "I know we're all ready to hear the results of today's Carolina Reaper World Record Competition! Am I right? Are we ready?"

Claps, whistles, hollers. I find Patrick in the audience, not far from where he was before. Where the hell was he when I came out of the bathroom? Why didn't he come find me? Why wasn't he streaming me? He probably wanted to make sure he kept his spot for when the winners were announced, so he could give our viewers the best view possible. A consummate professional. Whatever.

There's chickenleggy. Jackdaw2000. I'm sure there are other people here, other viewers, who haven't made themselves known. All these eyes watching me, and all I can do is stand here. Casper is in the audience now, too. In the back over there, on the left. I grimace, pushing him out of my head. I can't be preoccupied up here in front of all these people, bright hot lights beaming down on me from the ceiling. I just can't.

"In third place, we have Christopher Tyrrel from Staten Island, who ate six grams of pure, vomitous fire! That's one extra-large Reaper. It's better than zero, right? Right? Maybe? Let's give the man some respect for giving it a shot!"

Fedora steps forward and bows. The audience claps and claps. Me, I'm holding my breath. If someone told me last week that I could win a competition like this, I would have slapped them across the face. If someone told me that I'd meet my fundraising goal and then some, I would have backhanded them in the other direction. But now I'm here.

"In second place," the announcer continues. "We would have had Yevgenia 'Gene' Makarov of Brighton Beach, who came in at a whopping thirty-seven grams of Reaper! That's nearly eight peppers! An impressive show, if I do say so myself. But unfortunately, she was disqualified. Don't let it fool you, that minute of waiting is much harder than the minute of eating. But that's okay. Maybe next year, right, Gene? Promise me you'll come back next year? Let's give a round of applause for Gene!"

She doesn't bow, more of a head twitch, a nod, and I wonder if she regrets it. Running offstage like that. If she wishes that she could have waited out the fire for just a few seconds longer. I remember my ranking rocketing up, up, up as my arm burned. But it's not bravery that makes someone do that, or even a high pain tolerance. It's stubbornness, and a good deal of self-loathing that not just anyone has.

The announcer clears his throat. It's hard to stand, my stomach is cramping up so bad, but I force myself to stay on my feet.

"In second place, from the kitchens of hell themselves, we have Dell Danvers, who kicked some serious ass with a backbreaking thirty-two grams of Reaper insanity!"

My insides go white, and then a fuzzy yellow, as the audience screams and hollers. Second place. Not first. Not third. Second fucking place. I pump my fist for the audience and for Patrick's camera, feeling moderately dejected, until they announce first place and my disappointment turns into bewilderment, absolute wonder.

"And that means that our winner today is Cadmus Hussain, who came in at a nasty, disgusting, revolting seventy-six grams of Reaper! That's over fifteen Reapers in a single minute. While we have not broken a world record today, seventy-six grams is an absolute feat of inner strength and willpower. Congratulations, Cadmus! You're our winner today, and as our winner you'll be receiving a huge check in the mail: a grand prize of twenty thousand dollars and all the bragging rights that you can manage!"

I clap for Cadmus, feeling myself one of the audience now. Seventy-six grams of Carolina Reaper. I wasn't even close, and I can't be mad about it. That guy is a tank.

When the clapping finally dies down, we all make our way offstage. The audience disperses slowly, amoebic in its patterns, until soon the expo hall seems overlarge and empty. I don't see Casper anymore. But I do see Patrick, over at the bar cradling a beer, phone nowhere to be seen. He must have ended our stream.

"Hey," I say, bounding up to him. "Can you believe—"

The look on his face shuts me up.

"What is it?" I ask. "What?"

"You lied," he says.

"What?"

"You weren't raising money for your sister. You lied. You were raising money for yourself."

"Patrick, what are you—"

"Now, I don't care what you do on your own time, you know? I don't care what you say or what you do. I try to give people grace and the benefit of the doubt. But you made a fool of me. You made my viewers lose trust in me. I took you under my wing because I cared about you and your story, and you completely—"

"Hold on."

"I don't—"

"Please, hold on a second," I say.

"Okay." He shakes his head. "So, what then?"

"That guy was here tonight. In the audience. I blocked him and he's been stalking me ever since and tonight he threatened to dox me and destroy my life. He cornered me outside the bathroom. He's trying to ruin me, Patrick. There's a reasonable explanation for all of this."

Patrick picks up his plastic cup of beer as if to drink, then pauses and throws it away. "What were you even going to do with the money?" he asks.

I open my mouth, but for once, I don't have the right words. I could make something up. Do what I always do. Piece together a story that would explain everything. But the way he's looking at me now, the disappointment—nothing will make him unsee me for what I am.

Patrick waits for me to respond, then just shakes his head and turns, walking out of the expo hall and into the midday sun.

•   •   •

There's a sharpness below my sternum that doesn't go away. A despotic gurgle in my gut. A pinch of the spine that cracks me over when I get back to my apartment.

I reach for the floor and bring it to my face. Splintery wood on cheek skin, knees cut against the gaps of grain. Fuck. Fine. He told all of them. Crabbybob direct messaged me to ask where my moral compass

went. Forget moral compass. I'm on a different fucking moral planet.
But I'm suffering for it. I have never not been suffering for it. Fuck. My
stomach pain is sharp overlaid with a diffuse groan, a slurping spasm,
like a pyre burning in my esophagus. Pain. A white sheet of pain, empty
in its fullness. I imagine the ulcer spreading and spreading until my
insides are just one big hole, a cavity big enough to devour me from the
inside out.

There is no longer a room around me, a building around me. There
is only the fact of my body, the fact of this suffering. The pain is turning
me into a simpler organism, all sensation and no cognition. And in that
sensation there is anger. Yes, I lied. I admit it. But all these other people
with streams for different causes, are they telling the truth? They're not
paying themselves out at the end of the day? You seriously want me to
believe that someone else, in my same circumstances, would let themselves get evicted?

The white sheet of pain singes at the edges. That guy who raised
half a million dollars to rebuild his family home in Florida. What makes
him better than me? Give it a year. Another hurricane is right around
the corner.

The most someone made during a streamathon was $1.4 million
dollars in a single month. Of course, he was LiveCast's number one
streamer at the time. But still. I don't need a million bucks. Not even
close.

And besides, I put work in. I gave my viewers a show every single
day. I inserted a foreign object into myself. I lit myself on fucking fire.
I'm damn good at eating hot peppers and I was paid well for it. So what
if I injected some drama, a human interest element?

So a hospital can charge exorbitant, life-ruining fees and get away
with it—tell me that isn't a scam. But these things are not punished. There
are no consequences for gaming or rigging the system. Not if you win.

I wasn't always like this. I was earnest. I meant well. I did my best.

But if I'm already beyond redemption, then nothing I do should matter at this point. At least not to anyone that matters. The people that I truly care about, that really matter—where are they? They're certainly not here now. The only people here are my viewers. You.

I can't fathom a world where Daisy isn't here. That's always been true.

I grimace as another crack of pain rocks through me. Would I feel better if I ate something? I stuff a slice of bread into my mouth and chew slowly for a moment, then spit it out. I can't swallow. My body won't let me. The floor is slippery against my bare, sweating feet as I gyrate around, laying on one side and then the other and then curling up in a ball, trying to find the least excruciating position.

I should just delete my LiveCast account. Withdraw my funds and run for the hills. But Casper messages me and says he's going to dox me if I don't pay everyone back in twenty-four hours.

The pain gets inconceivably worse. Breathing is suddenly an over-complicated process, each inhale and exhale a separate tremor of torment. Air has to travel down to somewhere, and in this path, it moves other things. The lungs expand downward and push the liver and stomach, then contract back in and stretch them upward. Agony. And when the needles start to subside I find that I have to breathe again. Always have to breathe again. Why? So laborious. My viewers don't have an answer for me. They don't want to talk to me. There are only a hundred and fifty of them here now. My LiveCast ranking rocketed up briefly when the fuming hordes heard about the scammer and came to spew their toxicity at me, then tanked back down to a dismal 280,938. But I'm in too much pain to care. The viewers I have left, a lot of my original viewers and some others, are here to watch me die.

pklrik: give me my money back
chillnessa: wtf cabrón

pklrik: it wasnt even my money
pklrik: it was my parents money
kirk_equivalent: this is a criminal offense

"You will all get your money back," I try to say. But what comes out through the pain is: "Okay? Okay?"

Twenty thousand dollars. At a different point in time, that money could have changed everything. Saved everything. I turn my phone off and shove it away. I've had pain before, but this is something else, this is an ocean I can drown in. But it seems that there's still something left inside of me that wants to get out. I don't know how I make it to the gym downstairs, only that I do. There is someone at the front desk. I don't even glance in her direction. I get to a stall just in time, and before I flush, I look down and see an oil slick of blood in the toilet, black as tar.

• • •

This isn't happening. It's been hours and I'm still doubled over, a pulsating star of pain. After a long time on the toilet trying to stem the bleeding, I was able to make it out of the gym and back up to my apartment. I turned my phone back on momentarily. Bad idea. Texts and calls from my mom to make plans for tomorrow. A torrent of messages from my dwindling viewers. Chats. Direct messages. Emails. LiveCast ranking 461,842. I've been reported for violating the LiveCast community guidelines. My account is under investigation. Fine. Investigate me. Hate me. Vilify me.

Fine. Fine. Fine.

In the past hour, I've guzzled the rest of my Pepto, downed all of my manifold antacids: Gaviscon and Tums and even the minty, chalk-dust Rolaids I haven't touched in weeks. Nothing has helped. The pain should be subsiding by now. But instead, it's getting worse. I wish I could peel my skin off in a clean sheet, like the neat ribbon of a red apple.

With my skin gone, my muscles would slough off easily enough, and my brain plant would be able to escape this silvery pain and float, float, float to a weatherless place.

I need help.

I remember when my apartment was full of plants. I could hardly see the walls or the floor or anything else for all that rampant life. I used to have a nerve plant on my mini fridge: veined leaves, cupped, eager palms. It took up so much space and interfered when I tried to eat, swatting the food right out of my hands. I put it in the corner of the room as a punishment, face turned toward the wall. It twinged in anger, its leaves reaching across the apartment to shake their coiled fists in my face. I put it back on top of the mini fridge then and it seemed to relax. I sold it for twenty-five dollars.

I crawl across the floor, hooking one arm over the other and dragging my legs along with me. Finally, I can reach far enough to knock on the wall between my apartment and Lee's. I knock again and again and again. I knock until Lee is at my door. A vision, standing up so straight it hurts to look at them.

"What the hell?" they say. "Are you okay?"

"I'm bleeding out of my ass," I say.

"Excuse me?"

They kneel down and put their arm on my shoulder. I start weeping then. Not just because of the pain, or the fact that they're actually talking to me, being kind to me, or because all of my money has to be returned, but because of all of it. "You didn't have to change your locks," I cry. "You didn't have to change your locks."

Lee sits on the floor with me until the ambulance arrives.

SUNDAY

LiveCast Ranking: 555,942

A lingering nightmare that I can't remember. My mom is asleep in a chair beside me. There are windows in this room. Natural light. I'm not in my apartment. I'm in a hospital bed. I'm in a hospital. I sit up and wince, then lay back down. The air smells lemony and antiseptic, and I don't want to muddy it by breathing too much. My mouth tastes like old cat food. I'm in a hospital bed. I look around. I'm not at Mount Babel Hospital. I don't know why I would be, but it suddenly strikes me as odd that I'm not. I don't know where I am, or why my mom is here. I had stomach pain last night after the competition. I have stomach pain all the time, but not like that. Lee called me an ambulance.

Where is Lee, anyway?

I don't have insurance. I can't afford an ambulance. Irony of ironies. Why didn't Lee order me a taxi or something?

Forget the ambulance, I can't afford to be in this hospital at all. Did I get here late last night or early this morning? Staying in a hospital overnight costs more money. What time was it when Lee called the ambulance? I don't think it was after midnight, but it must have been close. Does the clock start when you call the ambulance, when it picks you up, or when it checks you into the hospital? Either way, I can't afford any of this. I have to give all my viewers their money back. I can't afford any of this.

I try to sit up again and the pain is blinding. There is a small bandage on my stomach. I try to lift it off my skin but I'm tired, too tired to commit to the effort.

"Mom," I say. She opens her eyes slowly, and then jumps up in her seat.

"I must have fallen asleep," she says, removing her hair tie and putting it on her wrist. Her hair is smooth and wiry at the same time, and explodes out like the end of a broom when she lets it out of its ponytail. "You woke up a few hours ago and then you went back to sleep. You were still out of it from the anesthesia."

"What's going on? Why are you here?"

"How are you feeling?" she asks.

"I don't know."

"You got surgery last night."

"Oh," I say. "Right." My heart is racing, apparently. I can hear it on the monitor. I'm attached to things. Cords and such, an IV attached to a tube inserted in the top of my hand. "I'm in a hospital."

"They called me late last night. I'm your emergency contact. Your friend brought you in?" she says.

"Where are they?"

"Who?"

"My friend. Lee," I say.

"Oh. I didn't meet them. They were gone when I got here. Are you in pain?" my mom asks but doesn't wait for a response before getting up to find a doctor. I look up at the ceiling when she leaves to rest my eyes. My heart monitor is a chant that distorts the more I focus on it. This hospital room looks nothing like Daisy's. There's a light orange curtain slicing the room in half, and I can faintly hear someone on the other side of it, on the phone, or whispering to themselves. No television in the corner. I can't see the view from the window to the right of my bed, but I can hear birds. I do a mental inventory of the hospitals closest to

JUST WATCH ME | 253

my apartment. There's Northwell Health near Central Park, Cornell Medicine on the Upper East Side, Sloan Kettering by the East River. I look around the room for any logos, labels, clues, but I find none. I suppose it doesn't matter where I am. Still, it would be nice to know.

Soon my mom returns with my doctor.

"Good morning," she says. Her voice is downy, brighter than expected from her small mouth in her round face. Such a soft, nice tone of voice that I think I might cry, because I'm exhausted and want to be unwitnessed but also fed and tucked in, and no one can do that for me, not really.

"How are you?" the doctor asks, coming over to read my vitals. "Feeling good?"

"Where am I?"

"You're in the hospital. You came in last night with a perforated ulcer and we had to perform emergency surgery."

"But where?"

"The ulcer? It was in your stomach lining."

"No. Never mind."

My mom sits back down beside me as the doctor goes on. "A severe, untreated ulcer can sometimes burn through the walls of the stomach, allowing digestive juices and food to leak into the abdominal cavity. You were experiencing severe blood loss when you came in last night."

I learn that the mortality rate of a perforated ulcer is up to twenty-five percent, as high as fifty percent for those of advanced age. While the doctor is speaking, I can only look at my mom, who can only look at her hands. Her palms splayed open in front of her like pages: a birth certificate, a death certificate. She shouldn't have to be here, in a hospital again. She shouldn't have had to get that call in the middle of the night.

"We did a gastrectomy, which means we cut away a section of your stomach where the ulcer was located, then surgically closed the gap and reconnected your stomach to your small intestine. Everything went well. You should be able to leave in a couple of days, and then you can expect a four-to-eight-week recovery."

Her smile is a tide pool that laps at her eyes, nearly getting there.

"Can I leave now?" I ask. I hate that I'm in a hospital right now. I hate that my mom is here.

"How are you feeling? Your vitals are good. Are you in pain?" the doctor asks.

I shake my head. "Only when I move or breathe."

"We're going to keep monitoring how you're doing," the doctor says. "I'll have the nurse bring you some clear fluids. Later on you can try some light solid food."

"Fine, but I need to leave. I don't have insurance. I can't pay you," I say. But even as I speak, I know that I won't leave. I feel like an ass but I'm not ready, in any sense, to get out of here. Each uninsured day at a hospital can cost thousands of dollars, but there's nothing to be done about it, and that's probably chump change compared to the ambulance and surgery fees anyway.

"Try to eat something tonight and see how you feel, okay?" the doctor says. "Do you have any other questions I can answer for now?" I shake my head. "Let the nurses know if you need me. I'll stop by in a couple hours to see how you're doing."

I shouldn't have gotten back onstage so quickly yesterday. I should have taken a fucking second to do damage control. Found Patrick and talked to him in person before he read the chats. Kneed Casper in the balls and shoved a Reaper up his rectum, see how much he likes it. When my mom goes for a walk to the hospital gift store, I scroll back and relive the damage for the first time. Casper posted Daisy's death certificate, and then began his rampage. My LiveCast ranking has plummeted to 555,942 and is still dropping quickly.

fr13ndlygh0st: MADEMOISELLE_DELL IS A LIAR
fr13ndlygh0st: SHE IS NOT RAISING MONEY FOR HER SISTER
fr13ndlygh0st: SHE IS RAISING MONEY FOR HERSELF
fr13ndlygh0st: THIS HAS ALL BEEN A SCAM
fr13ndlygh0st: HER REAL NAME IS ODELIA DANVERS
fr13ndlygh0st: GIVE US OUR MONEY BACK ODELIA DANVERS

Aside from Daisy's death certificate and much of my personal information, Casper shared my social media profile with all my viewers. He
shared a middle school picture of me from the depths of the internet.
He shared a piece of news coverage about my sister's incident. Everything except my address and phone number. That's coming next, if I
don't pay up by the end of the day.

I should've blocked fr13ndlygh0st the very moment I recognized
Casper in the audience at the expo hall, the very instant that I made
the connection between his real name and the screen name I'd seen
floating around my viewer list. He would've made another account, but
it would have bought me time. Maybe even enough time for the Live-
Cast team to block his IP address. But would that have been enough,
or would he have found me and my viewers some other way? Would he
have kept trying forever until he took me down?

Would any of this have happened if I hadn't shared my online
marketplace link on my first day of streaming? If Casper hadn't found
my full name and been able to do all the internet stalking his heart
desired?

If I had just paid him back his meager couple hundred dollars when
he first asked?

There are twenty-seven people in my stream now, which has officially been live for one hundred and forty hours. It's my seventh day of
streaming and I need to rest. My audio and video are turned off. But the
chats keep coming. All my OGs, asking for their money back. Demanding their money back. Talking about reporting me, doxing me, ruining

my life. A bunch of little excelsior404s running around with torches and pitchforks. I send a few messages in the chat.

> **mademoiselle_dell:** I already told you that you would all get your money back
> **mademoiselle_dell:** but i'm in the hospital
> **mademoiselle_dell:** I got emergency surgery last night
> **mademoiselle_dell:** so give me a little bit of time
> **chillnessa:** mentirosa
> **redtimepolice:** no way ur in a hospital
> **jackofnotrades1:** bitch
> **crabbybob:** you owe me $28
> **MSRN273:** i never donated tg tg
> **jackofnotrades1:** KILL YOURSELF
> **mademoiselle_dell:** i'm sorry that i wasnt who i said i was

My brain is scrambled eggs. My guts are scrambled eggs. I take a deep breath and click on the button on the corner of the screen: "End Stream."

• • •

The ancient Greek word *sparagmos* means to tear, rend, pull to pieces. I took Greek mythology my freshman year of college, the rare class I actually enjoyed. Sparagmos was a Dionysian rite. People would be ripped apart for the gods. Shredded in penance and devotion. With their organs laid out one by one on a stone altar, people found themselves turned into symbols. Beyond the shock value, there's something else there. It's like sometimes you have to take everything apart in order to understand it.

I feel relief when I end my stream, but also a deep and frenzied worry. "She's a lucky girl," the doctor says to my mom before she departs.

Soon I'll be discharged and this bed will be occupied by another body, and then another, and then another. I eat a single saltine cracker and it goes down with only mild discomfort. Tomorrow morning I'll try two. If I don't experience pain, I can try to incorporate other soft foods.

Nothing with texture, and certainly nothing spicy. And now there's a part of me, a few inches of stomach, in some medical waste bin somewhere. An excised bit of ulcer, a gaping lack where there once was something strange and rotten. The doctor tells me I'll be okay, but she doesn't know about the plant in my ear. It's not a seed anymore. It's fully grown. Long, fragrant roots that itch at the insides of my nostrils.

Every few seconds I have the urge to check my stream, then remember that I don't have one. Mademoiselle_dell was mostly a lie but not quite. An impression of an impression of an impression of me broadcast out, a camera obscura of my life. Despite everything, I became rather attached to her, to the way she let me turn back time for a brief moment. For a couple of days, Daisy was still alive, and everything was fixable.

SUNDAY

A Week Later

My mom pushes me out to her car in a wheelchair. It hurts a little when I move or laugh or breathe too deeply, but I feel okay. Not lucky, but okay.

It's nearing evening as we drive away from the hospital, which was, ironically, Mount Babel after all, a second location farther north and farther west. Wherever you go, there you are. My mom asks if I want to go back to my apartment and I say no. She asks if I'm too tired to visit Daisy and I say no. We drive into New Jersey as the sun sets, across the subaqueous Lincoln Tunnel, winding quietly across the state before finally pulling off the highway into the parking lot of a small and well-maintained cemetery.

It doesn't take long to find Daisy's grave. I've never been here before but I spot it instantly: the cleanest headstone, the freshest flowers. While my mom sits on the grass with an arm around Daisy's shoulders, I lay down at her feet, a facsimile of our arrangements when we would visit Daisy at the hospital. I lift my hair off my neck and spread it in a corona around me on the dirt. The sky is dark and well-starred.

"We saw it, right?" I ask. "Her hand moved?"

"Oh, yes," my mom says, and then: "I don't know what I saw."

"I lied about visiting Daisy the other day, when I texted you."

"I figured," she says. "I can't believe you let things get so bad."

"I know."

"You got emergency life-saving surgery, Odelia," she says.

"I know."

"You always know everything," my mom says.

I snort, and the action is accompanied by a small shock wave of pain. "Then why do I make the worst decisions possible?"

My mom brushes nothing off of Daisy's tombstone, brushes nothing off of her pants. "It only feels that way right now."

I put my head in my mom's lap and let her stroke my hair. We sit in silence for a while, deep and replete with nighttime music. I dig in my left ear, reaching around with my nails until I catch hold of the plant's stem. It's thick enough now that J don't have to worry about severing it by accident. I give a tentative pull and feel a slight give, a suctioning feeling in my brain that isn't unpleasant, only tingly. I pull a little harder, and then a little harder, applying firm pressure, and the roots slowly come free of my creased and crinkled lobes. The sensation is slightly uncomfortable but it mostly tickles. Slowly, the plant emerges. A bright yellow marigold, blooming red at the edges like a sunset, a buoyancy of leaves surrounding its silken center. It wasn't a jalapeño seed after all.

I never propagated marigolds in my apartment. Maybe the seed flew in my ear while I was outside on a walk, carried by the wind. Or maybe it was planted a long time ago, and laid dormant, waiting for a confluence of variables to align. There is no way to know. My brain slips back into place when the flower is loose, and settles nicely, with plenty of room to cogitate. It's ironic that I can think clearly here and now, of all places and all times, but not something I feel the need to question.

I show the flower to my mom, like a magic trick. She laughs and then cries and then laughs again. She has the same mouth as me. That's something. The shards of her heart swim up her spine and glimmer behind her eyes, which are not my eyes. I place the flower on Daisy's grave. We sit together for a little longer, but not too long. Soon it's dark and the katydids shoo us away. Endangered, dancing fireflies circling our hair. My mom helps me up slowly, and I use Daisy's gravestone for support. My mom's car is the only one in the parking lot when we leave, and she drives us home, to my childhood home, and helps me into bed, which is my childhood bed, in the room I shared with Daisy, though her bed isn't there anymore. Now instead there is a desk, and on the desk is a single flower in a glass. And in my childhood bedroom in my childhood home there is a window which looks out onto a big, affectionate elm tree, with leaves as big as my head.

"Are you going to sleep?" my mom asks.

"It's early," I say, and it is. Not even nine. And yet it does feel like time for bed, time to end this day once and for all.

"I'll go grocery shopping in the morning?" she says. "So there's some food you like in the house?"

"Soft foods," I say.

"Sleep in and I'll have some things ready when you wake up. We can have breakfast together. Something soft, like eggs, or yogurt."

"Pancakes?"

"I don't think pancakes are a soft food," she says, smiling. "I suppose you could really soak a pancake in maple syrup and it would go soft after a while." She pauses in the doorway, as if she might say something else, but changes her mind. "Good night."

mademoiselle_dell: hey
mademoiselle_dell: did u get my deposit
mademoiselle_dell: i sent it on Monday
hot_pat_of_butter: yeah
mademoiselle_dell: its all the money u donated to me
mademoiselle_dell: i paid everyone else back too
mademoiselle_dell: including your viewers
mademoiselle_dell: its took me hours
mademoiselle_dell: its a manual process lol
mademoiselle_dell: i did it one by one

mademoiselle_dell: thanks for believing in me
mademoiselle_dell: ive never said anything that lame so u should know it means something
mademoiselle_dell: with ur brother and everything
mademoiselle_dell: i hope u can understand, out of everyone
hot_pat_of_butter: i don't
mademoiselle_dell: thats fine
mademoiselle_dell: thanks for answering anyway

During the course of my streamathon I received donations from seven hundred and sixty-two unique users. It took me over five hours to pay them back on Monday, partially because of all the clicking, and partially because I was exhausted and achy and had to take breaks every couple of minutes. It was slow going at first, but once I got the hang of it, it was almost nice to zone out and go through the motions. Zoning out also helped me deal with watching my LiveCast balance shrink from over twenty thousand dollars to a neat and tidy zero dollars.

I let down people who believed in me. I messed everything up. If I were smarter, I could've figured out a way to have my cake and eat it, too. I could've recognized excelsior404 for who he was and dealt with him early, got him off my back, or better yet, got him on my side, whatever that took. Then I could've solved a lie with a lie and told everyone that Daisy died during the course of the livestream. I could've thanked my viewers for their overwhelming generosity and said I was going to use their donations to pay for her funeral, or her hospital bills, or something. Surely my viewers would've been okay with that, wouldn't they?

But if I were smarter, I wouldn't have been in this situation to begin with. Daisy would still be here.

I didn't pay my rent, for obvious reasons. I'm not going back to my apartment, not even to get my things. What things? I'm happy to leave it all behind. I texted my landlord and told him to consider my lease broken. Normally, a lease break would cost a couple months of rent, but he knew I wasn't good for it, and he seemed enthusiastic about getting a tenant who would actually pay on time.

I didn't pay my phone bill or my utility bill. I didn't pay my student loan bill or my credit card bill. My medical bills haven't come in yet from the hospital, but I'd be surprised if they were under fifty thousand dollars for an uninsured ambulance ride, emergency surgery, and a week in the hospital. I will absolutely not be paying those. Not for a long time, anyway. I'm going to stay here for a little while to sort things out. And it feels good to leave the city. Like sometimes the places you haunt end up haunting you.

Pancakes in the morning. That'll be nice. My stomach is stronger now, the bad bits excised, the viable bits strung back together. I'm sure my mom will ask me how I'm feeling, what I'm thinking, how long I'll stay at her place, if I'll try to go back to NYU in the fall. But there will be pancakes, and that's nice.

I call Lee and thank them again for everything, let them know that I'm at my mom's. We texted a bit when I was at the hospital. I let them know that I was okay, that I was sorry, etcetera. The sound of their voice now moves me nearly to tears. They offer to come by and say hello. Not tomorrow, not sometime next week, but tonight. A miracle. An hour later, they're on a train from Port Authority to New Jersey. My mom is asleep in her room. I don't want to disturb her, so I send her a quick text instead.

I walk carefully down the stairs, slowly and awkwardly so as not to irritate my wounds. I grab the car keys out of the bowl by the door and start my mom's car. Driving isn't too bad, I can get by without moving my midsection at all. It's nearly midnight when I pick Lee up from the bus station, but I'm not tired and neither are they.

"Thanks for coming," I say. "I know it's late."

"Yeah. It's fine," they say. "I'll call in sick tomorrow."

They would call in sick to work tomorrow, just like that, as if it's nothing, when I know that it matters to them. Showing up for people, doing what they say they're going to do. I guess, at least in this moment, I matter more. I want to reach across the car and pull them into an embrace, but I start the car and drive instead. They're the greatest person I've ever met, and I'd probably be dead without them. They know it and I know it.

"I'm sorry," I say. "For everything I put you through."

"It's fine," they say, and I wish I could see them better, wish I weren't looking at the road so I could parse their body language, the shape of their mouth, the texture of their gaze as they speak.

"Is it?"

"It's very difficult to be angry with someone who's just had a medical emergency."

"But you are? Angry with me?"

"Of course," they say. "But I'm here, aren't I?"

"I paid everyone back."

"I know." They snort. "I got your twenty dollars."

"Your twenty dollars."

"You didn't have to pay me back," they say. "Is that guy leaving you alone, then?"

"We'll see. I deleted my LiveCast account after I paid everyone back, so I can't exactly ask him if he's over it. I haven't heard anything all week, but if he doxes me I'll probably be the last to know about it."

"Right," they say. "God."

"It's so quiet," I say. "Not out here in the suburbs. I mean, it is. But now that I'm not streaming, it just feels so quiet all the time."

"Bad quiet?"

I consider for a moment. "No, not bad. I guess I'm okay with it. I could've died last week but I didn't. But I probably can't eat anything good for a long time while my stomach recovers, which is lame."

"I was so scared when I saw you on the floor like that."

"Oh," I say. Lee isn't looking at me. If they are upset, it's impossible to tell. "I'm sorry. I'm sorry you had to help me." They shake their head as if to say: don't be silly.

A few minutes later, we pull into my mom's driveway. I turn the car off but don't get out. I look at Lee in the passenger seat, the way they can curl their feet underneath their tall frame with such ease, look comfortable contorted into nearly any position. Calling in sick for me. That's pretty cool.

"Did you bring weed?" I ask. They shake their head, then remember something and reach into their bag.

"I brought your mail," they say. "I figured you'd want it since you're not coming back. When was the last time you picked up your mail?"

Lee hands me a thick stack of envelopes, at least thirty of them.

"I don't know," I say. "I never check my mail. It's all junk." Coupon, coupon, catalog, credit card offer, coupon. And then a letter from a name and address I recognize. I rip it open and inside is a check for $408. I've never been paid by check before at Juice Body, only direct deposit. The check is signed by Nik and dated to last Tuesday. He probably had a change of heart after I visited him at the store but before I hacked into Juice Body's social media account.

"Shit." I laugh.

"What?" Lee asks.

I wave the check in their face.

"My sister is dead, but I have four hundred dollars."

"Oh, come on," Lee says.

"She's dead, and it was probably my fault, but at least I have four hundred dollars."

I'm laughing but Lee isn't. Their face is calm, their fingers tracing shapes on the dashboard. "Do you want to talk about it?" they finally ask.

"Maybe later," I say. "Not tonight."

"Okay," they say, and then we sit quietly for a while, listening to the way the suburbs sound at night, how still the air gets just miles out of the city. Still but not stagnant, quiet but not voiceless. The air smells like fresh-cut grass, with only the faintest hint of skunk. I close my eyes and lean back into my seat. The quiet is smothering but nice. I have made my uneasy truce with it. It won't devour me, not just now.

When I open my eyes, Lee is closer, just a little bit closer, arm resting on the console between us. I hold their gaze. The moment stretches out, the wingspan of a second longer than I thought possible and infinitely more precious. "I'm glad you came," I say.

"Of course I came."

"You can be mad at me for as long as you want. I know I haven't been a good friend lately. Maybe not ever. Just don't hate me, okay?"

The fizzing, crackling corners of a smile. "I don't hate you," they say. "I could never hate you. You're too pathetic to hate. Especially now."

"Asshole."

They laugh. "And if you get tired of suburbia, you can come back and stay at my place. At least until you get your shit together."

"Maybe," I say. And I know they mean it, their offer to put me up, but I would never take them up on it, no matter how nice it would be. More than nice. But I can't be indebted to them in that way. I'm indebted enough as it is. My future is an unknown quantity, and in the present moment I have no solutions and no desire to come up with them.

I start the car and pull back out of the driveway. "Let's drive around a little longer."

New Voice Message, 1:27 AM
Hey, Dell, it's Mom. I woke up and you weren't here. I mean, I got your text, and then I immediately went to check your room, and you

weren't here. You should be in bed, like the doctor said. Apparently you went to pick up your friend from the station, but that was over an hour ago. It's half-past one in the morning now. I just want to know if you're okay because you're not answering my calls. Maybe your phone is on silent, I don't know. If you're driving, then maybe it's good that you're not on your phone. But still, I'm worried. You shouldn't be driving. You just got surgery. Why wouldn't you just wake me up? I would've picked up your friend for you. Or your friend could've come tomorrow, during the day? Wouldn't that have made more sense? Send me some kind of sign that you're okay so I can go back to sleep.

•   •   •

New Voice Message, 1:39 AM
God, I really need to go to bed. I called out all of last week at the pharmacy when I was with you in the hospital and I have to work double-shifts now to catch up. You have the car or else I'd probably go and look for you right now. Why is your phone off? Call me.

•   •   •

New Voice Message, 1:45 AM
Do you remember when you were six or seven, and you got your Betty Boop toy stuck in the tree in the backyard? And you wouldn't let me help? You were out there for at least an hour, trying to get it down with sticks, rocks. You even threw your shoes at it, and one of them got stuck, too. It was so hard to watch you struggle like that. I wanted to help but you were so determined. You were so frustrated. When you started climbing I ran out and you yelled at me not to come closer. But you got them down, didn't you? The toy and the shoe, too. You looked so grown up then. I guess that's who you are. Always so stubborn about figuring things out on your own.

•   •   •

New Voice Message, 1:57 AM
I don't like worrying about you in this way, Dell. I know you're an adult and you've lived on your own for a while, and I know you haven't even

been home for a day yet, but you need to tell me what you're doing and where you are. A text isn't enough, especially not tonight. I don't need every detail but enough so that I don't have to worry about you like this. Okay? I mean, I'm allowed to be a little overprotective right now, so don't make me feel bad about it. Because I know I said I don't want to be that mom, the one that demands access and intimacy, but I feel like this is much more basic than that, so I'm not going to second-guess my judgment here. It's been over two hours since you texted me and I'm sure you're just driving around with your friend and maybe you went to the diner or something but it's still nice to know where you are and if you're safe and if you're okay, especially if you're going to live at home.

• • •

New Voice Message, 1:59 AM

I'm so happy that you're home right now, don't get me wrong. I've missed you. It's not something I want to put on you, but it's been so hard to be home alone without Daisy. She went away for a weekend and never came back. I dropped her off and never picked her up again. I think about that all the time. It's been over two months since she died, but sometimes I still feel like she'll appear at the front door with her weekend bag. I really do feel like that, like the doorbell is about to go off. I can almost hear it sometimes. Almost. And once in a while it does ring when I think it will, but then it's always someone else: a delivery, a neighbor. But I always run to the door. Always.

Sorry that I'm crying. I shouldn't be crying like this on a voicemail. Just call me, okay? Just come home.

• • •

New Voice Message, 2:06 AM

This is not okay, Dell. This is absolutely not okay. Where are you? I'm glad you're home and I don't want you to feel like you can't do what you want. But if you are going to live at home for some period of time, then we have to talk about ground rules, we have to talk about boundaries, we—

Oh, I think that's you. Pulling up in the driveway? Yes, I see you. There you are. Look at you, with your friend. You're both laughing.

I love your laugh. You're so good, helping them with their overnight bag. You're so good.

And your friend, this is the Lee person who called you an ambulance? Well. I guess I'll know in a moment. Anyway. I don't know how to delete this so I'm just going to hang up now and get the door for you. Bye, Dell. Love you.

ACKNOWLEDGMENTS

This book would not have found its way out onto your shelf, dear reader, if not for the support and love of the following people: Aram Fox and the team at Massie McQuilkin & Altman; Lauren Wein, Amy Guay, Chris White, Caroline McGregor, Rhina Garcia, the entire Simon & Schuster team across continents; Erika Krouse and my Book Project cohort; and my lifelong friends from my NYU MFA. Thank you for believing in me and this story. I am humbled to know you and grateful beyond measure.

And finally, thank you to Dell—the little demon in my ear—who I probably wouldn't like very much in real life, but who I've come to love all the same. Thank you.

ABOUT THE AUTHOR

LIOR TORENBERG received her Master's in Creative Writing from New York University and is a member of the Lighthouse Book Project. Learn more at www.liortorenberg.com.